The Voice of the Corpse

by

Max Murray

Dover Publications, Inc.
New York

TO THE CITY HALL, NEW YORK
WHERE I MARRIED MAYSIE GRIEG,
AFFECTIONATELY

This Dover edition, first published in 1985, is an unabridged republication of the edition first published by Michael Joseph, London, in 1948. The dedication is taken from the American edition, first published by Farrar, Straus and Company, New York, in 1947.

Manufactured in the United States of America
Dover Publications, Inc., 31 East 2nd Street, Mineola, N.Y. 11501

Library of Congress Cataloging in Publication Data

Murray, Max, 1901–1956.
  The voice of the corpse.

  Reprint. Originally published: London : M. Joseph, 1948.
  I. Title.
PR9619.3.M84V6 1985   823   85-6842
ISBN 0-486-24905-0 (pbk.)

I

EVEN in death there was something arty and crafty about Angela. The grim reaper had caught her as she sat at her spinning wheel, at the moment when she was taking the first steps towards converting a heap of unsavoury hair that she had plucked from her Chow into a pullover for Celia Sim. She had died a thoroughly unnatural death, and in spite of all the skill in her cunning fingers, she could not have done it herself. Somebody else had hit Angela on the head. If Angela had not thought it necessary to sing appropriate folk songs as she sat at her spinning wheel, she might have heard her approaching end. But on this occasion, as the saying goes, she never knew what hit her.

That certainly made a change for Angela. It was the first time in many years that someone had done something in her vicinity about which she was not thoroughly informed.

When considering these matters it is not an unusual thing to consider who benefits by the death. Celia Sim naturally, because Celia was going to dislike wearing a pullover made of Chow's hair even more than she disliked the donor of the raw material. And in Celia's view Angela's Chow was not everybody's dog. But let it be said now that Celia, benefit or no benefit, did not remove Angela.

But back to the corpse.

Back indeed to Angela Mason Pewsey in life. At the time of the incident she was forty-nine years old, and had been waiting for some years, so she said, for an individual named Richard to get back from Ceylon. They met on a boat it appears, and he told her that a little woman made all the difference to a man's lonely solitude and could she wait till next he came home on leave from the plantation. That was fifteen years ago, and as he had been rather long in the tooth

5

at the time, he was now probably dead. Anyway, he hadn't come back on leave, and Angela was really much happier without him.

Her cottage faced the church, and one of the few of those circular burying grounds in the country, obsolete now, of course. The modern one was in a convenient swamp half a mile away. But apart from the church, Angela could see from her window and spinning wheel quite a comprehensive amount of the life and habitations of the village. She could and she did. When she was not at the window, she was attending one or other of the sources of slander and collective endeavour, such as the Institute and Mothers' Union, or the Church Guild. She knew something about everybody and everything about some, and in every case far too much.

She was arch about it. Whether the knowledge concerned a mild flirtation or incest a few arch references were enough to give the victims a clue to her knowledge. The method of these revelations was in itself enough to make most reasonable people feel capable of murdering her, particularly the gay little giggle. So somebody did murder her at half past three on a fine afternoon. The time was established by a neighbour who noticed that a particularly trilling note broke off suddenly almost at the moment the church clock chimed the half hour.

The body was discovered by Mrs Tilling, who came in to make the tea, as she always did at four. Mrs Tilling looked thoughtfully at the body; her hands folded comfortably over a lap that existed even when she was standing up. She was not unduly disturbed by the sight of the victim. What did make her sound nervous when she broke the news was that she never could abide the telephone. But she had to telephone the police and she knew that the police in times like this were to be had for the asking.

'You better get on your bike and come down to the churchyard,' she shouted. 'Somebody's done in Miss Pewsey. What's that? Well I do know, because I just see her. What did you say I was to do . . . sit in the room with the body till

6

you get there and don't let nobody interfere?' Rather than bandy further words on the telephone Mrs Tilling hung up.

She went back to the lounge and picked up an Elizabethan poker and carried it back and put it where it belonged on the hearth. But she gave it a rub over with a cloth first. There was nothing furtive about this. Mrs Tilling was a woman of tidy instincts. Or it may have been the rural instinct that every creature deserves a run for its money, even a fox.

Then she went back to the lounge and selected a chair not occupied by the corpse and sat down contentedly to wait. She had not long to wait either because Constable Wilks arrived not on a bike but on a motor cycle, as if he were afraid that the only body he had been asked to deal with would get away from him. But it was still there as immobile as Mrs Tilling.

Constable Wilks gave the impression that now that he had a murder he didn't quite know what to do with it. He regarded the body with proper decorum and then removed his hat. He looked at Mrs Tilling as if for inspiration, but Mrs Tilling was looking at the corpse.

'Life is extinct, I suppose!' said Constable Wilks.

Mrs Tilling nodded comfortably. 'Of course.'

The constable had never really doubted the fact himself. He had never come in contact with violent death before, but to recognize it in this case needed neither experience nor subtlety. Angela was dead all right, and somebody had been responsible.

'I wonder who done it,' he said, continuing this line of thought.

'The Vicar,' Mrs Tilling said.

The constable dropped his hat on the floor and his hands shook as he fumbled to recover it.

'You be careful, Mrs Tilling, you be careful what you're saying now. Remember this is a murder case and you're on oath.'

'No, I'm not.'

7

She was not on oath, of course, as she quite rightly said, but that didn't excuse her, anyway. 'Saying a thing like that. Somebody might hear.'

'Well, don't ask no silly questions then.'

The constable remarked appropriately as it seemed to him: 'Who would want to take the life of a helpless innocent old lady?'

'She weren't helpless, she weren't innocent, and she weren't old,' said Mrs Tilling. 'And don't ask me again who done it, because I shan't tell.'

The constable made no reply. According to instructions he was waiting in a state of suspended animation for the arrival of his superiors, particularly Sergeant Porter, a stern man, whose principal fear had been that Constable Wilks might begin an investigation on his own initiative. Sergeant Porter had once at the peak of his long career brought to book a man who had strangled his nagging wife after a long series of violent public quarrels. With this endorsement of his qualifications he felt competent to match the subtleties of his own mind against the darker ones of crime. Even at this moment he had got out his bicycle and was resolutely on the trail.

In the meantime Wilks, Tilling, and Angela maintained their tableau; Wilks, hat in hand, by the door, Mrs Tilling seated, and Angela suspended over the spinning wheel. Sound effects were provided by a wandering bee, which bumped its head doggedly against the window, and animation was supplied by the frilled net curtains, which rose and fell prettily on the delightful breeze. The setting was peaceful, charming, and chintzy. The jarring note, of course, was struck by the characters.

Wilks tried not to look at the body, and when he did look tried to keep his mind on ways and means of finding out who did it. Fingerprints . . . a smart man could make a lot of use of those things.

There'd sure to be fingerprints . . . couldn't help it, not rightly speaking. The whole place was crawling with them,

like as not, the victim's, the murderer's, Mrs Tilling's . . .
He would have slapped his thigh if it hadn't been for the
company. Between one bump of the bee against the window-
pane and the next, Constable Wilks solved the problem to
his own complete satisfaction. Here they were, all together
in one room. The victim, the murderer, and the instrument of
justice, and, of course, the bee. But the bee had no pre-
occupations whatever beyond the matter of knocking itself
unconscious.

As to the murder itself: Mrs Tilling's presence in the room
would have caused no astonishment, even if she had come in
with a blunt instrument in her hand. A housemaid mostly
was carrying a blunt instrument of some kind or another.
Why should Mrs Tilling use a blunt instrument on Miss
Pewsey? Maybe she was under notice, maybe she didn't like
folk songs or spinning dog's hair (most local people didn't
come to that). Anyway, she didn't like Miss Pewsey, because
she as good as said so herself.

Constable Wilks fell to wondering whether to tell the
Sergeant straight away as soon as he got there or to let him
get himself in deep water first and sort of play him like. Anyway, it was obvious that if he was to get any credit for his
piece of deduction it would be just as well to have a witness
when he revealed the murderer. It was Wilks' conviction
that nobody below the rank of sergeant ever got any credit
for anything. But if the inspector happened to be there when
he let the cat out of the bag that would be different.

If Mrs Tilling had any suspicion that the constable had
got his victim already she gave no sign of it. She was sitting
very much as she had when he arrived, quite comfortably,
quite contentedly, as if she were thinking among other
things how nice it was to take the weight off her feet, as
indeed it must have been.

'Dog's hair,' she said. 'I can't see myself putting my head
into one of those nasty smelly things.'

'You never know what you'll put your head into one day,'
the constable answered and fixed a penetrating eye on her to

9

see if she started at this subtle reference to the hangman's noose. But it must have been too subtle, for Mrs Tilling.

'Anyway, it won't be one of them,' she said. 'I shouldn't wonder if this doesn't put an end to all the lot of the whole nonsense. Dog's wool.' Suddenly at the recurring idea she gave a deep fruity chuckle. It shook the constable, though it confirmed him in the idea of her callousness.

But if it was processes of the mind that superseded action inside Rooks Roost, there was physical activity elsewhere. The train came in, dead on time, and Ted Mattock, the porter, was so impressed that he hardly noticed the only passenger. She handed him one half of a day return from London and disappeared. That is to say, she never came back. Also she passed from Ted's mind. It was so unusual for this particular train to be on time that he thought at first that his watch must be slow, and that was worrying considering what a wonderful good timekeeper she was. But the train was on time and there was no getting away from it. What caused this nobody rightly knew.

As the woman came out of the station yard she passed within a few yards of Sergeant Porter. He did not notice her particularly, either. Why should he? When it's murder you keep to the business on hand, and for the moment it was getting to the scene of the crime. The woman passenger moved on in the same direction as the sergeant, quite unnoticed. It is true that Eric Daw looked at her legs as he overtook her in his car, but all he remembered afterwards was a vague pair of legs that had failed to interest him. He had an impression too of blue crepe, a hard blue colour, popular but unfortunate for almost everyone.

The news of the murder was beginning to spread.

'I tell you she *is* dead,' spoken by a small boy. 'I seen her, I tell you. She's by the window. If you don't believe me come and climb the tree by the churchyard wall, then you'll see. Mrs Tilling is watching over the body. Constable Wilks is there, with is 'at in 'is 'and. She's layin' over the spinning wheel.'

'She's fainted, that's what it is.'

'Oh 'as she. She was 'it with a blunt instrument, that's what she was. I crept up to the window and heard them say so. Look, here comes the sergeant, now will you believe me.'

'So it is. All right, come on, let's get up the tree.'

Celia Sim may not have been the belle of the village of Inching Round, but if she was not, then Inching Round had not selected one. Of course, she was spoiled, but why not? She lived alone with her mother, but she was extraordinarily nice to her. She went out a lot and she was nice to the men who took her out, but not too nice either, certainly no nicer than you can be if you are a nice girl, and Celia was. She was a country girl for preference because she could go to town when she wanted to. But she liked the house parties in the country and the drives to dinner or cocktails, through the leafy winding lanes that linked the houses of the neighbourhood. She liked the point-to-points in the winter at which it was not out of place to wear silk stockings, a coat and skirt, a mink coat and fur lined ancient boots. She really did seem a part of both worlds. If you met Celia in a London street you'd know that she'd come up from the country, but you couldn't help feeling glad that she had. She was not tall, but she walked with that free gait that isn't schooled to the necessity of avoiding falling over somebody's feet. Her blonde hair was natural. Her brows were level and her head was poised so that her grey eyes trained naturally on the horizon. When she was angry, she was mad, but that was generally on someone else's behalf. When she smiled a light was dancing in her eyes. She was twenty-one.

Celia had an alibi for the time of the murder. She was sitting in a train with Firth Prentice, waiting to leave Victoria. Every train that left Victoria for Inching Round left from the most obscure platform available, as if one and all were thoroughly ashamed of it. From there it crawled out and stopped almost at once to wait for the more important train to cross the Thames. Then it bustled across and stopped with a self-satisfied hiss on the other side. From then on, in stations and out, it never stopped stopping till it got to Inching Round.

It was all right when you got used to it, but Celia's companion was not used to it and he began to get restless almost at once.

'I'd no idea that Battersea Park was so far away,' he said when he looked out and saw that they were there.

'We're doing well, considering,' Celia said. 'You wait till we leave London and get on our own ground.'

Mr Firth Prentice accepted this with courage but without enthusiasm. He had little enthusiasm for any train travel, and for little dirty trains that hung about the suburbs, like a boy at a fair, he had none at all. Nor did he like the country, nor particularly the job he had let himself in for. But he did like Celia, although he would have been the first to confess to himself that he was hardly her type. But she had come to him in anger and distress, and he had found her irresistible.

He wished now that he hadn't.

'I still can't think what you expect me to do,' he said.

Celia answered impatiently: 'How can you think till you get there?'

'But I'm not a detective, and what's more, I'm not going to pretend to be one. If you wanted a detective, you should have let me hire one.'

Celia looked at him pityingly. 'Do you expect me to entertain a private detective for days on end?'

'All right, why not put him up at the village pub?'

'Firth darling, how do you suppose he'd describe himself at the village pub?'

'How do I know? Anything he fancied, an artist, or a fertilizer salesman.'

'Fertilizer salesman . . . what would he do then?'

'How should I know? Take his samples from house to house, I expect.'

She shook her head again. 'They would know all about

him in one day. Have you ever seen a stranger mixing with the natives in the " Merry Harriers" at Inching Round?'

'I can't say that I have, no.'

'When the stranger isn't talking you could hear a pin drop. You, of course, will be different.'

'What will cause the change? Has the village run out of pins?'

'You'll be staying at the house.'

'Yes, I've been wondering about that. Is there any good reason why I should be staying in your house?'

'Don't be ridiculous, Firth. You're the family solicitor, aren't you?'

'Up to a point, I suppose I am. Anyway, the firm, that's to say father, is.'

'Well, why shouldn't you stay in the house?'

'Your mother may begin to wonder if there is something wrong with your family estate.'

'You can tell her that there isn't.'

'Yes, but she may think that just to tell her that hardly merits an extended stay.'

'Mother won't think anything of the kind. After you've been there a few days she will think you are another boy friend. She's quite vague.'

'Yes, but she still might think vaguely that it's a little odd. Specially in view of your engagement to this Graham Ward chap.'

'I'm not engaged to Graham Ward. At least not any more. Not after yesterday.'

He shook his head. 'Yes, but getting rid of this Graham Ward one day and bringing me home the next must seem a little quick even in a metropolis like Inching Round.'

'Mother won't give it a second thought,' Celia said impatiently. 'She's used to seeing men wandering about the place. When there's no one there she keeps wondering what's missing.' She looked at him suspiciously. 'Look here, I believe you're sorry you came.'

He protested mildly. 'Came where? We aren't in

Clapham Junction yet. No, I'll go through with it. But it does seem to me like looking for a needle in a haystack, you know.'

'It isn't,' Celia said, 'it's like it is: Looking for an anonymous letter-writer in a village.'

'Has nobody expressed any views as to who it is?'

Celia bit her lower lip. 'Nobody has mentioned it,' she added bitterly. 'Nobody, of course, but Graham and me.'

'Hum . . . perhaps you and Graham are the only ones who have had them.'

Celia's head was turned to the open window, but she was not looking at South London. She was passing in review her neighbours and friends in Inching Round.

'No, a lot of other people have had them too. You can tell. There's something in the atmosphere. There's something furtive about it: the way they look at each other as if they were wondering, suspecting; and then their eyes slide away as if they were ashamed of their thoughts. It is pretty awful.'

Firth tugged impatiently at his tie. 'But I can't understand two apparently sane people like you and Graham letting yourselves be taken in by all this . . . by a lot of stupid lies in an anonymous letter.'

Celia looked at the floor. 'You see they weren't complete lies. I mean it was the way they were said that made them so awful, the implications. Graham expected me to deny the whole thing – naturally, I suppose.'

'And of course you refused to discuss it?'

'Yes, I was angry because he asked for an explanation. I hadn't asked Graham for one.'

'You had a letter too, of course?'

She shivered. 'It was horrible. I started to read it and then burned it.'

Firth laughed. 'How sporting of you, Celia. I always think it does help the dear criminal so when you burn the evidence.'

'I couldn't bear to think of it being in the house.'

'Did Graham know you had it?'

'Yes, but I didn't talk about it.'

'You should have done, it might have taken his precious mind off his own. Did he burn his too?'

'I think after he had shown it to me, he put it back in his pocket-book.'

'Was he going to take it to the police?'

'Of course not.' She spoke as if the idea was quite out of the question.

'Why not? Surely that would be the sensible thing to do?'

She protested. 'It would be dreadful. They know us and we know them. It would be unbearable to have them hunting up all those letters, knowing what was said about us all, keeping records.'

'The police don't talk about what they hear.'

'It's obvious you never lived in a village.'

'No, I've been spared that. All right my village maiden, your friend Graham is not going to give the note to the police; what is he keeping it for . . . a souvenir?'

She looked away. 'I don't know.'

'Well, it's not the sort of thing I personally would wear next to my underwear for preference. He may be keeping it to remind him of his past follies. He may be keeping it for purposes of self-torture. Or,' he looked at her with a slow grin, 'he may have an idea of changing the address and sending it on to your next beau.'

It was a scandalous suggestion, but the idea of rubbing out the address and passing the odious thing on like a chain letter made her laugh.

Firth's grin widened. 'When he hears of this visit, he may even send it on to me. It would be one way of getting the evidence, wouldn't it?'

'Fool!'

'How true. And yet . . .'

'Yet what?'

He laughed. 'Well, perhaps not quite yet. You might bear it in mind though. I am one of the few really attractive men who are still at large.'

Celia said quite seriously: 'Yes, I suppose you are. I suppose you can be damned attractive when you put your mind to it.'

'From scraps overheard and a hint here and there I understand that in certain quarters I have a widish public.'

'But you're smug.'

'No, realistic. Why pretend one doesn't know? You can't help it if you are more than eighteen and not a saint or an imbecile. And I'm neither. But why go on, it can't possibly interest you.' He untangled his long legs and put his feet on the cushion opposite. 'If we are to spend the rest of our lives in this mechanical snail we might as well be comfortable.' He leaned back and she had the indignant feeling that he was about to go to sleep.

He was right, of course, she thought irritably. Women would make asses of themselves over him. She noticed that the lashes that were lowered over his eyes were long, and thick, like a girl's. There was a wave in his brown hair too, that was wasted in a man. And his features were regular and fine drawn without being thin, and there was generally a suggestion of a smile lurking somewhere in the corners of his widish mouth, that made you wonder whether he was going to laugh with you, or at you, or both. You would certainly have to be more than average to make him take you seriously . . . really seriously. He was slim, but she remembered for no particular reason, the casual way in which he had lifted her heavy suitcases on to the rack.

She heard herself saying: 'Why couldn't it possibly interest me?'

'What's that?' He seemed to have difficulty in recalling that she was still there.

'I said: "Why couldn't it possibly interest me?"'

'Oh yes, I heard you, but it took me a while to pick up the threads.' Without lifting his head from the cushions he turned to look at her. 'Because you aren't my type. I mean, of course, I'm not your type.'

'I see, so I have a type?'

'Oh, quite a comprehensive one, of course. I mean it would cover a wide assortment, tall, thin, brawny, bookish, hearty, quite a choice, I should say. But, Celia dear, you would never, never live in London.'

'How do you know?'

'Oh, you'd come up, of course. You might even take a house for a while. It would be a house, mark you, it always is; never a flat. But of course you'd only really live in the country.'

'And you, of course, wouldn't?'

He shook his head and smiled. 'No. Not even for Celia.'

'So now we know where we stand.' She hoped he noted the nice blend of sarcasm.

But he nodded comfortably and said, 'Yes, don't we. It's nice to be understood.' His long lashes drooped down to his cheeks and Firth fell asleep, calmly, gracefully, but he did fall asleep. And what is more he stayed asleep throughout the whole interminable journey. And, as if that were not enough, she had to shake him as they approached Inching Round.

'It's over? Celia, how wonderful. Did you have a nice sleep too?'

'I read, thank you.'

'Well, every man to his taste. I get impatient in trains when I read.'

'You snored.'

He shook his head. 'No, Celia, no. I can bring a whole covey of witnesses to swear that I never snore.' He sat up reluctantly. 'From the violence of the motion I suspect that we are gradually drawing from dead slow to a stop. Do I prepare to be met, or do we make our own way home?'

'We walk.'

'We do? Who carries this wardrobe trunk we have with us?'

Celia laughed. 'Don't worry, dear. It's one of the traditions of the village that our porter Ted Mattock delivers all luggage in his own time on the railway company's barrow.'

'Ah tradition, and what's more, good old Ted.'

Ted was the sole occupant of the platform when they got out. He was replacing his watch with the comfortable assurance that this train at least was normally late. But the gentleman who alighted with Miss Celia shook him a little. He said familiar like, 'Good evening, Ted.'

Ted replied, 'Good evening, sir,' not knowing as he said later what else he could rightly have said.

'Take the luggage up on the barrow in the usual traditional way like a good chap, will you.'

'Good evening, Ted.' (If it hadn't been for Miss Celia I should have thought I was hearing things. Imagine knowing about my barrow away up in London like that. Things do get round, don't they?)

'Good evening, Miss Celia.'

'Everything under control?'

'Well, since you ask things have been happening, Miss. There's been a murder like.'

'A murder,' Celia laughed. 'You're pulling my leg.'

'Well, somebody hit old Miss Pewsey over the head with a blunt instrument, and she's no more. Some would call it murder, Miss.'

Celia stood stock still. Firth, too, was suddenly completely immobile, alert, listening.

'Miss Pewsey, murdered?'

'Yes, no doubt about it, Miss Celia.'

'But why . . . I mean it isn't possible!'

Celia felt Firth's hand under her arm. 'Murder is a strange thing, Celia. It happens and very seldom anybody is expecting it. When it happens you think first quietly and talk afterwards. Have a nice journey with the bags, Ted. Good night.' He guided her out into the roadway.

It was a still, clear night. They could hear the little train, making its dogged way to the next stop, the sounds

18

growing more remote as it moved on, making way for the smaller, more furtive sounds of the neighbourhood. It seemed to the girl that the friendly atmosphere she had always known had changed. The soft breeze seemed to be whispering secretively. For the first time in her life she was glad of companionship in the short overhung lane between the station and the village. It was ridiculous . . . Simply because somebody had died . . . no, somebody had been murdered. That was different; that meant that there was a murderer. Somebody came by stealth, entered without knocking, and then slipped away again, leaving behind them, death.

Firth said quietly: 'It seems that I might have saved myself a journey, doesn't it, Celia.'

'Why, what do you mean?'

'The mystery is solved.'

'You mean that . . .'

'When somebody is writing anonymous letters and somebody is murdered, it's not hard to guess who was the author of the anonymous letters, is it?'

'Miss Pewsey . . . Angela . . . I.'

'Are you surprised?'

Celia spoke as if the admission surprised her. 'No, no, I suppose I'm not really. She was rather a fearful old . . . Oh, but she's dead.'

'Yes. She underestimated one of her neighbours.'

'But why should it have been Miss Pewsey?'

'From the moment you heard you had no doubt in your own mind that this was connected in some way with the letters, had you, Celia?'

'No, it must be. It's the obvious thing. The atmosphere has been like that, but . . .'

'So that's that, isn't it.' He sounded relieved.

'But, Firth, who murdered her?'

'That, of course, is a job for the police. I hate to remind you, darling, but it was a job for them from the very beginning.'

'You think if I had gone to them, she would be alive still?'

He shook his head in the darkness. 'I should think a lady like Miss Pewsey would have been digging her own grave for some time. No doubt at the time she thought she was having fun. Is that the pub ahead?'

'Yes, would you like a drink?'

'Why not? We've solved our mystery, we might as well relax.'

2

IF Firth had come in alone to the 'Merry Harriers' he would have been treated as a stranger. When he came with Celia he was still a stranger, but one under good auspices. Roughly twenty patrons had a look at him, not blatantly, of course, but in each case it was a good look. He was a city man and he looked one, but there was nothing to be said against him for that. It was they that came from the city and tried to dress up like countrymen that nobody couldn't abide. Proper caricatures most of them.

The landlord of the 'Merry Harriers' was a small man, and when he wanted to say anything confidential he had to stand on tiptoe to lean over the counter. Celia introduced him to Firth . . . Thomas Tiptree.

'How do you do, sir.' His sharp little lined face broke into a smile. 'We're always pleased to meet a friend of Miss Sim's. Nice young gentlemen, every one of 'em.'

Firth smiled gently at Celia, as he pictured the procession of nice young men of whom he was the latest.

'It's nice to be one of such a goodly company. What shall we drink?'

Mr Tiptree brought their drinks and consented to join them with half a pint.

'You're crowded to-night,' Celia said.

'Yes, more than usual for a week night,' Tom replied. 'You been up to Town, Miss Celia?'

'For the day.'

'We've had a regular day down here.' Without seeming to listen, the other patrons were waiting for Tom to break the news. It was his place to, of course, being landlord.

'We had a fine day in London too,' Firth answered, seeming to miss the point, 'for a change.'

Tom addressed Celia again. 'You didn't hear the news then, Miss Celia?'

'Ted down at the station said something.'

The audience in the bar was disappointed. Something of the expectancy left their faces. They thought of Ted, strategically posted at the station, in a position to see everyone first.

'It was murder all right. Poor old Miss Angela Pewsey. I didn't have any cause to like her, as we all know. But murder . . .'

'Some wouldn't call it murder.' The voice came roughly, harshly from the group at the other end of the bar. Celia and Firth turned quickly. All the faces were blank. It was impossible to guess the owner of the voice.

Tom Tiptree said quickly: 'The sergeant calls it murder, anyway,' his voice sharpened. 'And it was murder, whether it was convenient for some or not.' He sipped his beer, holding his glass with three fingers and with the other one raised, appreciatively, landlord fashion. 'The sergeant has his own ideas on that.'

Celia gave a little gasp. 'He knows who did it?'

'Aye, Miss Celia . . . a tramp.'

'A tramp, a stranger of forbidding appearance has been seen in the neighbourhood?'

'What's that, sir?'

Firth laughed. 'I've got a silly habit of talking to myself. Do you think we might have the same again?' He lighted a cigarette for Celia and one himself. 'Is that what the sergeant thinks, Mr Tiptree?'

'That's what he says he thinks. He was quite set on it, it seemed to me.'

'Then all he has to do is find his tramp. It was quick work, wasn't it? That will be a great relief to everyone.'

'Some more than others.' Another voice spoke from the group and there was a soft murmur this time of agreement.

Tom Tiptree stuck to the tramp as if from a sense of obligation. 'There's plenty of tramps round here, this time of year; lots more, if you count the gypsies. Your change, thank you, sir.'

The door burst open and a man obviously in a hurry, habitually in a hurry, bustled to the bar.

'Good evening, Tom. Good evening, everybody. Why, hello, Celia, I thought you were in Town.'

'Hello, Eric. No, I came back this evening. Firth, this is Dr Eric Daw.'

Firth found himself shaking hands with a little man, full of vitality, and yet with an odd suggestion of exhaustion about his bearing, as if he were run down but kept running at full speed. A little man with a cheerful bedside manner who at the same time was too rushed to indulge in the niceties. His eyes shone with eagerness and yet they were bloodshot with weariness. Firth recognized him for what he was, a good general practitioner, without time to do justice to his practice.

'Won't you join us?'

'Thank you, can't stay to return it, I'm afraid. The usual please, Tom.' He flashed an almost apologetic smile at the landlord.

Tom had already poured out a large whisky and pushed it across the counter. He watched the doctor drink gratefully, and his expression was more like that of a benign doctor than the doctor's own. And the doctor, too, seemed to relax a little as the spirit took hold and soothed him. He seemed to realize that he was not in such a hurry after all.

'Whew, what a day.'

Celia smiled at him affectionately. 'They always are with you. You're tired?'

He nodded. 'Of course. To-day was the end.'

'Why to-day especially?'

He leaned towards her with mock drama. 'The murder, dear.'

'She was a patient of yours, wasn't she, Eric?'

He answered 'Yes,' and then not to be rude, 'She called me in at odd hours.' He laughed shortly. 'She didn't call me in to-day, however. That was the police.'

'You seem to be very much in demand, doctor,' Firth said.

Dr Daw laughed. 'Demand is a good word for it. When you have every minute taken up, a couple of hours given to the police means that you are a couple of hours late. I still have six calls to make.' He looked at his watch. 'Still, Celia, we don't often meet like this, shall we have the other half?' Already Tom Tiptree had reached for his empty glass and was holding it under the measure.

Celia shook her head. 'Firth will, I'm sure. The journey down from town must have worn him out.'

Firth smiled. 'I had a disturbed sleep. Perhaps I do need a little sustenance. Is the cause of the death a secret, doctor?'

He laughed. 'A secret, in Inching Round? You don't know us! Miss Pewsey was hit on the head with something heavy and hard.' The doctor gave the description almost with relish. 'Somebody stood behind her and she was struck down from the top note of a song. A folk song,' he laughed shortly, and then looked uncomfortable at his own outburst.

'So, the tramp we are looking for was powerful, stealthy, and no lover of folk songs.'

'A tramp?' The doctor caught himself up quickly. 'Oh yes, the sergeant did say something about a tramp. Well, the tramp that hit Miss Pewsey did so with every intention of hastening her from this world.' He raised his glass and said absently: 'Here's luck.'

'Did the job as if he hated her, in fact.'

The doctor looked towards Firth quickly and looked away again. 'Or was afraid of her.' He might have been speaking to himself.

'Yes, the effect can be the same, can't it?'

'Sometimes,' he looked at Firth thoughtfully. 'Are you here for a stay, Mr Prentice?'

Firth shook his head. 'Almost no time, I expect.'

Celia said quickly: 'Firth is the family solicitor ... I mean his father is. He's here on business. I call it business and pleasure, but you'd never get him to agree.'

'Oh, but I do,' he laughed. 'The business has almost faded from my mind already. Shall we push on, darling?'

The little doctor made a move as if to go with them, but it was half-hearted, and as they went out Firth noticed that he turned back to the bar again. Firth thought it would be a harsh judge who blamed him. In spite of the forced energy, the drooping shoulders spoke for themselves. He tucked Celia's arm comfortably under his own as they stepped out into the lane. She had not forgiven him entirely, but it was comforting to have him striding along at her side.

'This village is not what it used to be,' he said.

'Oh, since when? And how do you know?'

'Since this morning, darling. They are nice people, but they feel that they are confronted with nasty goings on. You realize, of course, Celia, that this business has only just begun.'

'But Firth, if they catch the tramp.'

'Do you believe in the tramp, Celia?'

'Why shouldn't I?' She sounded defiant. 'If the police think so ...'

'What is one police sergeant against so many? Even I, stranger that I am, could feel them disbelieving him. No dear, there's no tramp. There never is. The tramp is always a pious hope.'

'But, Firth, if it isn't a tramp,' her voice sank, 'it must be someone in the village ... one of us.'

'Yes, tiresome, isn't it.'

'But it's impossible.'

'Maybe. But you'd find it difficult to get Angela Mason Pewsey to agree with you.'

'But who could ... who would do such a thing?'

24

'That is what your sergeant will have to ask himself . . . when he has run out of tramps, that is.'

'But what will they do – the police, I mean. How will they find out?'

'I expect the anonymous letters will come to light first. You may be sure that you and Master Graham are not the only ones who've had them. They will collect them, and I suppose try to make up their minds which villager had the most provocation to commit murder.'

'I'm glad that I burned the one I had.'

'Why? Would you say that it offered enough inducement to make Graham a candidate?'

'I told you, he didn't see it, so he couldn't know what it said.'

'He couldn't be sure. On the other hand he might guess what it said.'

'You mean the things in the letter might be true? That's ridiculous!'

'Probably, but you can bet your life Miss Pewsey was murdered because what she wrote in one of her nice little letters happened to be the truth.'

'But how could she know these things?'

'How did she know about you?'

'It wasn't true about me. At least it was half true. I did go away for that week-end, but there were four of us. It was her innuendoes that were so sickening.'

'Don't get excited, Celia dear, innuendoes always are.' He added lightly: 'If you had gone away alone for that week-end, it would have been all the same to me. I don't know what causes it, but I have a quite childish faith in you.'

There was no particular reason why a few lightly spoken words should make her feel better about things, but they did.

Celia and Firth had reached the churchyard and were following the circular road that surrounded it. As they approached Angela Pewsey's cottage, Celia found herself moving closer to the churchyard wall on the other side of the lane. The blinds were drawn and no light was showing.

'That's her house.' In spite of herself, Celia's steps were quickening.

'So I guessed from the guard outside.'

Celia had not noticed Constable Wilks. But she saw him now, walking slowly up and down the path outside. She supposed it was usual, but it looked almost as if they expected death to pay a second call.

To Celia it seemed that the distance between Rooks Roost and her own house had never been so short, too short a distance from what had happened in the open daylight of this fine afternoon. Rooks Roost was beside the road, but Danescroft, where Celia and her mother lived, was approached by a curving drive, shadowy and secluded. Once again she was ridiculously glad that Firth was with her.

Celia had been wondering how her mother had been affected by the news. But she need not have worried. If somebody came along and murdered Angela Pewsey, no doubt they did so for reasons of their own, excellent ones, no doubt. This was an unorthodox view to take, but then Angela's mother was unorthodox in many things. But unorthodox be it understood in the nicest possible way. She was small, vague, and slightly deaf, and could, if need be, be almost totally deaf. Added to this, she was remarkably pretty, with golden hair and straight brows and grey eyes.

'Oh, there you are, Celia,' she said. 'Ted brought the bags along from the station, so I knew you'd come in. You've brought somebody with you, how delightful.'

'Mother, you know Firth Prentice, surely?'

'Of course.' Mrs Sim shook hands. 'How nice of you to come.' But she had obviously no idea who he was.

'He's the family solicitor, dear. You must know him. Anyway, his father.'

'Oh, of course, how is your father, Firth? Such a persistent man, about details, I mean, and so painstaking. But I'm sure that underneath it all he is as bored as I am. Does he still wear that extraordinary ribbon on his glasses?'

Firth smiled. 'I don't recall that he ever did wear one.'

'Of course not, how silly of me. That was Mr Hoover, wasn't it?'

As Firth had never heard of a Mr Hoover, he supposed she might or might not be right.

'Your father, of course,' she added, 'was the one who had the white piping on his waistcoat.'

She might have gone on, but Celia intervened. 'Firth has come on business, mother, something about the estate.'

'Poor boy, how dull for him. Never mind, he mustn't let it interfere with his holiday. Now run along up to your rooms, both of you. Dinner will be ready as soon as you come down. Please don't be long, Celia dear. You know where your room is, of course, Firth.'

'I'm afraid . . . '

Celia laughed. 'Now don't try to explain that you've never been here in your life, because that will be a waste of time. Come on, I'll show you the way.'

'Oh Celia,' her mother called. 'There is a letter for you from Graham.'

Celia halted abruptly. 'From Graham?'

'Yes, I'm sure it was from him. He called about an hour ago, when I was out, and left it.'

Celia found the letter on her dressing-table, with her name hastily scrawled on the envelope. The note itself was equally hurried.

Celia darling

I had to write to tell you what a fool I was the other day. It was really stupid and I'm more sorry than I can say. Please forgive me. I was upset by that beastly letter.

I've just heard of the murder in the village, so it doesn't need a detective to guess who wrote the note, does it? You can understand anyone feeling murderous in the circumstances. As soon as I heard I chucked that letter of mine in the fire, and I can tell you it was a weight off my mind to watch it burn. There is no point in you and me being mixed up in this business and I'm sure that the quicker we forget the whole thing the better. I'm sure you've destroyed the letter you had about me, and this one too, by the way, after you've read it.

27

You will forgive me, won't you, darling. Anyway, I'll be over to-morrow morning and I thought we might drive down to Larkhaven and lunch at the Sailing Club. So till then my love...

Graham

Celia folded the note and was about to tear it up. Then she decided that a safer thing would be to drop it in the dining-room fire. She slipped it into her bag. Graham was right, of course, there was no point in being involved with the police. It might be horrible.

3

WHEN she came out of the bedroom Celia found Firth idling at the head of the stairs. He smiled at her gently as she came up.

'Hello, did you have a nice letter?'

Celia coloured. 'Why, naturally.'

'So he has burned the horrid old anonymous letter and all is well again?'

She looked at him in astonishment. 'How did you ... what do you mean?'

'I knew he had, of course, hence the hurry to get in touch with you.'

'Don't be ridiculous, Firth.'

'Did he ever write in such a hurry before?'

She tried to laugh. 'I say, is that a cross-examination? You are behaving just like your father.'

'Yes, aren't I? Something tells me that the letter suggested that you let bygones be bygones, and forget everything, especially that anybody ever wrote to either of you and didn't sign their correct names.'

'Is that so silly?'

'That depends on who asks you to remember.'

'Or who asks you to forget.'

'Ah yes, of course.'

She turned to the stairs. 'Well, now you know.'

Celia led the way to the drawing-room and indicated the cocktail tray. 'Mix me one too. I shan't be long.' She went to the door.

'Going to destroy some more evidence?'

She stopped suddenly. 'Don't be ridiculous.'

'But, my dear, if you didn't burn the note, all your deceit might be brought to nothing. It wouldn't have been a bit in the tradition of conspiracy if the note hadn't ended with something like: "Burn this," would it?'

'Sometimes, you can be quite insufferable.'

'It must be the lawyer in me. I hate seeing good evidence going to waste. We may need that note one day.'

'You have ceased to be funny.' Celia went out and closed the door.

'Ah, there you are. And you are making a cocktail, isn't that sweet of you.' Mrs Sim smiled at him vaguely, and he was sure she was wondering who on earth he was. 'Is Celia down yet?'

'Yes, indeed. She left the room only a second ago.'

'Oh, of course, she went to the dining-room to burn Graham's letter, didn't she?'

His jaw dropped. 'She told you that?'

'Of course not.' She smiled at him. 'But she would, naturally. He must have been most disturbed to have written it at all, and then to bring it himself . . . murders can be most upsetting. Everyone feels so guilty. But I do hope Graham didn't do it; if he did I'm afraid even the local sergeant would be capable of pinning the guilt on him.'

'But he didn't, so we don't have to worry.'

'No, I must say that worrying does not help at all. In fact, it can be a definite handicap. The vicar is coming in for bridge, by the way.'

Firth could see no connexion between worry and the vicar's bridge, but he supposed there must be one. Celia came in and relieved him of the necessity of wondering what it was.

The vicar was one of those sound bridge players who hum and haw their way through a series of conservative bids to modest victories. Celia was good: Mrs Sim so startlingly brilliant that Firth could see only two alternatives: either she cheated, or had second sight. But the fact of the matter was that she concentrated on the game.

After one particularly brilliant game she looked up at Firth and smiled as if she guessed what he was thinking. 'I find it so much easier to be absentminded as a rule,' she said. 'Otherwise people do expect you to concentrate on so many things that aren't worth while. But really we are quite an intelligent family, as you'll discover after you are married to Celia.'

'Mother,' Celia's protest burst from her. 'How can you say such things.'

'Oh yes, of course, it's Graham Ward, isn't it? How tiresome I am. Let me see, vicar, it's your deal, isn't it?'

The game ended with Mrs Sim a considerable winner and the vicar a small one. Mrs Sim put her winnings on a corner of the mantelpiece and obviously forgot them at once. The vicar placed his carefully in his waistcoat pocket. Then he took out a neat little black notebook and recorded the date and the amount won. He looked at Firth half shyly, half roguishly and said: 'At the end of each year I give my bridge winnings to the church. I never can be sure whether I should be praised or blamed.' He gave a little self-conscious laugh. 'It really is such a foolish world, isn't it?' Yet Firth had the impression that the world he termed foolish was something very dear to him, his own small world, that clustered about his church. He was neat, trim, and precise, but when he said good night his handshake was warm and firm.

Mrs Sim came back from walking with the vicar to the door. 'What a nice little man he is,' she gave a brief sigh. 'I'm sure that if anything happened to him, he'd be quite incapable of taking care of himself.'

Celia laughed. 'But, dear, in a place like this, what possibly could happen to him?'

'But it did happen to Angela Pewsey.'

'Yes, of course.' Celia's voice had an odd note of surprise in it. 'So it did.'

'And Angela, one would have thought, was quite capable of taking care of herself.'

Celia turned to stare angrily at the fire. 'But not capable of minding her own business. If you want to know what I think . . . '

Mrs Sim interrupted with such gentle finality that Firth wanted to laugh. 'But we don't want to know, darling, not about Angela and not at this time of night. Firth has had a long and tiring day, haven't you, my dear?'

Celia snorted: 'He had a long and uninterrupted sleep, if that's the sort of thing that wears him out!'

'Yes,' he said. 'But that was hours ago, way back in the afternoon.'

'And to-morrow,' Mrs Sim said, 'he has the mystery to solve.'

Firth started. 'What's that?'

'Of course, it's all part of the anonymous letters and you did come down to see about those, didn't you?'

Firth looked in bewilderment from Celia to her mother. 'But who on earth told you that?'

She laughed. 'My dear boy, why should one have to be told things. I know, of course, that your father is much too sensible to send you down here just to talk about the estate.'

In a rather subdued voice Firth said: 'I suppose what you mean is that if I find out who knew that Angela was the anonymous letter writer, I'll know who killed her?'

'Oh, but I knew that.'

Celia gasped. 'You knew . . .?'

Mrs Sim gave a nod of annoyance. 'But I only realized it this morning. It was most stupid of me.'

'But, mother,' Celia was genuinely disturbed. 'But don't you see . . . '

'That the police will think I did it? Yes, I suppose they will – if I tell them. On the other hand, if I don't tell them

31

and they find out for themselves, they will be quite sure. And of course once Sergeant Porter is sure of anything he is quite positive. Happily at the moment he is preoccupied with tramps. Oh well, we will see what the morning brings.' She went vaguely towards the door. 'Good night, Celia dear. You won't keep Graham up, will you? I know what young love is, but it really is rather late. Good night, dear boy.'

She drifted out of the room and left them gaping like two handsome fishes.

Firth turned slowly to Celia. 'Did I once hear you suggest that your mother was not always aware of what was going on about her?'

'Yes, that's what I said.'

'I thought it was.'

'I seem to have been wrong.'

'Yes, that's how it seems to me, too.'

'Perhaps it's because she's interested,' she ended on a note of self-justification. 'After all, she did call you Graham.'

'Which would seem to imply that she is not interested in me, doesn't it?'

'Yes, but I mean it's more like her true form, so to speak.'

'You should know. She's your mother.'

'That's true, and she said I mustn't keep you up. You must be exhausted.'

'I am. It must be that young love your mother was talking about.'

'But that was when she thought you were Graham. So there's no excuse whatever for keeping *you* up.' She meant it too. At least at that moment she thought she did.

Firth was not so sure. He put one finger under her chin and tilted it up so that he could look into her eyes.

'Young love . . . Hum . . . well, there may be something to be said for it after all.' He kissed her lips and then turned and strolled away out of the room.

If anyone had asked Celia how she felt about all this, she might have said that he left her feeling like an angry jelly.

Firth reviewed his first impressions as he undressed. The

people he had met were an interesting lot ... nice **was** another word you could apply to them. Nice people in **a** nice quiet country village. One of them had brought about Angela Pewsey's end with almost indecent haste. No matter how nice they were, one of them had no doubt done it. Probably it was one he had still to meet.

He drew aside the curtains and leaned out of the window. To his surprise he saw that he was overlooking the church, and then he remembered that this was the back of the house. The church itself rose softly and mistily in the moonlight, and the old white tombstones stood out from the dark shadows of the trees. He picked up the quaint shapes of the housetops, whose eaves stood shoulder to shoulder as they ringed the churchyard. Angela Pewsey's cottage was almost touching the garden wall.

The murderer's cottage was where? Somebody under one of these roofs would be lying awake reliving the experience of taking a life. Perhaps they were hearing again the high note of that ridiculous song, the last one. Perhaps they were finding the memory horrible. Or was that to them perhaps the funny side, and were they chuckling? The village murderer was hard to visualize. It occurred to Firth that, at that moment, the murderer might be sleeping, secure at last after months of torment, sleeping dreamlessly perhaps, after endless wakeful nights. It was possible, anything was possible, even that Angela Pewsey had been bumped off by a maddened tramp.

4

I T would be unfair to Inching Round to say that its inhabitants enjoyed the aftermath of Angela Mason Pewsey. On the other hand, there was a background of excitement to the whole business that made quite a nice change. The tradesmen's carts took twice the time in making their rounds.

People in quite different social strata stopped and spoke to each other just like they do in wartime. Several little boys had fights. No one else would go so far as Ted Mattock and say the village was well rid of the old bitch, because Ted was an outspoken man whose views always did take him too far. But without a doubt there was a trace of buoyancy in the air.

Firth Prentice was not sharing in this buoyancy; being a stranger, he could not be expected to share in it. He was, in fact, feeling something of an ass. Two people at least were calmly assuming that he would let them know the name of the murderer of Angela Pewsey, a nasty-minded spinster whom yesterday he had never heard of. When they gave him fish for breakfast he had a horrid feeling that Celia's mother arranged this with a view to stimulating his brain.

But Celia's mother made no mention of this topic at breakfast. She seemed to have forgotten what he was there for and even asked Celia if she had arranged for him to visit any of the local beauty spots.

'No, mother,' Celia answered.

'Oh, well, I'm sure he's quite familiar with the same sort of thing elsewhere. I do think our English places of historic interest are apt to be repetitive, don't you . . .?' She looked in doubt for a second, and then added with a kind of triumph . . . 'Firth.'

'Birthplaces especially,' he said.

'Speaking of places of interest,' said Celia. 'What time do we start work?'

'Work?'

'That's it. Do criminal investigators keep office hours; or do they wait till they feel inspired?'

Mrs Sim said conversationally: 'Sergeant Porter was at work at seven-thirty. But then I imagine he was setting a good example to Constable Wilks.'

'On the other hand,' Firth said, 'he may have thought the best time to catch a tramp is before he gets up.'

'The papers,' Celia answered, 'say that the police have

34

thrown a net over the whole county, so I suppose you'll leave the tramp angle to them.'

Firth answered firmly. 'I'm going to leave all angles to them. I am going back to London.'

Celia looked startled. 'You can't mean that?'

'I most certainly do. What possible reason is there for staying here? I don't know these people. I didn't know the victim, and in a couple of hours the police would be regarding me as an interfering busybody.' He added emphatically: 'Angela Pewsey tried to interfere in other people's affairs and look where she ended up. I'm sorry, but I have work to do in London.'

Mrs Sim said gently: 'It's perfectly all right, my dear boy, you mustn't upset yourself at all. I spoke to your father this morning.'

His jaw dropped. 'You did what?'

'Yes, of course. I'm afraid he was rather irritable when I had him called, but when I told him we were in danger of being arrested, of course he said we must have a legal representative near us.'

Firth could only stare at her. 'You told him you were in danger of being arrested?'

'Well, dear, aren't we?'

'Of course not, it's ridiculous, why ...'

She smiled at him and shook her head. 'You really hadn't thought of it at all. But it's quite different when you do, you know.'

'But how could you possibly be in danger of arrest? ... People like you ...'

'My dear boy, you don't know people like me and Celia. I, for instance, would be the last person to stand by quietly and let Celia's life be wrecked by somebody like Angela Pewsey.'

This, of course, was true, but Firth's reaction was a feeling of frustrated rage. 'If you and Celia are going to have yourselves arrested for murder, I suppose there is nothing I can do to stop you. But I may tell you, Mrs Sim, it is no part of the duty of the accused to conduct his own prosecution.'

Mrs Sim threw back her head and laughed. 'You are an irritable boy. So like your father. There is one very odd thing about solicitors, they do loathe being told what is perfectly obvious to everyone else.'

In the distance a bell rang, and as is the habit with all country people nobody spoke. They sat waiting to find out who rang.

'It's the police, madam,' Mary's voice was filled with awe. Yesterday she would have said with a note of patronage: 'Sergeant Porter would like to have a word with you when it's convenient, madam.' But now, Sergeant Porter had become twice as large and ten times as imposing. He was a man after a murderer.

'Very well, send him in here please, Mary.'

There was an odd feeling of suspense. They could hear the murmur of Mary's voice and the slow squeak, squeak of Sergeant Porter's boots as they crossed the parquet floor of the hall. Sergeant Porter approached slowly as becomes a man of poise. Firth could almost feel the lines of his own face smoothing out into that dead expression which is so appropriate to proceedings in court.

Sergeant Porter was a big man, very big, which tended to make his head look smaller than it really was. His helmet had pressed the hair in a tight circle round his head, which made it seem smaller still. It grew and expanded as it descended to the eyes, the cheeks, and the jowls. It was a Toby jug sort of face without the joviality. The first joints on all his fingers were all fat and crowded like a row of thighs. None of this, of course, was the fault of Sergeant Porter. He was born that way. It seemed to him that the destiny that shaped him must have had the police force in mind, so he became a policeman.

He placed his helmet in the crook of his elbow, and said: 'Good morning, Mrs Sim. Good morning, Miss Sim. Good morning, sir, it's a fine morning, isn't it?'

They muttered what he seemed to take for agreement, and he continued: 'I'm sorry to trouble you so early, madam, but when it's in the way of duty, I know you'll understand my position.'

Mrs Sim answered for the house: 'Oh yes, indeed, Sergeant Porter. Do sit down, won't you?'

'Thank you' he said, moving to a straight-backed chair, at the same time shifting his helmet from elbow to knee.

None of this ponderous manoeuvring did anything to ease the tension. Firth was thinking that once the berthing operation was complete anything might happen.

Mrs Sim tried again: 'Won't you join us in a cup of coffee, Sergeant? It's not at all hot, I'm afraid.'

'No, thank you, madam, not at the moment, thank you.' It seemed to be a kind of reproof, but that again may have been just his way, and they may have been feeling over-sensitive. Mrs Sim said: 'Yes, of course,' rather quickly, as if she realized her mistake and there was another pause.

Then Celia in a hard bright voice said: 'Have your investigations led you to us, Sergeant?'

Mrs Sim placed one hand slowly over the other on her lap. Firth was suddenly as still as a pointer.

'Well,' said Sergeant Porter as if unaware of everything but his own timing. 'Well, you might put it that way, miss. I'm endeavouring to follow the movement of a certain individual in whom we are interested.'

'How interesting,' Mrs Sim said, without quite knowing why.

'I wonder if you saw anyone loitering or lurking about as you might say.'

A brighter man might have noticed that the atmosphere changed considerably. Mrs Sim unclasped her hands and touched her handkerchief to her lips. Celia lighted a cigarette and inhaled deeply. Firth said with a kind of sigh: 'The tramp!' But he recovered quickly and added: 'So this might be described as a routine inquiry, Sergeant?'

'I'm making inquiries in the neighbourhood. This is my twentieth call, sir.'

'I'm afraid I can't help you,' Celia said. 'I was in town all day. That's what you call an alibi, isn't it?'

'If you needed one, it would be, miss. And you, madam, were you in town?'

'No, I was in the village all day.'

'And you saw nobody?'

'Of course, I must have seen lots of people. But I must say I don't remember offhand who they were.'

'But you would remember anything suspicious?'

'Oh, I don't know about that. It might not seem suspicious.'

'But a tramp, you'd have noticed him, wouldn't you, Mrs Sim?'

'Well, really, I don't know. One so seldom sees one nowadays. I suppose they dress differently and one does notice them. But then of course everyone else is so shabby I expect a tramp would look quite well dressed. One almost never sees anyone well dressed now except, of course, Celia's fiancé.' She paused to smile at Firth. 'But then of course he is City, and I understand they get extra coupons because the Government expects them to look prosperous.'

Sergeant Porter returned doggedly to the business on hand. 'I'm sure you'd have noticed a tramp, madam. It would be someone you didn't know.'

'Someone I didn't know,' Mrs Sim devoted her mind to the events of the day before.

'Someone I didn't know. There was the vicar, of course.'

'But you know the vicar, madam.'

'Oh, quite well.'

'I was asking about strangers.'

'Yes, I know. The vicar must have had some sort of meeting. There were several cars. Miss Fitch and Miss Rankin went, but I don't recall a tramp. Have you asked the children, Sergeant? They are so good at these things.'

'They were in school, more's the pity.'

38

'I'd ask just the same, if I were you. They see everything.'

Sergeant Porter answered with a sort of desperation. 'Not a soul saw a single person go into Miss Pewsey's cottage.'

'But Mrs Tilling went in, because she found Angela.'

'But nobody saw her. I asked, just to check up on the time. It's my opinion there could have been fifty tramps and nobody would have seen a thing.' Sergeant Porter almost blushed at this outburst and endeavoured to rectify it with a retreat into officialdom. 'If you have nothing to add to what you have already said, madam, I will be getting along.'

'Oh, I'm so sorry I've been so unhelpful. I know how tiresome it is looking for someone. I remember when Celia was little she was continually disappearing. But I'm sure he'll turn up sooner or later, Sergeant.'

'He will, madam, never you fear.' The sergeant spoke with more confidence than he felt. Why couldn't someone have seen the tramp and come forward and admit it? His footsteps as he recrossed the parquet floor sounded a little slower and a little heavier. The group in the dining-room listened and felt sorry for Sergeant Porter. They were sorry because he looked hot and tired and because there was no tramp. But there was nothing to be done about it. It was one of those things that Sergeant Porter would have to find out for himself.

And this plodding, hot but purposeful Porter intended to do. He had given it as his dictum that a tramp had done this thing, and if it had been obvious from the start, it was obvious now. It was his flesh that was weakening, not his convictions.

He turned from the Sims' drive into the road and a few yards farther on he turned through the door of a walled garden. Only the upper floor window of Impy House could be seen from beyond the high wall that shut it in.

The garden itself was neat, formal, and strictly disciplined, and looked as if it might be slightly cowed by its master.

The house itself was Georgian, simple, honest and charming.

Sergeant Porter braced himself as he approached the door. He knew Major George Torrens would resent this call. But then he knew also that Major Torrens resented most things, particularly those over which he had no control, or didn't understand. He was proud to say that he could tell the difference between black and white. He had come to Inching Round ten years ago, apparently to retire from the army, and aggressively associated himself with local affairs. He bore down heavily on such organizations as seemed to merit his support, and in due course became secretary of the local Conservatives and the Hunt. The back of his neck was thick. His face was pitted and red, his eyes protruded. His ginger moustache was thrust forward as if his tongue were kept under his upper lip.

Sergeant Porter asked to see Major Torrens, and the maid hesitated and then went off as if she refused to be held responsible.

'What does he want?' Sergeant Porter could hear the loud and locally famous voice. 'Well, why the devil didn't you ask him? What's he mean coming round here at this time in the morning? No, no, never mind, I'll go and see what he wants myself.'

Major Torrens appeared brushing the crumbs from his moustache with a napkin. He was wearing a shooting coat that seemed to Sergeant Porter to be mainly pleats, pockets and leather. He wore gaiters that came half-way up to his knees.

'Hum,' he said mildly. 'Come in, Sergeant; inexcusable leaving you out there in the sun, come in.' He led the way into his study.

'I hope I'm not keeping you from your breakfast, Major.'

'No, no, finished long ago. Drinking cold coffee, wasting my time over *The Times*. What's the trouble?'

'It's this murder ...'

'God damn it, don't tell me you still don't know who did it?'

40

The Sergeant tried to be funny. 'Don't tell me that *you* do, now, Major?'

'Suppose I did? I wouldn't tell you if I did know.'

'You don't want me to take you seriously, I'm sure.'

'God damn it, man, why shouldn't I want you to take it seriously? I don't give a damn who killed Angela Pewsey... Except that I'd rather like to shake hands with the feller.'

'Murder is murder, none the less, sir.'

'"Murder is murder," poppycock! Do you mean to tell me it's doing a useful service to find and hang the man that rid the world of that caterwauling old bitch down the road?'

The Sergeant was genuinely shocked. You simply did not talk about dead people like that; and especially about people who had been murdered in cold blood.

'Now, now, Major, that's no way to talk.'

'My dear chap, you didn't know the woman.'

'I know she was the innocent victim of a cowardly attack.'

'How do you know she was innocent?'

'Everybody is innocent till it is proved to the contrary,' said Sergeant Porter virtuously.

Major Torrens treated this piece of nonsense with the contempt it merited. 'She was a born trouble-maker. Do you know what she asked me to do once?'

'No, sir,' admitted Porter reluctantly.

'Wanted me to take part in one of her damned folk dance festivals.'

The Sergeant accepted this statement solemnly and then for no obvious reason he began to laugh. He gave his thigh a slap that would have broken a weaker man's leg and literally roared. Major Torrens sat looking at him with undisguised astonishment.

Sergeant Porter knew that he was being undignified but he couldn't help it. Every time he tried to pull himself together he had a fresh vision of Major Torrens folk dancing in a home-made costume.

'For God's sake,' said Major Torrens at last, 'shut up.'

That cured him, especially as Major Torrens added: 'I

would have expected a man investigating a murder at least to have tried to be serious about it.'

Sergeant Porter accepted the rebuke as no more than deserved. If that were possible after his recent exhibition, he coloured a deeper red.

'Yes, sir,' he said, 'there are one or two questions I would like to ask.'

'Then for God's sake get on with them.' Major Torrens was not a man who easily forgot being laughed at.

The Sergeant steadied himself by making a slow study of his notebook.

'I want to know first,' he said, 'if during the course of yesterday you met with, or heard of any suspicious characters.'

'Suspicious characters? What do you mean?'

'What I said, sir. Any character that aroused your suspicions.'

'There are one or two that always arouse my suspicions. I can't say that I saw them yesterday. What time yesterday?'

'Well, at any time during the day. I can narrow it down later.'

'No.'

'You mean you didn't.'

'That's what I said. No.'

'Were you out and about at all, sir?'

'What do you mean, was I out and about? I don't want to tell you how to do your own job, but if you want facts for the love of God ask questions that will produce them.'

'Right,' said the Sergeant grimly. 'Did you leave the house yesterday?'

'Yes.'

'Where did you go?'

'Into the garden.' The Major was inclined to sit back and regard that answer with some satisfaction, but the Sergeant gave him no time.

'Where else?'

'What do you mean, where else?'

'Where else did you go?'

'I also went to the stable, and the chicken-house and the orchard and the garage and the lavatory . . . anything else?'

But Sergeant Porter was on top now. Sneers and blustering were right up his street. Year in and year out he encountered them from petty thieves, wife beaters, rogues, vagabonds and motorists. He wrote it all down in his book and it was no longer abuse but evidence. Major Torrens was giving an account of his movements and he was not liking it.

'Yes?' said the Sergeant blandly.

'Yes, what, man? Yes, what?'

'Yes, what next, Major. Where else did you go?'

'Haven't I told you?'

'Did you leave the grounds?'

'Of course I left the grounds.'

'Where did you go?'

'Listen, is this the third degree? If it is I won't put up with it.'

'You are not obliged to answer my questions, Major Torrens.'

'And if I don't, you'll run to whoever you do run to and tell them that I obstructed your inquiries.' Then he said violently: 'All right, for heaven's sake get on with it, man.'

'You were about to tell me where you went.'

'I went into town and called at my bank. I went to the Conservative Club and looked at the correspondence and had a drink and came home to lunch. And I stayed at home.'

'And during that time you saw nothing to arouse your suspicions?'

'Damn it, man, what sort of suspicions? I've told you I'm suspicious of hundreds of people, including the whole of the present Government and all their damn fool supporters.'

'I mean,' said the Sergeant, who thought he had a better chance of an increase of pay from the Socialists, 'I mean suspicious with regard to the matter in hand. I am looking for somebody who might look like a tramp.'

43

'My God, do you mean to tell me that you are going to try and pin this on a tramp?'

'It's my belief,' said Sergeant Porter heavily, 'that this crime was committed by a stranger.'

'And I tell you you're wasting your time. Whoever killed that old singing snake had known and hated her for years. Somebody quiet, somebody respectable, somebody who did it once and won't do it again.' He stood up. 'And I for one hope you never find out who it is.'

Sergeant Porter rose. 'And now, sir, if you don't mind, I'd like a word with the servants.'

The Major looked at him in surprise. 'The servants?'

'That's it,' he smiled judiciously. 'Servants have eyes as well as their masters. And often enough they're more curious as to what goes on about them.'

'I have only two servants in this house, Watson and his wife. They can't help you.'

'I'd like to find that out for myself, sir, if you'd be so good as to let me see them.'

'Watson and his wife were not in the village yesterday. They spent the day in Tonbridge with his sister. They caught the first bus in the morning and got the last one back at night.' He fixed the sergeant with a protruding eye. 'Would you care to verify that or are you prepared to take my word for it?'

The sergeant picked up his hat. 'If you say they were out of the village for the day, sir, I have no reason to doubt your word.' He said good morning and went stolidly down the path and out into the road, hunting still for the elusive somebody who had seen the suspicious character.

5

THAT other unwilling sleuth, Firth Prentice, strolled into the churchyard and sat on the tomb of some departed stalwart of Inching Round. It was very pleasant, shaded from the sun, fanned by the gentlest of breezes. Somewhere not very far away a hen was announcing the advent of an egg, at greater distance a tractor was fussing over some ploughing.

He could, of course, have stayed indoors, but he could not escape the feeling that Mrs Sim expected him to be up and doing. It was comforting to him that the tombstone was out of sight of the house. He fell to wondering about the resident over whose remains he was now seated. There was nothing to be gathered from the inscription because time had obliterated it. And then he thought that pretty soon Angela Pewsey would be having a tomb of her own. He wondered idly what they would write on it. 'Loved and Respected' or just simply 'Bumped Off'. What did one remember about women like Angela Pewsey, the unloved ones, who peered and pried and raked over the dead past; who fawned and hated and who hated with a smile? Perhaps it was better not to write anything on her tomb, except simply: 'Departed this Life' and the date, and let her neighbours forget her with gratitude. His mind hovered about the circumstances of the death, but he was reluctant to come to grips with the affair. It was too unpleasant, too close to people who had excited his respect. That policeman, smouldering in his tight serge uniform, was looking for a tramp. Firth was simply not looking.

A small boy hopped past on one leg, kicking a tennis ball. This might have seemed an absorbing occupation, but it was not. The boy was interested in Firth. He actually hopped back and forth several times before he essayed the kick that landed the ball at the stranger's feet.

'Hello,' Firth said.

'Hello,' said the small boy. 'My sister's got chicken-pox. Ten spots.'

'Interesting.'

'I can't go to school, but I play with boys that's had it.'

'Had what?'

45

'Chicken-pox. I can play with them and they can't get it no more. Old Miss Pewsey had a hole in her head bigger than this fist.'

'How do you know?'

'I seen it.'

'No you didn't.'

'Well, Jackie Day did.'

'How?'

'He got up that tree over there and he could look right into the room. Blood too.'

'Blood?'

'That's right. Constable Wilks got some on his boots. We saw it.'

'No you didn't.'

'Well anyway, Jackie Day, he seen it.'

'What Jackie Day seen ain't evidence,' Firth answered.

The small boy looked at Firth defiantly. 'I seen him and he told me he seen it. Blood. My name is Alfie Spiers.'

'Who cares?'

'I'm waiting for Jackie Day now.'

'I hope he doesn't delay you,' Firth said. 'Or perhaps you'd like to wait somewhere else?'

'It's all right.'

The little boy sat beside Firth and took off one of his shoes. 'You see that blister?'

Firth eyed it with reluctance. 'Yes, now that you point it out, I can; miserable little one, if you ask me.'

'I bet you don't know where I got it though.'

'I don't care either.'

'I got it from Old Pewsey.'

Firth stared at him. 'You got it from Miss Pewsey?'

'That's right. I got it from her old Maypole dance. We were practising for the fête. We went round and round and I got a blister.' He slipped his foot back into his shoe and sang: 'Pewsey's dead with a hole in her head, hole in her head, hole in her head. Pewsey's dead with a hole in her head on a cold and frosty morning.'

46

'Little boy.' Firth spoke so loudly and emphatically that he caught the little boy's attention. 'Shut up.'

The little boy picked up the ball and began bouncing it on the gravestone, and Firth thought how maddening it must be for whoever was underneath it. At the same time he could see Alfie Spiers' lips moving, and they were obviously forming the words: 'Pewsey's dead with a hole in her head,' thereby establishing the liberty of the subject, without interfering with the right of his neighbour. Firth would have preferred him to say it out loud.

A rather desperate situation was relieved by the arrival of Jackie Day. Jackie was a thin freckled young boy, obviously very agile. He had untidy yellow hair and sharp blue eyes.

He stopped, lifted up his sweater, underneath which, astonishingly enough, was a waistcoat. He obviously regarded this garment as a very worthwhile piece of attire. Every pocket was put to some use or other. After examining the contents of a bottom left, he turned his attention to a bottom right. From this he brought out a piece of paper, which he unfolded and examined with care.

'What's that you got?' asked Alfie as he was expected to do.

'Evidence.' He was refolding it when Firth held out his hand. 'Let me see.'

Jackie hesitated, then handed the paper over to Firth. It was the lower half of a torn sheet written over in a back sloping long hand. Firth turned it over.

'Why is it evidence?' he asked distastefully.

'Because it was written by Pewsey,' said Jackie Day at once.

'I see.'

Firth had the indescribable feeling that this business of Angela Pewsey was being pressed on him by a malign fate. All he wanted to do was to sit in the sun, forget Angela Pewsey, and in due course go back to London.

'The trouble with you two is that you have morbid imaginations.'

47

'What are those?' Jackie asked as if he might be interested.
'In other words, you should mind your own businesses.'
'What does it say on the piece of paper, please, Mister?'
In spite of himself, Firth smoothed out the creased paper and read:

. . . Been one of my really best days. Such fun. Of course when I told him what I knew I laughed gaily as if we were sharing a joke. But the really funny thing was his face, which was absolutely like death. And of course he couldn't speak at all. I really did laugh . . . . It *is* thrilling to feel that you have power over people's lives. I mean really the kind that destroys . . . To-day for the first time I felt safe to deliver one of my shafts actually in person, and really watch the reaction. Of course I had often imagined what it would be like when I sent my little secret missives out. But to-day I was actually there . . . I saw his face! He offered me money. Which really made me laugh joyously. It's the really wonderful sense of power . . .

Somewhere on another page Angela Pewsey's revelations continued. Firth turned over the fragment of paper in his hand. Somebody had killed her and here perhaps Angela Pewsey was writing about her murderer. Her murderer? It seemed to Firth that he could hear Angela Pewsey's high-pitched laugh.

He hated Angela Pewsey. The idea that in death she could impose on him like this was an affront. He wanted nothing to do with Angela Pewsey. He wanted to sit in the sun and leave the wretched female corpse to Sergeant Porter and his tramp.

But the two little boys were watching him, with that steady intentness that children have. He wanted to roll the wretched Pewsey manuscript into a ball and throw it away. He could not do that, and he could not give it back to the small boys. When a boy brings a piece of vital evidence to a responsible adult, that adult does not throw it away or even give it back to the boy.

He folded the torn sheet of paper and put it in his wallet. 'Thank you,' he said with all the finality he could muster.

He lighted a cigarette, waved the match out, took a deep puff and looked up to find the situation unchanged. The two little boys were still looking at him.

'Well,' he said. 'Don't let me keep you.'

It is, of course, very effective to say that sort of thing to an adult. Children are not impressed. These two merely waited.

Firth began to think that a village that could produce these two and Angela Pewsey must be sinister in its own right. It was almost a relief to him when Jackie Day decided to break the silence.

'Are you going to find out the murderer?'

'I am not. Sergeant Porter is going to find the murderer.'

'No, he ain't.'

'Who says so?'

'My dad.'

'What does your dad know about it?'

Jackie laughed. 'He knows about Sergeant Porter.'

'I see, so your dad has been mixed up with the police, has he?'

'No, but he should have been if it hadn't been for Sergeant Porter. He locked up a gypsy instead of my dad.'

'Well, he should be grateful to Sergeant Porter.'

'The gypsy ain't grateful. He says he's going to cut out Sergeant Porter's heart. The sergeant's gone to look for a tramp now.'

'Don't tell me,' said Firth, 'that it was your dad again.'

'What, that done in Miss Pewsey?'

'Yes, you seem a bloodthirsty lot.'

'No.' Jackie denied it with some reluctance. 'My dad couldn't have done it. He was watching the coal 'opper at the brickworks.' He added in the terms of one who has reserved judgement: 'My dad says you're a detective.'

Firth threw his cigarette angrily to the ground. 'You tell your dad that I am nothing of the kind.'

'He saw you in the pub last night and he told my mum how you'd been brought down about the letters old Pewsey used to write.'

Firth opened his mouth, closed it, and opened it again.
'Letters?'

'That's right. She wrote and told everyone what they done. That's why she got her head bashed in.'

'I see. I wonder why you and your dad haven't told all this to the police.'

'My dad won't go near the police. It's asking for trouble, he says.'

'But the same inhibition would not necessarily apply to you.'

'What?'

'There's no reason why you shouldn't go to the police.'

'I've given the paper to you. Alfie and me's going to help you.'

'Help me to do what?'

'Detect. Alfie and me knows everything that goes on, everything, don't we, Alfie?'

'Yes, everything. We knew all about the big hole in Pewsey's head, didn't we, Jackie?'

'I seen it from the tree. I was as close as close and no one didn't see me. There was a fly . . . '

'Listen.' The violence of Firth's interruption startled even himself. He modified it as he continued: 'I don't want to know anything of the appearance of the late Miss Pewsey's remains. I don't want any help in tracking down her murderer, because I am not going to track him down. I simply want to be left alone. Good-bye.'

'But you'll give the police the paper, won't you, sir?'

'You may be sure that I shall place the paper in the hands of the police.'

'But that's nothing,' Alfie said. 'We seen Miss Pewsey sneaking out of Major Torrens' back door.'

'Well, why didn't you tell the police?'

'I told my dad,' Jackie said. 'And he give me one on the ear and told me to keep my nose out of other people's business. But he laughed too.'

'He would.'

'From the way dad laughed he must have thought the Major and Miss Pewsey was canoodlin', but the Major wasn't there and Miss Pewsey was tiptoeing and looked pleased.'

'Did you tell your dad that too?'

'No, because he seemed to like to think of the Major and Miss Pewsey canoodlin', so I didn't tell him.'

'We know lots and lots more,' Alfie said, eager not to lose grip of their audience. 'Lots and lots.' And he looked at Jackie in the confident hope of further revelations.

'Miss Pewsey had some papers in her hand when she come out of Major Torrens'. Most always she had papers with her.'

With painful reluctance Firth put his first real question.

'On what day was this?'

'Thursday last week,' Alfie said quickly. 'It was on the first day I had to stop home from school.' A good witness, prompt, sure of his facts.

'Probably,' he said, 'Miss Pewsey was collecting money for the women's institute or something.'

'Well, this was at seven in the morning.'

'Well,' he said angrily. 'No doubt she wanted to catch him before he went to work.'

'He never went to work, sir.'

'All right then, to London.'

'He went to London the night before. Alfie and me saw Miss Pewsey say good-bye to him when they met near the station. She said: 'Have a nice time in Town.'

'Well, what if she did? Miss Pewsey may have gone to call on his servants.'

'They always go away to Tonbridge on Wednesday nights and have the next day off. And the Major he goes up regular on Wednesday nights. Dad says he stays at his club ... anyway, that's his story dad says, and laughs.'

Firth was not laughing. He was unreasonably angry. Here, without the slightest inconvenience to himself, there was placed in his hands information of a vital character, supported by facts and corroborated by a witness. He was

51

angry because he felt himself being propelled into something he wanted to avoid.

They were still standing before him waiting for his next question, ready to answer any challenge to their facts.

'You and your immediate associates know such an awful lot about this,' he said. 'Why not tell me who murdered Miss Angela Pewsey and have done with it?'

'We can't do that,' Jackie said.

'No,' said Alfie.

'No, why this access of modesty? Why can't you tell me who murdered her?'

'We don't know.'

'But surely you have some idea?'

They shook their heads and for the first time they seemed to lose some of their confidence. They looked, in fact, like two small boys, suddenly shy.

For the first time since he had made contact with them, Firth felt a touch of sympathy.

'Now you two run off and don't bother your heads about this at all.'

Jackie looked up. 'I'm sorry we didn't see who done the murder, Mister. Dad says we mustn't say we know unless we actually seen it.'

His anger returned. 'Oh, so you do know who did it?'

'We mustn't say.' There was a pause and Jackie said: 'You aren't going to give the paper to Sergeant Porter, are you, sir?'

'Of course I am.'

'I mean not just yet you ain't . . . Not till Alfie and me have done some more detecting, are you? All you have to do is to just sit here quiet in the sun and we'll do all the work.'

'I see. And did your dad tell you that too?'

'No,' Jackie answered. 'My dad said give you the paper and let nature take its course. He said if you passed it on to Sergeant Porter you wouldn't be fit to investigate this here murder, anyway.'

'You tell him the place for that paper is in the hands of the police.' But he knew now that he was not going to put it there . . . at least not for a little while.

6

GRAHAM WARD drove towards Inching Round and the state of his mind was confused.

Angela Pewsey was dead, stone dead. She wouldn't write any more letters. She wouldn't constitute again that menace that had seemed to blur the future and possess the past. All that menace in old Angela Mason Pewsey; it was difficult now to credit it. Angela Pewsey, trilling and spinning in her Olde Worlde cottage, a twentieth-century witch. A few centuries ago they would have got rid of her by ceremonial burning. The more modern victim of her sorcery had walked into the cottage and under the clatter of spinning and song had hit her a crack with a blunt instrument. The results were the same, and in Angela's case they were satisfactory to Graham Ward. He might have said that from his point of view the outcome was the only possible one.

As he drove, Graham whistled through his teeth. They showed white between his parted lips. They looked strong, like everything else about him, about his square, good-looking face, with its rather sullen droop, about his great shoulders and long limbs. You felt that later on he might become a little pompous like a number of other good men. You felt that his vanity would be hurt before his body. This dark, slightly sullen young giant would find it hard to face humiliation.

Graham had an Achilles heel and Angela Pewsey had located it, which, had she but known it, was a dangerous thing to do. His face turned dark as he faced again the realization that she had written to Celia. Written what? Celia had torn up the letter and thrown it into the fire, but how much of it had she read, and what had there been to read? Celia would put it out of her mind. She would decide that to remember anything that was written in an anonymous letter would be unworthy of her. But would she be able to avoid remembering? It was easy enough to use words like 'Oh, let's forget the whole thing.' But whoever did forget?

She was dead, but if it all came out it would be like Angela Pewsey's accusing voice speaking from the grave.

Whatever Graham had been thinking on the drive over he was cheerful enough when he arrived. Too cheerful, according to Firth's judgement, and not quite in character. None the less, as he watched Graham talking to Celia the depressing thought kept recurring to him. 'Just the type . . . Just the type.' And he was not thinking that Graham was just the type to commit a murder. Oh well, he hadn't come down here on a love mission, so why worry.

He was not awfully keen to go down to the sea for lunch, but they insisted. Celia, it seemed to him, was particularly anxious for him to make the trip, but he was not convinced that that had anything to do with his personal charms. She didn't want to have another heart-to-heart talk with Graham . . . not just yet at any rate. Celia, dear girl, was probably still too sore about the recent past.

It was Graham who put the topic of Angela back into circulation. They were sipping pre-lunch cocktails at the local hotel, and he said after a brief silence, 'They tell me she was singing.'

Celia looked at him in surprise. 'Who was?'

Graham in his turn was also surprised. 'Why, Angela Pewsey.'

'She was, I understand, but we weren't talking about Angela Pewsey. I thought we were trying to forget her for a bit.'

'But Prentice here is trying to find out who killed her, isn't he?'

Firth said: 'No, the police.'

And Celia said in exasperation: 'Don't be tiresome, Firth. We know you are.'

Firth answered her patiently. 'All the investigating I have done is through the gory eyes of two little boys. All I've learned is that Pewsey had a ruddy great hole in her head, which I don't believe for a moment, and that Constable Wilks put his foot in her blood. One hardly knows what to believe, does one?'

'I wish you wouldn't act the fool,' Celia said. 'And tell me what did you find out . . . that is if we have to talk about it at all.'

'We don't,' Firth said quickly.

'The idea being,' Graham interrupted, 'to put our heads in the sand and wait for the police to come and hawk one of us off to the cooler.'

'Well,' Firth answered. 'Presuming, as you say, that one of you is guilty, what else do you expect?'

'It's an outrage that anyone should be arrested on her account. Whoever killed Angela Pewsey was a public benefactor.'

Firth looked at him mildly. 'It's very difficult to find justification for a murderer. And very difficult indeed when the murder is planned.'

'But, Firth,' Celia said, 'you just didn't know Angela Pewsey.'

'I'm beginning to know her better. To-day I was reading a piece of her autobiography.'

Silence seemed literally to fall into the space between them. Firth waited. He saw Graham's hand, which had been reaching out for his glass, come back slowly and rise to press against his mouth.

But when Graham did speak his voice was almost gentle.

'You mean she left something in writing?'

'I should say she left a great deal.'

'Probably a book,' Celia said. 'She was just the sort of frustrated old thing who would write a book. Nobody would publish it, of course. Probably she was going to call it *Flowers from a Village Garden.*'

Firth shook his head. 'No, this wasn't that kind of writing. It wasn't for publication.'

'You mean,' Graham said, 'she kept a diary, or some other such sort of rot?'

'Some other such thing.'

Graham said quickly, almost eagerly: 'But where is it, what have you done with it?'

Firth shook his head. 'Nothing. I haven't seen it, and I haven't the least idea where it is now.'

'If you haven't seen it, how do you know it exists?'

'I don't.'

Celia said impatiently: 'Oh, darling, I do wish you would tell us what you *do* know instead of continually harping on what you don't.'

'Yes,' Graham said, with a kind of angry conviction. 'How can you assume the existence of something you haven't seen?'

'I have to assume the existence of lots of things I've never seen. Otherwise I'm afraid my existence would be most prescribed. I'm convinced that there is or was a diary kept by Angela Pewsey.'

'How do you know?'

'I read a page that had been torn from it.'

'Firth,' Celia gasped. 'Wherever did you find it ... when?'

'I did not find it. Please don't think I have been working on this case, Celia. I have not been and will not be. It was forced on me, this morning.'

'But how do you know it was Angela Pewsey's writing? You don't know it. Why, you said so yourself.'

'No,' he said patiently. 'I don't know the writing. I only know the things she used to write about.' He added gently: 'There wouldn't be another like her in the same village.'

Graham said stubbornly: 'But why should it be part of a diary, why not just a random note?'

'Because it was in a style that diary writers develop . . . taking themselves into their own confidence as it were.'

Graham spoke again; this time he gave the impression that he was asking because he had to know and yet was reluctant to ask.

'You said that only Angela could have written what you read.'

Firth nodded. 'That is true.'

'Why, what did she write? Was it . . . well something to do with her murder?'

Firth smiled briefly. 'It could have been, but presumably Miss Pewsey was not aware of it at the time. She hadn't known then that her murder was about to take place.'

Once again Celia interrupted impatiently. 'But, Firth dear, what did it *say*?'

He moved his hand towards the pocket where his wallet was, but changed his mind.

'It recorded the interview with a man. It recorded the great pleasure the interview accorded to Miss Pewsey. The pleasure was inspired by the painful impression she was able to make on the other party, the evidence of her power over another human being. She laughed.'

'The fiend,' Graham said. 'The old fiend.' His voice was low, but the venom in it brought a protest from Celia.

'Graham!'

'Why not say it? Why pretend? She was a monster and we all have good reason for knowing it. Of course she was well out of the way.'

'As a statement to the police,' Firth said gently, 'that would sound almost like a confession.'

Graham's face darkened and he swung round in his chair.

'You aren't accusing me by any chance, are you?'

'No,' Firth said. 'But presumably the police are looking for those with a reason and the will to get rid of the old girl. This is not the time for idle chatter about how glad you are that she's gone.'

'I take it,' Graham said after a pause, 'that you had the

good sense to get rid of that piece of nonsense from her diary.'

'In my profession,' Firth answered, 'we are taught never to "get rid" of papers that come into our possession. It becomes almost a religion.'

'What are you going to do with it?'

'I should have handed it to the police.'

'You aren't sorry for the poor devil it was referring to?'

'Not if he killed her.'

'Well, I am.' He added quickly: 'And I don't give a damn whether he killed her or not! Thank God I'm not bound by the totem worship of the legal profession.'

'Graham,' Celia said mildly, 'will you stop being an ass?'

'Oh,' Firth laughed. 'I imagine he's right in a way.'

'Of course I'm right. Presumably the name of the man was not mentioned in this precious document of yours?'

'No, there were no names.'

'Well, what possible use can it be, handing it over to the police? Start them raking over the past of *anyone*.'

'I seem to have heard something like that before. To people with a past everything must look like a rake.'

Again the angry flush mounted to Graham's temples.

'Just what do you mean by that?'

Firth was impatient now. 'Oh, for heaven's sake what does it matter what I think? All this business is no concern of mine whatever.'

Suddenly without warning Celia laughed. 'That's what you think, chum. Don't tell me you've forgotten what mother said at breakfast!'

'I tell you once more, Celia, I'm not interested in what your mother said at breakfast.'

'But surely, darling, from your clients' point of view you must be glad that the other person mentioned in the Pewsey document was a man.'

Graham was looking at her curiously. 'Is he acting for you and your mother in this business?'

She laughed again. 'Yes, much against his will, and in spite of what he says, he is.'

But Graham was not laughing; he was thinking over what she had told him.

'In that case,' he said presently, 'if he is looking after your interests, perhaps it might be a good idea if he looked after mine as well.'

'No.' Firth's reaction was brief and emphatic. 'I'm sorry, but I can't.'

'Why not? You're not afraid you'll have a murderer on your hands, are you?'

'I'm not afraid of anything. I've simply had more to do with this case than I care to have.'

'I'm not blaming you,' Graham said after a pause. 'I can see that you can't act in the best interests of everybody.'

'Thanks.'

He went on reasonably: 'Presumably because there is a man mentioned in that document, it is in the interests of your women clients that you are handing it over to the police. I'm sorry I was so stupid about it.'

Once again Firth was conscious of a rising anger. 'I feel there is no need to take any action whatever in the interests of my women clients. They are not menaced.'

'Of course not, old boy. But it would be only a reasonable precaution.'

'Listen,' Firth said patiently. 'This has nothing to do with my clients or anybody else; but hasn't it occurred to you that when they get the torn piece of paper they'll want to find the diary itself?'

'Oh,' Celia's hand flew in a kind of panic to her lips. 'Do you suppose that it will be all written down there?'

'Presumably. One gathers from the literary style that writing it all down was part of the fun.'

'Names as well.' Graham spoke as if he was making a reluctant admission.

'I should expect so. Some diarists of this type have a little habit of referring to others by their initials, or little symbols, or such references as the "Old Crawley Cat". But it's ridiculously easy to find out to whom they are referring. This is because they themselves are compromising. They don't want to be quite open, and yet they like to think the references are so cunning that they could refer to no one else.'

'But, Firth, where is the diary?' Celia was in no doubt now that it did exist, or had existed.

He shook his head. 'I haven't the least idea.'

'But where did the page come from?'

'Two small boys. Presumably they found it somewhere. I can't imagine them stealing it. I would put nothing past them, but I don't think they did that.'

'In that case,' Graham said, 'I suppose you've decided that someone else tore out the page?'

'I don't even say that. She may have torn it out herself ... not satisfied with the literary style, or thought it was too compromising to leave in the diary. Once having enjoyed the thrill of putting her feelings in writing she may have decided to get rid of it. I don't know. Without knowing her, I can't say how she'd act.'

'She'd act in the way calculated to do the most harm. You can be sure of that,' Graham said. 'Even now she is dead she seems capable of hunting us.'

'Yes,' Firth said. 'Killing her doesn't seem to have done. the trick.'

'I wonder,' Celia said, 'if the police have found the diary?'

Firth shook his head. 'If they had, I don't imagine Sergeant Porter would be wearing himself out in a hunt for the elusive tramp.'

'I hope to God he finds him,' Graham said. 'Why shouldn't there be a tramp?'

Firth sighed. 'Why indeed? Sergeant Porter believes there is presumably, but of course he is in a hopeless minority.'

To Celia this was an obvious diversion.

'If they didn't find the diary,' she said, 'it must still be in the house.'

'Unless the murderer took it.'

Graham shook his head. 'He wouldn't want to be seen carrying a big black book like that about with him ...' He stopped abruptly, appalled by what he had said.

'Graham,' Celia said in a strange voice. 'You've seen it?'

'Well, suppose I have?' He tried to cover his mistake by a burst of anger. 'I saw her writing in a book, if that's a crime.'

'But when? I didn't know you'd even been to the cottage.'

'Who said I'd been to it?'

She shook her head. 'Oh, very well ...'

'I have never been to the cottage. What I saw inside I saw through the cottage window.' When they didn't reply he went on: 'Two weeks ago the car packed up outside her house. There was a block in the petrol pipe. I told you about it, Celia, you remember I was late.'

She nodded with a quick sigh of relief. 'I remember.'

He gave a short laugh. 'You'd better, I may need you as a witness. I saw the old creature through the window. She always keeps the window open so that she won't miss anything that's going on. She was writing in this wretched book. It looked like a ledger and I remember thinking how damned silly it was to keep accounts when you had only yourself to bother about. Nice to think now that she might have been writing God knows what about me.'

Firth nodded. 'Miss Pewsey found it amusing, no doubt. It was like a small ledger, you say?'

'Yes, much thicker than a school exercise book. Of course,' he added, 'she may have been doing just what I thought, making her accounts.'

'You say it had a black cover?'

'Yes.'

'How did you manage to see that if it was open at the time she was writing in it?'

Graham's face darkened with anger. 'I see, so you're going to take care of Celia and her mother by trying to set traps for their friends?'

'Graham!' This time Celia was angry, angry and oddly frightened.

'Well, what else am I supposed to think he's doing, helping me?'

'I'm helping you to get your story straight, certainly. You wouldn't be making a very good showing if *I* happened to be the police.'

'You may not be the police, but it seems to me you're doing your damnedest to do their job for them. Personally, I'd rather have my dealings with the real thing.'

Celia jumped to her feet. 'That's about the meanest thing I've heard from you to date,' she said. 'And lately I must say your gems have been falling thick and fast. I'm going.'

But before she could move Graham was standing by her side, holding her hand. Firth was startled by the change in him. He was smiling down at Celia. It was a shamefaced, lopsided grin, and he looked like a schoolboy who had been teasing his little sister and realized that he had gone too far.

'Of course, you aren't going, my darling, because honestly and truthfully I'm going to behave myself.' His grin widened as he looked down into her eyes. 'From now on I'm going to be one great simpering mass of charm.' He jerked his head towards Firth. 'Even to him. Now let's all sit down again.'

Certainly when Graham wanted to he could be very hard to resist. Celia did not even try. She allowed herself to be pressed gently back into her chair.

This time Graham had himself and the situation in hand. He smiled across at Firth ruefully, but from the way he shuffled his wide shoulders back comfortably into his chair it was obvious that he was completely at ease.

Firth had a feeling that he would have to change his views about Celia's friend. He might make mistakes, but it would take a skilled opponent to profit by them. Almost against his will he found himself sharing in the mood of the moment. There was a party spirit abroad and it was Graham's party. It was Graham who signalled the waiter.

'Bring us the same kind of thing again, will you please? I'm ashamed to say I should have ordered them before.'

'Better late than never, sir. I'll be right back, and they'll taste so good you'll be forgiven.'

'It's nice,' said Graham, 'to have a friend.' And the waiter strutted off feeling pleased with life and himself.

'Now where were we when Celia said her Exit line?' He paused, then went on: 'Oh yes, I was playing the part of cornered rat over the Pewsey diary. I said it was black and the counsel for the crown asked me how I knew it was black when, from my own account, Pewsey was writing in it and it was therefore open. Well,' he paused as if for effect, 'I also saw it when it was closed.'

The way he said it left them no option but to laugh. At the same time the fabric of suspicion that had seemed to surround him disappeared. Firth had an odd feeling that Graham was laughing at them both. He waited for them to say something and then went on:

'I'm sure it's only your good nature that stops you from insisting on a more elaborate explanation. At the risk of making another blunder I'll give it. Pewsey, as you all know, lets nothing happen within her orbit without being aware of it. That a man, *any* man, should halt unseen by her window, would be out of the question. Pewsey saw me and at once her silvery laugh began to shatter my ear drums.' He added with a sudden return of savagery: '*That laugh!*' It was a flash of anger that came and went. He was half smiling as he went on.

'But I see now that what she was writing must have been damned important to her, because she actually went on writing.' He turned to Celia. 'You know Pewsey, so you know what that means.'

'Yes,' Celia said. 'It must have been terrifically important. She'd hardly ever let a woman go by, but a man, never. Oh...' she broke off ashamed as she remembered how newly the subject of her conversation was dead. 'I'm a beast. There was no need for me...'

Graham broke in again. 'It's no use, Celia. If we've got to talk about her, and obviously we've got to, we aren't obliged

63

to pretend we loved her. That I for one can't do.' He paused, and then turned back to his story.

'After a while she must have finished, for she leapt up with one of those glad cries of hers and presently she came darting outside. She was wearing red sandals with a green frock that was meant to represent some medieval period. Her hair was in ringlets like Queen Victoria as a girl, only Pewsey wasn't a girl. I tell you this because her appearance out of doors both impressed and startled me.'

'Was she friendly?' This from Firth.

'Oh definitely ... in fact she was arch. She shook her ringlets at me, and said, whatever would the neighbours think, seeing my car at her door.' His brows lowered. 'When anyone passed she did her best to give the impression that I was having some sort of assignation with her.' Graham put on a flutey imitation of the late Pewsey. '"The whole village will be in a flutter. I do hope that Celia doesn't mind."'

Celia laughed, but Graham said: 'I don't know if either of you have experienced the urge to strangle anyone with your bare hands.' He stopped abruptly.

Firth said gently: 'Someone preferred a blunt instrument, it would seem.'

7

DR ERIC DAW had been held up by the inquest. It was funny how everyone in the country seemed to have ample time on their hands with the one exception of the local doctor. The coroner had time to chat to the local police. Mrs Tilling had ample time to relish her role as that of identifier of the body. If only, the doctor thought, Angela Pewsey could have taken part in the proceedings to establish the cause of her own death, she'd have loved it. Or would she? Surely there had been an air of satisfaction in the little courtroom as the doctor himself had given evidence.

He had explained, as doctors do, half in layman's, half in

technical terms, what he had found when he examined the body.

'You knew Miss Pewsey, did you not, Doctor?'

'Yes.' Yes, he knew Miss Pewsey.

'You were, in fact, her medical adviser?'

'That is so.' Up to a week ago . . . but there was no need to go into that.

'Would you say that she was a person of robust constitution?'

'For a woman of her age, I should have said that she was in a very satisfactory state of health.'

'What would you say as to her nervous condition, Doctor?'

'I don't quite follow you. There was no nervous condition such as would affect her general health.'

'I was rather considering the possibility that she might have contemplated taking her own life. Have you any evidence of that?'

'No.'

'She had no worries that you were aware of?'

'No, none that I am aware of concerning herself.'

'Does that mean that she had, had *other* worries?'

'Miss Pewsey seemed to worry a great deal about other people's affairs.' He regretted that immediately. Quite apart from everything else it was ethically wrong. But he could not help hearing the sudden growl of approval that came from the body of the court.

The coroner glanced quickly at the public. He was a man of wide understanding. The murmur he had just heard was not evidence, but it gave him a quick insight into the character of Angela Pewsey.

He hesitated and put his next question.

'Is there any further evidence' – he stressed the word evidence – 'you would care to give as to these worries, Doctor?'

'No.'

'You do not connect them in any way with her death?'

'I don't follow you.'

'I'll put it another way. Were these worries in your opinion such as to cause her to take her own life?'

Someone in the court laughed, a single, mirthless bark.

This time the coroner did intervene. He reminded them caustically that there were places of amusement more appropriate than a coroner's court. Not even their stupidity would condone those who thought that these proceedings were a joke. He turned to his witness.

'We will proceed to the question, Doctor.'

'The possibility was never in my mind that Miss Pewsey might take her own life.'

'Thank you. It is a possibility we must consider none the less.'

The doctor nodded. 'Yes.'

'You were called to the cottage immediately after the discovery of the body, I understand?'

'Yes.'

'You are satisfied that the head injuries you have described were the cause of the death?'

'Yes.'

'In your opinion could the injuries you have described have been self-inflicted?'

He saw the faces in the body of the court lean towards him.

'In my opinion that would have been impossible.'

With a kind of communal sigh the audience leaned back in their seats.

'Would you please explain to the jury how you have arrived at that opinion?'

'It was a blow on top of the head. Sitting as she was with the encumbrance of the spinning wheel before her it would have been physically impossible.' He paused and added, 'The hands were clutching the threads she was weaving.'

Suddenly, to the doctor, the questioning seemed wearisome, futile. The woman was dead, his business was with the living – with Mrs Brooks, for instance, most likely by now in labour, alone with a distracted, clumsy sister, in an ill-equipped, airless room. There was the child with cerebral meningitis over at Upper Hadam, a child wearied of too much pain. But the next question was ready for him.

'Your opinion then was that the injuries were the result of an attack?'

'Yes.' In God's name what else could it be?

'Tell us now what in your opinion was the nature of the attack?'

'I came to the conclusion that one blow struck from behind and above was the cause of her death.'

'Would it have required a heavy blow to have caused the injuries found?'

'Fairly heavy. It would depend on the weight of the instrument used. The skull was not of average thickness.'

The coroner consulted his notes.

'Is there anything else you would like to add, Doctor?'

'Nothing else, I think.'

The coroner looked at the jury. A small thin man pulled his nose nervously and asked: 'Could a woman have struck that blow just as likely as a man could have, Doctor?'

'Yes, a woman of average strength.'

Another juror inquired: 'There was nothing in the angle of the wound to tell if it was a tall person or short, I suppose?'

'No, that would equally depend on whether the victim's head was raised, or bent over her work. I cannot help you as to that, I am afraid.'

There were other questions, but at last he got away and made his way out of the stuffy room into the sunshine.

He overtook Firth Prentice, who had paused to light a cigarette as he came out of the courtroom.

'Hello,' the doctor said. 'Been in to witness my performance?'

Firth grinned. 'Very nice too. I like listening to doctors, they're so cagey. You'd think the whole British Medical Council was listening to them.'

The doctor laughed grimly. 'So they are. When you

67

become a doctor the British Medical Council moves in to live with you.'

'Nice bedfellows.'

'Yes, as long as you behave.'

'You're not waiting for the verdict?'

'Too busy. I've attended Miss Pewsey for the last time, I hope.' He added quickly: 'I didn't mean to be callous; but in my job you learn to turn pretty quickly from the dead to the living.'

'Yes, I can see that.'

'You are waiting for the end, I suppose?'

Firth shook his head and smiled. 'No, I came to see the star. The rest would be an anti-climax.' He added: 'We all know what the verdict will be . . . murder against somebody unknown. Sergeant Porter's tramp, or somebody respectable in Inching Round. Which is it going to turn out to be?'

Dr Daw looked at him quickly. 'What do you think?'

Firth answered: 'I don't believe in fairies, so I don't see why I should start believing in tramps.'

'No? In that case it could be any of us.' The doctor turned towards his car. 'I'm passing through Inching Round, would you care to come along?'

'Thanks. I was wondering if I'd have to walk.'

Daw turned the car into the narrow main street of the little market town of Wilberforce. Firth was idly impressed with the doctor's obvious popularity. Women, men, old people and little children, waved or grinned as he went past. What made him popular? Was it his virtues or his shortcomings? Was it because he was an angel or a human? But the doctor he noticed was returning the greetings absently. His mind was on some inner preoccupation of his own.

'I suppose I should feel strongly about it,' he said presently. 'But I find it difficult, I must say.'

'You mean, of course, the late Pewsey?'

'Yes, or the manner of her going. The end was mercifully sudden.'

68

'Or in the words of the multitude, she never knew what hit her.'

'One unexpected blow and she had ceased to exist.'

Firth said dryly: 'The humane murderer . . . it sounds a bit odd, don't you think?'

'He may possibly have considered that he was doing humane work. Murder can be justified, you know.'

Firth turned to look at him with a new interest. 'My family have always in some way or another been connected with the law. We have a kind of instinct to put murder in a class by itself.'

The doctor drove thoughtfully for a while and then said reflectively: 'A doctor might feel justified in taking a somewhat different view. Of course, we all subscribe vocally to the theory of the sanctity of human life.'

'Vocally?'

'I was about to say that I myself have been an accessory to more than one murder.' There was nothing dramatic in the way he said it, but just a plain statement of fact.

Firth said: 'That's rather an odd statement to make, in the course of a social chat, you know, Doctor.'

'Is it?' The doctor smiled suddenly. 'It is not one I'd make before witnesses. But just the same it may help you to appreciate the background of some of the leading characters in this drama.'

'Why should I want to do that?'

'You are trying to get to the bottom of it, aren't you?'

'No, it's nothing to do with me. I don't want to know who killed Angela Pewsey. Why should I?'

'The reason is simple. Celia's mother has decided that that is what you are going to do.'

'Celia's mother is talking nonsense.'

The doctor laughed. 'You are quite wrong there. What Celia's mother says often sounds like nonsense, but it never is.' He laughed again. 'So there is another item of background for you.'

'I'm learning fast. Tell me some more about this murder sideline of yours.'

'I don't think of it as murder, as it happens. What I intended to say was that I've known many people, whose sufferings have become insupportable, to find sudden release. It has happened, for instance, that tablets have been left within the patient's reach. As the murderer walked from the room the eyes of the victim were filled with gratitude.'

'You are telling me this for some reason, of course, something to do with Angela Pewsey. If Pewsey had any last minute feelings, I'm quite sure they weren't those of gratitude.'

'I'm sure not. I'm not suggesting they were. But although Angela Pewsey was playing a leading part in this drama, she was not the only character by any means.'

'No, I know that. There was the villain presumably.'

The doctor shook his head. 'I take the view that the villain was the one who died.'

Firth said irritably: 'I'm only a simple Londoner, I don't understand all these nice gentlemanly murderous activities you indulge in down here. And what's more,' he added violently, 'I am having nothing whatever to do with this business, so let's talk about the crops.'

Without answering the doctor pulled into the side of the road. He opened his wallet and took out an envelope. He handed it across to Firth.

'When you have read that,' he said, 'we will talk about anything you like.'

Firth looked at him suspiciously. The doctor lit a cigarette and sat looking impassibly at the road ahead of him.

With a deepening feeling of anger that he could not explain Firth unfolded the letter. He had suspected before he saw the writing who the author of this letter was. Now before him were the same twists and twirls that had covered the page of the diary . . . Angela Pewsey, whose acquaintance he was making so rapidly. The letter was unsigned, but there was no real attempt at disguising the writing.

My dear, dear Doctor:

Oh dear what a naughty wicked doctor you are and all this in spite of your virtuous ways. And to think that of all people it should be that dear dutiful Joyce Everard, who so cleverly drove her husband to drink.

And you did think you were both keeping it so dark, didn't you, dear Doctor? But it was no trouble at all to find out all about the little trip to London you made and where you stayed and everything. Why, you foolish man, you didn't even go under an assumed name, but she did . . . Oh dear, yes . . . Mrs Daw, and that was not at all clever of you, was it now?

But you were clever about the husband, or rather you thought you were. Imagine putting him in that dreadful home for a month on the pretext that you were going to cure him. But, of course, he wasn't cured, he was just put out of the way, and, of course, when it's convenient you'll just put him out of the way again. Or will you? Now that's just the point. He's such a jealous and violent man, and only too delighted to make a scandal over anything.

Shall I drop him a little note, or shall I not? Shall I? Shan't I? Oh dear, I can't make up my mind.

Oh Doctor, I do so want you to think of me sitting by the fire or lying in bed at night trying to make up my mind. The British Medical Council are so tiresome about things like this, aren't they, and I do so want to do what's right.

But you will think of me trying and trying to make up my mind, won't you, Doctor dear? It will put you so much at your ease when next you go to betray your patient's trust!!!

The letter was of course unsigned, but it seemed to Firth sitting in the sun that he could hear the echoes of Angela Pewsey's laugh. Without speaking he folded the letter and passed it back. But the doctor shook his head.

'No, I'd rather you kept it, if you don't mind.'

'What do you want me to do with it?'

Without looking at him the doctor answered: 'Anything you think fit.'

'But you know perfectly well that it should go to the police.'

'Then no doubt you will give it to the police.'

The rage that had been taking hold of Firth flared up. 'You know perfectly well what should be done with this letter!'

'Do I? I'm afraid you are wrong. I don't know.'

'You prefer me to take the responsibility, that's it, isn't it?'

'That's it.'

'Damn you. Damn the whole bloody set of you. I tell you I will *not* be dragged into it.'

The doctor didn't reply. He pressed the self-starter and drove on steadily towards Inching Round.

Firth said presently: 'You obviously wanted to talk to me about that letter, otherwise you wouldn't have given it to me to read.'

The doctor shook his head. 'There doesn't seem much one can say, does there?'

'It's all true, I suppose?'

'Not all. Enough of it is true. Enough to put me down and out, certainly.'

'You a doctor, to let yourself in for this. You must be mad.'

'Perhaps. Yes, I suppose there is a kind of madness, when the kind of love I feel for Joyce Everard takes possession of anyone so disciplined and repressed as I am.'

'Well, I'm glad to hear it wasn't just a boyish prank on your part. That would have been too much.'

The doctor raised his head with a suggestion of pride. 'Joyce and I have loved each other for three years, ever since we met. We did nothing about it, except just that once.'

'Unfortunate, to say the least of it, that you had the husband put away like that.'

'That was his own idea entirely. He wanted to cure himself, but he couldn't, of course. He just didn't have the guts. Joyce tried to help him, with the result that he hated her. He hated her because she was strong and clean and everything that he was not.'

72

'It would have been simpler in that case to have got a divorce.'

'Divorce! The idea that she wanted to get away and couldn't delighted him. You see, Prentice, he did know about us. I mean he knew what we meant to each other. But he made it quite clear that if we tried to do anything about it, he would ruin me. I was ready to face it. Joyce said it would be hopeless for us both . . . She was right, of course.'

'Did he know about the London trip?'

'No, if he had it would have been just what he'd been waiting for. He'd have brought me down, but he wouldn't of course have divorced Joyce.'

'You could have gone away, both of you, out of the country.'

'I don't know if you know the medical profession – probably not. Otherwise you wouldn't talk about starting somewhere else. You could never start again, anywhere.'

'All this means that you had a very good motive for murdering Angela Pewsey.'

The doctor pulled to a stop by the gates of Danescroft. 'Yes,' he said. 'I had an excellent motive.'

Firth got out and leaned for a moment on the door of the car. 'Why did you tell me all this?'

The doctor smiled. 'Because,' he said, 'it would have been dangerous not to have told somebody. I have a suspicion that there is a diary somewhere, I may be mentioned in it.' He smiled again. 'So I told you.'

'You must know perfectly well that I'll have to give this letter to the police.'

The doctor gently let in the clutch and the car began to move. 'That I must leave entirely in your hands.'

What Firth was feeling as he watched the little car move sedately on its way was beyond print. What did these people think they were? What did they think he was? A well-meaning, meddling fool who was going to risk his career by withholding evidence? There were two obvious things to

73

do. One was to stop the first policeman he saw and hand over the letter and the scrap from the diary, the next was to get back to town, and stay back.

Then he saw Celia walk idly across the lawn and drop into a deck chair in the shade. The sight filled him with frustrated rage. Why should he be driven away from here? Why in God's name couldn't they leave him alone ... Or anyway alone with Celia Sim?

There was a thud beside him and he turned to see Constable Wilks dismounting from his bicycle. While his sergeant was at the inquest Constable Wilks was carrying on with the task of picking up the trail of the tramp.

In spite of his own dilemma, Firth couldn't help feeling sorry for the constable. It was bad enough pedalling about on a hot day pursuing inquiries that might conceivably lead to somewhere, but when they were heading straight for a dead end there was something quite pathetic about it.

'Still at it?'

'We are following a line of investigation, sir,' Wilks said without enthusiasm.

'Somebody said it is better to travel hopefully than to arrive.'

'They couldn't have meant riding round on a bike on a hot day,' observed Wilks.

'Have you found any tramps?'

Wilks took off his helmet and wiped the inside with his handkerchief. 'I am not in a position to reveal the point to which our investigations have taken us, sir.' Constable Wilks was obviously pleased to have brought off such a well-rounded and official sounding rebuke. Sergeant Porter himself could not have done better.

'Constable Wilks,' Firth replied, 'you are a natural born sergeant.' He added with a show of irritation: 'You realize, of course, that in this particular case you are wasting your time?'

'That may be how it appears to the layman,' answered

Wilks. 'But due to ignorance of police procedure much of our routine work must seem a waste of time.' Wilks replaced his helmet with a feeling that in spite of the heat he really was in good form. He had made two really good retorts, one on top of the other.

Firth himself was quite impressed. It was a joy to find one so young who could run so true to form.

'Beautifully spoken, Wilks. Beautifully.' But then it occurred to Firth that if Wilks was wasting time, so was he. Unconsciously he put his hand over the wallet in his inside pocket.

'You are searching for a myth, Constable.'

'No, I'm searching for a tramp. I've never yet come across a female tramp.'

'A female?'

'Well, you did say a miss, didn't you?'

'No, my boy, I don't lisp. I said myth.'

Constable Wilks pondered on this. 'You wouldn't be trying to teach us our own business, would you, sir?'

'I might offer to help you solve this case.'

Now there is nothing a policeman learns to run away from so quickly as a layman who wants to help him with suggestions and advice. And here was a smart Alec from London if you please, who didn't know the country or the people or the deceased even, coming along with an offer to put the local constabulary on the right track.

'We can get along very well without any outside help, thank you, sir,' Wilks said with dignity.

'Nonsense,' Firth said. 'You'll get bogged down so far in all this you'll need a periscope to see the evidence.'

'You think so?' Wilks was really getting on his dignity. 'You think so, do you? Well, I may say we'll thank you not to interfere or obstruct.'

'Suppose I told you I had some vital evidence?'

This, of course, was where Wilks made his first real mistake. He let his indignation rule him. 'I want no help from *you*, sir.'

Firth prodded him again. 'I see, you think you can blunder through this without my help, do you?'

'Yes, I do.'

Firth emitted what he felt should be a bitter sarcastic laugh. 'Let me tell you, Constable,' he said, 'I have been following a certain line of investigation of my own. I am quite sure that what you are doing is nothing but a waste of time. I am prepared to co-operate with you and I will place in your hands all the evidence that has come into mine up to the present moment.'

'And what I say to that, sir, is to keep your certain line of inquiry and your precious evidence to yourself and let the proper authorities conduct their inquiries in the proper way.'

'I could, for instance,' said Firth with maddening superiority, 'place in your hands certain evidence. A little boy, for example, has brought me a torn scrap of paper which I should hand over and suggest that you test it at once for fingerprints.'

'Fingerprints, eh!' Wilks hoped that his sarcasm was as glittering as a diamond. 'The scrap of paper was no doubt torn from an exercise book.'

'Exercise book, ledger, diary, or something of the sort.'

Wilks laughed. 'Now, sir, you just put two and two together and say what the little boy brought you was something torn out of his exercise book and forget about the whole thing.'

'In fact, Constable Wilks,' Firth said with dignity, 'you refuse my help?'

'Yes, sir. But I will tell Sergeant Porter that you're ready to put him on the right track any time he looks you up.'

At that point, to their mutual surprise, Mrs Sim popped her head over the garden wall.

'Really, Firth,' she said. 'I have been listening to every word you said. If you had a rebuke from Constable Wilks, I must say that you brought it on yourself.'

Firth looked hurt. 'You heard him refuse the evidence I offered him?'

76

'Of course, I did. I'm sure it is most annoying for the police to have strangers trying to take part in their investigations.' She turned to Wilks. 'You mustn't mind him, Constable. These tiresome little interfering ways of his are something he has inherited from his father, a most domineering man . . . or was it his uncle?'

Constable Wilks had a glowing sense that his wisdom had been vindicated. 'As far as I am concerned, madam,' he said, 'I would be prepared to forget the whole thing.' His voice took on a sterner note. 'But you must understand the incident will have to go down in my report to Sergeant Porter.'

'I quite understand, Constable,' she answered. 'And if this young man earns for himself a rebuke from Sergeant Porter, it will be no more than he deserves.'

Constable Wilks saluted smartly and mounted his bicycle, and his shoulders were squared significantly as he rode away.

Mrs Sim came out of the drive and linked her arm through Firth's. 'You know, young man, I have come to the conclusion that you have a great deal more brains than I gave you credit for.'

He smiled at her slowly. 'So you heard him refuse to accept my evidence?'

'Of course. So now we can suppress it with a clear conscience, can't we?'

'A clear conscience! You know I'm rapidly coming to the conclusion that a lot of people round here haven't any conscience at all!'

They walked along the drive a while in silence. Presently Mrs Sim said: 'You know, Firth, Dr Daw may be a very foolish young man, but he's a very lovable one.'

He looked at her sharply. 'Why Dr Daw?'

'I saw you talking to him by the gate.'

'But you weren't listening then, were you?'

'No, I was merely thinking. I was thinking that if a letter written to him got into the wrong hands, it would be the greatest tragedy.'

'Do you know something to his discredit, Mrs Sim?'

'Oh, Firth my dear, I know something to the discredit of nearly all my friends! I've known about Eric Daw and Joyce Everard for a long time. One could see it in their eyes.'

'The snag about all that is that she has a husband and he is a doctor.'

She sighed. 'You really must hurry up and find the murderer, dear.'

'I see, and what if the murderer turns out to be one of these many friends of yours?'

'Then you must forget about the whole thing and go back to London at once.'

'And do nothing about it?'

'But my dear, of course. Angela Pewsey was easily the most hateful woman I've ever known. I have known for some time now that she had to be killed.'

Firth stopped and faced her.

'Listen, Mrs Sim. There comes a time in everyone's life when they have to face up to realities. Even *you* have to face them this time. These are the facts. I am not investigating the murder of Angela Pewsey; the police are doing it. When Messrs Porter and Wilks fail to find their tramp, somebody more skilful will take over.'

'But dear, that's just what I said. You are far more intelligent than Sergeant Porter and Constable Wilks. Besides, I am going to help you. For instance, I may even tell you where the diary is.'

Firth almost jumped out of his skin. 'What?'

'Oh dear, have I said something wrong?'

He answered in a deadly voice: 'I think you said something about a diary.'

'Oh yes, of course. I suppose I should have mentioned it to you before.'

'What you should have done, and what you must do now, is to hand it to the police.'

She nodded thoughtfully and he noted how the sun glinted in her shining hair.

'Yes, yes, I'm sure that is what I should do. Of course they will ask me where I found it.'

'Naturally. Well, where did you find it?'

'Well, you see, Firth, that's the trouble. I found it in the cottage.'

'You mean you went in there and took it when Angela Pewsey was out?'

She shook her head. 'No, dear. I went in and took it when Angela Pewsey was dead.'

Dumbfounded he stared at her. 'You mean the police had not found it?'

'No, the police had not arrived.' She looked at him as if to apologize for the worry she was causing him. 'So you see what a problem it is, don't you?'

Problem . . . To call it a problem was most definitely an understatement. And what was more, he wasn't even sure that she was telling the truth.

8

CELIA really did look nice, as she lay back in the deck chair. She looked so right. But of course, Firth told himself, of course she would look right. This was her setting, this country garden with its bobbing flowers and great lazy trees, but then he remembered that she had looked pretty good in London too.

He took a cushion from a garden chair and tossed it down and sat on it with his back to the tree.

She smiled at him. 'Worn out from a hard morning's detecting?'

'I haven't decided which one of you is going to hang. Personally, I don't think it matters.'

'Now, that really is unkind. Anyway, for business reasons, you can't let them hang Mummy or me.'

'I suppose I could at a pinch prove that you personally didn't bash the old girl on the head. Your mother, no doubt, can prove that she didn't do it. At the moment, however, she seems to feel that a better time would be had by all if I proved that someone else did do it.'

'Well, that does seem to be a sort of good idea, doesn't it?' She added lazily: 'Don't let me keep you if you feel you should be up and doing.'

'Ah, but you see, darling, there's a snag. When I find out who did it, your mother and I have to decide whether they should be hanged or not.'

'That seems reasonable,' Celia answered calmly. 'Surely that's not what puts the domineering note in your voice?'

'I suppose there might be advantages in having a murderer among your many friends. You could always ring him up and say: "Oh, my dear, Mrs Juggins is really too tiresome, I wonder if you'd be an angel and do her in for me?"'

Celia said: 'But, of course, whoever did that to Angela Pewsey wouldn't make a habit of it.'

'Possibly not. But you'd find after a while that you began to mistrust that speculative look of theirs. Personally I never think they make good pets, but you robust country folk may feel differently.'

'Surely,' Celia said reasonably, 'the best thing would be to find out what sort of murderer ours was, and then make up our minds?'

'Ah, but of course, find the murderer, ask him what his plans are for the future, and if they don't include any more murders we dismiss the whole matter. The police will then proceed to hang him and arrest us as accessories. Don't ask me how I know all this. I just know it instinctively.'

Celia laughed. 'It might have been fun having you here if we hadn't had all this trouble.'

'If you hadn't had all this trouble you wouldn't have invited me.'

'Perhaps not. But now that we are in trouble I'm not so sure that we ought to be pleased that you are here.'

'Any reason?'

'We might have been better suited by someone a bit more manageable.'

'Listen, Celia. I'm the most manageable, reasonable creature in the world.'

'Maybe it's just that you don't love us?'

'By us, do you mean you?'

'Maybe.'

'Ridiculous.'

'Yes, I was afraid you might feel that way about it.'

'I mean ridiculous to suggest that I don't love you. I love everybody, even Graham Ward.'

'It would be ironical if it was your noted zeal that brought about *his* arrest, wouldn't it?'

'Do you think he did it?'

'Do you?' The question was lightly put, but Firth saw that her eyes were afraid.

'He might have done . . . But so might anyone else.'

'Of course, it's all ridiculous, the question, the answer, everything. I shouldn't have asked you. It was disloyal.'

'It has formed a habit of cropping up though, hasn't it?'

'What has? I don't know what you mean.'

'The question. Did he? Or did he not? Awkward question at awkward times.'

She turned to face him and her voice trembled as she spoke. 'Firth, you don't really believe that I think Graham had anything to do with this, do you? You don't *really* think so, do you?'

He reached over and took her hand lightly in his. 'You can't turn your thoughts on and off like a tap, darling. They simply arrive and make themselves at home.'

'But you must know that I don't think Graham did this. If I did, why am I urging you to find out?'

'Because, darling, one way or another you just have to be sure.' He asked suddenly: 'Do you love him, by the way?'

'I suppose I do,' she said. 'Yes, of course I do. I must.'

He grinned. 'Don't talk yourself into it if you're not sure, my angel.'

'Of course I'm sure.'

'In another minute you'll be certain.'

'All right then, I'm certain.'

Firth leaned back against his tree and lit a fresh cigarette.

'Nuts,' he said.

Celia said angrily: 'Ha, so the great brain has conceived another reason for my emotional approaches to my boy friend. If I kiss him ardently, that isn't love. If I adore him, that isn't love either. If I want to marry him and have kids, that isn't love at all. It's all just one of those things a little country mouse like me wouldn't understand. You make me so mad sometimes I could – could strangle you with my bare hands!'

'There now! Speaking of love – there you have the fundamentals of love. Your desire to come close to me, to hold me with your hands, to take possession of my life . . . To these . . . '

Celia hurled the remaining cushion at him and stalked into the house.

Firth got up and walked slowly out of the drive and round the curve to the churchyard. He was satisfied that if he was to do any thinking it would be easier for him when Celia was not at hand.

Firth walked slowly down the lane towards the 'Merry Harriers'. The heat had gone out of the sun and a gentle evening breeze was blowing the scented sea air up from the coast. The inn itself was nestling in the shelter of a group of giant chestnut trees. Nothing could have been more peaceful.

A hundred yards farther on the little self-important train was leaving Inching Round on its momentous journey to the Capital. To Firth the departing train was a symbol of his abandonment. London was only a few hours away even by that crawling little train, but it might as well have been a thousand miles away.

He went despondently through the door of the 'Merry Harriers' and asked Tom Tiptree to join him in a beer. He swallowed it, watery and warm as it came out of the barrel. Tom, on the other hand, inspected the fluid in his glass against the light. He seemed undecided whether to drink it or bask in its reflected glory.

'Very nice condition,' he said. 'Very nice drop of beer. Here's to your very good health, sir.' He took a swallow that showed a nice balance between thirst and appreciation.

The door opened and a man came in carrying a small black Gladstone bag. He was wearing a bowler and a dark overcoat with a velvet collar. He had a long face, long nose and long limbs. His name was Inspector Thomas Fowler. Naturally his associates knew him as Long Tom.

Firth watched him enter with a marked increase in his feeling of depression.

Inspector Fowler placed his black bag on the counter, removed his bowler and placed it beside the bag, then he leaned forward supporting himself on his long fingers and asked for a large gin.

'Anything with it, sir?'

'Neat, if you please.' He looked at it unhappily, drank it in one swallow and replaced the glass. Then he said as if carrying on from where he had left off: 'Well, it's unexpected to see you in these parts, Mr Prentice.'

'I suppose,' Firth answered, 'I should say the same to you.'

'But you can't, eh?'

'I must confess I expected something of the sort. Not necessarily yourself, of course. How is London?'

'Quiet, Mr Prentice. Quiet. So quiet that they were able to spare me to come down here.'

Firth laughed. 'Things must be quiet if they can spare you for a one-horse job like this.'

'No. They'll manage. I told them I expected to be back in a week at latest.'

'Easy as that, eh?'

'Well,' Inspector Fowler said tolerantly. 'You know how

it is with these cases. The local men can never bring themselves to believe that one of their neighbours would do such a thing. I'll bet the first thing they did was to start looking for a sinister stranger.'

'A tramp, I understand.'

'Well, if it keeps them happy for a day or so I won't grumble.'

He turned to Tom Tiptree. 'I'll require accommodation for a day or so if it's convenient, and in the meantime Mr Prentice and I will have a drink.' And to Firth he said: 'Will you have the same again?'

'No,' Firth said. 'I'll have a gin and French this time.'

'I agree,' said Inspector Fowler. 'I find that in conforming to local custom the consumption of local beer is one of the more difficult aspects. Landlord, I will repeat what I had before.'

He looked at Firth benevolently. 'I had a case last week before your Uncle, Lord Justice Prentice – assault and robbery. He gave the prisoner ten years, a most admirable man.'

Firth had never thought of his Uncle John as an admirable man. At home, he had always seen a jolly, rather mischievous, gnome-like creature, very old ever since Firth could remember. Later when he saw him in court he could never bring himself to believe that this dignified legal automaton was the same man. In fact, he was not the same. Very soon now, Firth thought quickly, Inspector Fowler would be producing somebody from Inching Round before somebody like Lord Justice Prentice. The personality of someone in Inching Round would lose itself under an impersonal cloak of evidence of fact. It was the business of Inspector Fowler to produce the prisoner. It was the business of Lord Justice Prentice to interpret the law and pass sentence. It was the business of the hangman to carry it to its conclusion. All this in spite of the fact that the world was well rid of Angela Pewsey.

'Have you any theories as to motive, Mr Prentice?'

'I have no theories whatever. I'm not interested.'

'That means, of course, you are interested.' He tapped with his long bony fingers on the counter and waited until Tom Tiptree was out of earshot. 'Now, what could the motive be? Love and jealousy? I've seen the deceased's picture, so I've ruled that out. Money? She hadn't a lot and what she did have goes to a cousin in Canada. Robbery? Nothing stolen so far as the police can discover. Revenge?' He tapped his long fingers more rapidly. 'It would depend on what you meant by revenge, wouldn't it? Revenge for what? Something old that had been rankling for years? Something new? Or, I wonder, if it was fear? You know, Mr Prentice, fear is a most powerful motive for murder. Fear's a thing to turn men into savages. Now I wonder what could have made anyone so afraid of Angela Pewsey that they had to kill her? Now how does anyone like Angela Pewsey make people afraid of her? Nine times out of ten, Mr Prentice, it's on account of something she knows.' He turned and looked down his long nose at Firth. 'Do you follow me so far?'

'It seems to me,' Firth said, 'that you have overlooked the possibility that somebody killed her as a public duty.'

He shook his head. 'Murder, except in the case of gang wars and robbery, is generally a personal thing as between one human being and another.'

'Well,' Firth said. 'It's your murder.'

'Oh, no, Mr Prentice,' Long Tom said unctuously, 'murder is everybody's murder.'

Firth shook his head. 'Not mine, Inspector. I like peace and quiet.'

'Ah, so you're taking a well-earned rest?'

'In a sense. I'm staying with a client of mine, Mrs Harriet Sim.'

Inspector Fowler looked at him quickly. 'Really, that's interesting now. Are you looking after her interests in this case?'

Firth laughed. 'That's what she says.'

The inspector leaned over and looked meditatively down at his feet. 'When did she call you in, Mr Prentice?'

'I left London for Inching Round on the morning of the day of the murder.'

Fowler's eyes bulged. 'What, before the murder?'

'Oh, definitely before the murder.'

'Looks as if she had second sight, doesn't it, Mr Prentice?'

'It would look very much like it. The only snag from your point of view was that she wanted to consult me about something else.'

'It must have been very important, Mr Prentice, to have brought you down to stay in the house.'

'Sounds like it, doesn't it?' He grinned at the inspector. 'But I'm a bit of a friend of the family.'

'There is a family?'

'There's a daughter.'

'Ah . . . '

'You must meet them.'

'In other words, you mean you want to be present when I interview them?'

'Are you going to interview them, inspector?'

'I can't help being interested if Mrs Sim and her daughter keep the family lawyer in the house when there is a murder in the neighbourhood. What was the business that brought you down, Mr Prentice?'

'Well, now, really, Inspector! That you with your experience should expect me to answer a question like that! It's unworthy of you, sir . . . Oh, Tom, may we have the same again, please?'

The inspector resumed his tapping on the counter and pointed his long nose at the wall. 'Perhaps Mrs Sim will be good enough to tell me herself.'

'Possibly. Mrs Sim is capable of telling you the most remarkable things. Whether you believe them all or not is your affair.'

'Now don't tell me, Mr Prentice, that you are casting doubts on the veracity of your own client?'

'You'll understand these things better when you have met my client. If you're as eager to get to work as you say you are, perhaps you d care to pop in and meet them to-night?'

'I think I should. Yes, that will suit me very well, if it won't be putting them out.'

'No, not at all. I'm quite sure they'll want to do their best to help.'

'Of course,' the inspector said amiably, 'you realize it would create a much better impression on me if I chat with them alone?'

Firth smiled. 'I'm sure it would. But it would hardly seem that I was earning my fees if I did that, would it now?'

'Have it your own way. If you insist on a formal interview, you do insist and that's that. It's not for me to tell you what's best for your clients.'

'Of course it isn't,' Firth said soothingly. 'You may find after all that you'll be glad of my help.'

'You know,' the inspector said without malice, 'I don't think you are even going to try to help.'

Firth pocketed his change. 'No, possibly not. On the other hand I may find myself in a position where I have to help you whether I like it or not.'

'Now I wonder what kind of a position that would be, Mr Prentice?'

'No, don't wonder, let's content ourselves with hoping it never arises.' He turned towards the door.

'Good night, sir. Hope to see you soon.'

'Good night, Inspector. Shall I tell Mrs Sim to expect you at nine?'

'That will suit me very well, thank you.'

9

FIRTH said nothing of the Inspector's visit till they were round the table. It was Mrs Sim who brought the subject up.

'You look very preoccupied this evening, Firth dear. Are you wondering whether to make an arrest or not?'

He shook his head. 'I'm afraid the playing time is over. There aren't going to be any more tramps and there aren't going to be any more little bits and pieces of amateur detecting. The murder is coming home to roost.'

'Really? How nerve-racking we are this evening. Whatever causes it?'

'Scotland Yard.'

'Oh.' There followed a dismayed little silence and then Celia spoke.

'But Firth, I thought the local police were making the inquiries?'

'Perhaps the local police thought so too, but the county headquarters is almost as far from here as London. I suppose the Chief Constable felt that it would be a good idea to have the thing off his mind.'

'How do you know all this?'

'I just had a drink with the man in charge. One Inspector Fowler. He doesn't believe in tramps, either.'

'I see, what does he believe in?'

'He knows how and when and where she was killed. He considered that his next move should be to find out why.'

'And when he knows why?' Mrs Sim raised her brows in mild inquiry.

'Then, of course, he believes he will know which one of you did the job.'

Mrs Sim shook her head. 'Which, of course, he won't.'

'Perhaps not. But he will know a great deal that one or two people have been trying to keep from being known.'

Celia sat looking ahead of her. 'Firth, how long will he stay here, going about inquiring into our lives?'

'That,' Firth said flatly, 'will depend on how long it takes him to find out what he wants to know.'

'But suppose he doesn't find anything?'

'Celia,' Firth said, 'by sitting on a gravestone trying my best to mind my own business I found out enough to know

88

to which group to look for the murderer. To get as far as that will be child's play to Inspector Fowler. I imagine he has got there already. He has moved into the "Merry Harriers". He's probably there now interpreting all the nods and grunts and growls; talking, listening and thinking. By the time he comes here he'll have a good working idea of who's who in the Pewsey circle.'

'"Pewsey circle" . . . Firth, I wish you wouldn't say that. It sounds somehow like a hangman's noose.'

'Really, Celia,' Mrs Sim gave a small exasperated laugh, 'I can't possibly have you suggesting that one of us is going to be hanged!'

'But, mother, one is, presumably. I keep on thinking which ones I would rather we kept.'

'We shall most certainly keep our friends. Firth, did I understand you to say that your Scotland man is coming here? How odd to call him a Scotland man.'

'Scotland *Yard* man, mother.'

'Oh, Yard, I must remember. You did say he was calling, didn't you, Firth?'

'Yes, I asked him. I hope you don't mind. I thought you might like to talk to him and get it over.'

'Of course we'd enjoy talking to him. You know that any friend of yours is welcome, my dear boy.'

'But he's not a friend of mine. I've seen him in court and talked to him and I know his reputation, but I wouldn't call him a friend.'

'I do hope we like him.'

Celia said grimly: 'It might be better to hope that he likes us.'

Firth smiled slightly. 'That won't help you. There is nothing a policeman likes better than hanging his best friend.'

Mrs Sim interrupted mildly: 'You know, Firth, I must confess that I'm mildly disappointed in you. You've had all the afternoon to find out all about this affair, and I'm sure you don't know who was responsible. Now I'm afraid that

89

by the time you know who the murderer is we may not have time to make up our minds.'

Firth opened his mouth, sighed, and closed it again without saying anything.

'You aren't sulking, are you dear?'

Sulking? One thing he did know and that was that his face was getting red. He could feel it. It may have been Celia looking at him in that slow speculative way of hers. The bell saved him. He stood up.

'That,' he said, 'will be the inspector.' He turned sternly to Mrs Sim. 'You don't have to answer his questions if you feel they implicate you. And you really don't have to talk too much. If you are in any doubt you must be advised by me.'

'Good gracious, what an extraordinary statement, my dear child. For a moment you sounded exactly like your father, Timothy.'

'My father was not named Timothy.'

'Really ... How odd.'

The maid came in to say that Inspector Fowler was in the hall. She seemed awed. But Mrs Sim told her to take him to the drawing-room and to have another coffee cup put on the tray.

Then she got up and went quite eagerly towards the other room, leaving Firth and Celia to trail rather lamely behind her.

'So this is it,' she said to Firth.

'The beginning of it, yes.'

'Well, you needn't say that with such relish.'

'Relish? I haven't even said "I told you so" ... not yet, anyway.'

'You will.'

'I notice already, with your perverse feminine reasoning, you have decided I am somehow to blame.'

'I didn't say so. Apart from a certain amount of time wasted while you meandered on the subject of love, I suppose you have done your best.'

He replied with feeling: 'I hope when the police find out what I have been doing they agree with you.'

Celia said with a surprising change of tone: 'Oh, I know. Honestly, Firth, I'm sorry we dragged you into this. It is sort of squalid, isn't it? And I really didn't want you to know about Graham and me and all the rest of it. If you go back to London now, that's all right, you know.'

He stopped, facing her. 'Do you want me to go?'

'I don't . . . I don't know why I don't, but I don't.' She seemed very young then, and he thought she might be about to cry.

He put a finger under her chin, bent over and kissed her lips. 'I don't really want to go myself.' Then he grinned at her. 'Come on, we've got to protect your mother from the law, or the law from your mother, I don't know which.'

The inspector was holding a delicate coffee cup with both hands and balancing it on his bony knees.

'Yes,' he was saying. 'Yes, they're very bad up our way too. My wife treats them with a preparation sold under the trade name of Bug-ho.'

'Really, Bug-ho? I must make a note of it before you go, I've been quite desperate about them. Oh, there you are, Celia. The inspector has been telling me about how he gets rid of those wretched things on the roses. I think you've not met my daughter Celia, Inspector Fowler.'

The inspector rose from the couch like an extension ladder and bowed to Celia from the neck.

Celia and Firth helped themselves to coffee and joined the others by the fire. There was no atmosphere of the interrogation about the gathering so far, but presently Mrs Sim sighed and said: 'It must be very tiresome for you to have to come away from your affairs in London to bother over our problems down here, Inspector.'

'Oh, it won't be any bother, I assure you, madam,' Inspector Fowler said airily. 'These country trips are more or less routine to us.'

She shook her head. 'Isn't it strange. What has happened

here is something that none of us ever expected to happen in our lives. You come and see us all at odds, during a few days of turmoil, and then you go away. All you will remember of our lovely village will be that you solved a murder there. Really, Inspector, you must promise to come and visit us again some day when we are all back in our dull and pleasant grooves.'

'I'd like to think I'll be able to do that, madam, I'm sure. I realize that this isn't a very nice thing for anyone, having a murder in the neighbourhood and the murderer still at large.' He added hastily: 'Not that I think you have anything to be afraid of, of course. This sort of murderer very seldom strikes again quickly.'

'Oh, I assure you, we're not at all afraid.'

But the inspector continued: 'In a case like this the victim is chosen with care, and the motive has to be a strong one. Of course, that does not console you for the loss of a friend.' He paused and waited.

Mrs Sim half smiled. 'We'd be untrue to ourselves if we pretended that Miss Pewsey was a friend, Inspector.'

Firth said quickly. 'A village is not like a city, you know. In a village one sees much more of a mere acquaintance than one would for instance in a bigger place.'

'Oh I know, I know,' the inspector said dryly. 'That's the reason why Londoners like you and me have to come to Mrs Sim when we want to know about the village.'

Mrs Sim smiled as she looked across at Firth. She was obviously enjoying herself. 'You mustn't mind my daughter's young man, Inspector. He guards the family reputation like a watchdog. One can't blame him, of course.'

'Mother,' Celia protested. 'Must you say things like that?'

'Like what, Celia?' Mrs Sim asked mildly.

'You know perfectly well why Firth came here.'

'The main thing,' said Celia's mother, 'is to try to remember that Firth is trying to do his best. I do always, however difficult it is.'

Firth grinned. 'You forgot to tell him that I am as tiresome as my father.'

'Oh no, Tim dear. I never said your father was tiresome. That was your Uncle Peter.'

'"Tim dear".' Celia repeated her mother with a kind of desperate resignation.

Mrs Sim looked surprised. 'Why, Celia, what is the matter dear?'

'Don't worry, Mrs Sim,' Firth said. 'It's just the little matter of my name. It isn't Tim.'

Gently Inspector Fowler passed his hand across his brow. 'With regard to Miss Pewsey, madam. Did I understand you to say she was not a friend of yours?'

'She was quite friendly, Inspector. She laughed a great deal when we met.'

'She must have been a gay little lady.'

'She was not little, Inspector. She was a rather angular person; her laughter was not gay. It was high pitched, and I found it rather loud. It was energetic, as were all her activities ... I do hope I am helping you?'

'You are indeed, Mrs Sim.'

'I suppose it's wrong to be so frank about her now that she has been poisoned; but I am sure it's important that you should know.'

'She was not poisoned, mother,' Celia said.

'I know, dear, she was hit on the head with something dreadful, but I prefer not to think of it. Surely, after all, the main thing is that she is dead.'

'The main thing.' This time it was the inspector who repeated her words.

Firth interrupted quickly. 'Mrs Sim means that the tragedy remains, no matter how it was brought about.'

'May I take it that that is what you meant, Mrs Sim?'

'Of course not, Inspector. The main thing is to forget about the whole wretched business as quickly as possible.'

'I assure you, madam,' Inspector Fowler said, 'you will all be left in peace immediately we have found the murderer.'

Mrs Sim murmured vaguely: 'Oh yes, of course, the tramp.'

The Inspector smiled. It was meant to be a tolerant worldly-wise London smile. It was something like one, but not a lot.

Celia for some reason giggled – perhaps she was feeling the strain. But the inspector seemed pleased.

'I see you agree with me, Miss Sim.'

She swallowed and said: 'Yes, of course . . . That is, I haven't any sort of an idea, really.'

'That has been one of Celia's difficulties, Inspector, since she was quite a little girl. Even in the choice of sweets. If you gave her two you could be sure she would eat neither owing to the difficulty of making up her mind which to eat first. It was the only thing that prevented her from becoming really fat.'

'I must say, mother, you never told me that one before.'

'Of course not, dear,' her mother said simply. 'I hadn't thought of it before.'

'You will be interested to know,' the inspector said, 'that I have no difficulty at all in making up my mind.'

'What a blessing you would be in this household,' Mrs Sim told him.

'I have made up my mind,' he said, 'that Miss Pewsey was not murdered by a tramp.'

'The inspector has told me,' Firth said, 'that what he is looking for now is the motive.'

'Good gracious, Firth, you told the inspector all about that, surely?'

Firth looked startled, opened his mouth to speak and closed it again.

'I hope for his own sake,' said Inspector Fowler, 'that he hasn't been holding anything back.'

'Oh, no,' protested Mrs Sim quickly. 'On the contrary, Inspector, he has been offering his services everywhere. Constable Wilks was quite annoyed about it.'

Inspector Fowler threw back his long head and laughed

quite heartily, and Celia remarked in passing that the inspector had false teeth.

'So our young friend here decided that he was going to solve the case himself, did he?' He shook his head. 'You should have known better, Mr Prentice.'

Firth permitted himself a sheepish grin. 'Don't tell me that you are going to refuse my help as well,' he said.

The inspector laughed again. 'I most certainly am.'

'You may be asking for it before you're through, Inspector.'

'I think not. No, I think I can give you my word as to that. Now these two ladies here, I shall be asking for a lot of help from them.'

'You forget, Inspector,' Firth persisted, 'I have a way with me. People tell me things that I am sure they would never tell you.'

The inspector's face clouded a little. 'If anyone knows anything I want to know, sir, I have my own ways of finding out what it is.'

Firth knew that however cocksure it may have sounded, Inspector Fowler was speaking something very like the truth.

The inspector turned now to Mrs Sim. 'You said something about a motive, madam. Knowing the people concerned you may be able to help me. The person who killed Miss Pewsey obviously had a good reason for doing so.'

'Yes, but you see, Inspector, I would be talking about my friends.'

'If one of your friends is at the same time a murderer, Mrs Sim, what would you say about that?'

Mrs Sim said with an odd kind of finality: 'I do not make friends lightly, Inspector. When I do, I give them my trust.'

There was a note of patient exasperation in the inspector's reply. 'But we are investigating a murder, Mrs Sim.'

Her answer seemed to shake him. 'I know very little of your business, Inspector, but from your manner I gather that the investigation of a murder is a matter of some importance. I am sure also that to murder somebody is

95

something in very bad taste, to say the least of it. But as to telling you who murdered Angela Pewsey, I cannot feel that it is my duty to do so.'

'Am I to suppose,' Long Tom Fowler said heavily, 'that you know who murdered the dead woman?'

'Perhaps.' She smiled at him as if to sustain him in his ordeal.

'And now, Mrs Sim, I ask you a second time to tell me who in your opinion murdered this woman?'

Firth half rose in his chair. This business had got quite out of hand. 'Now look here, Inspector . . . '

But Mrs Sim had raised a gentle hand.

'But, Inspector, surely we have told you?'

'Told me?'

'Why, yes, the tramp.'

'The tramp.' Inspector Fowler took out his handkerchief and passed it slowly over his brow.

'Firth, dear boy, would you please get the superintendent a drink? I know we are all most tiresome and he has had a trying day.'

Firth poured out a drink and the inspector accepted it without a word.

'Mother,' Celia said reluctantly, 'you know that the inspector doesn't believe it was a tramp.'

'No,' said Fowler dully. 'I don't believe it was a tramp. I was asking if there was anyone you know who had the motive and opportunity to have killed Miss Pewsey.'

'Really,' Firth said tentatively, 'I do think Mrs Sim has answered to the best of her ability.'

But Mrs Sim would have none of that. 'Now, Firth, you mustn't stop the inspector asking me questions if he wants to. What was it you wanted to know, Inspector?'

'Motive and opportunity,' said the inspector. 'I want to know if you knew anyone who had it.'

'But of course I do.'

'Ah . . . '

'I beg your pardon.'

'Who had motive and opportunity, madam?'

Mrs Sim laughed. 'Why, we all had. If anyone had felt that way, Angela Pewsey must have looked most tempting. She was sitting at her spinning wheel, preparing dog's hair for the knitting circle.'

'Dog's hair?' Dog's hair? He thought that his brain had stopped.

'Yes, indeed, Inspector Fowler. No dog with long hair escaped the attention of poor Angela. The owners of the dogs were not very pleased, because Angela wanted to organize them so that they plucked the unhappy animals at regular intervals. She said it was unpatriotic not to do so because she was reviving an industry that would provide warm clothes for all kinds of people. She was threatening to make Celia a pullover of chow's hair.'

'The donor of the hair,' Celia said, 'was the smelliest animal in the county.'

'She must have been a good friend of Miss Sim's,' the inspector said hopefully, 'to have gone to all that trouble.'

Mrs Sim shook her head. 'The motives that inspired Angela Pewsey's deeds could be very mixed. They were not always done with the desire to give pleasure.'

The inspector gave up that line. 'You were suggesting,' he said, 'that any of you could have seen her that day?'

'Seen and heard her. She had a loud warbling singing voice.'

'I see. I take it that the neighbours would be passing to and fro at fairly regular intervals?'

'Well, occasionally. Latterly I'm afraid some of the neighbours had actually taken to walking a longer way round in order to avoid passing Miss Pewsey's window.'

'Good gracious,' the inspector said. 'Why on earth should they do that?'

'I'm afraid after all we haven't given you a very good impression of Angela Pewsey's character. It was not only that she was excessively interested in our lives – she actually penetrated into them. She seemed in a way to live beneath the surface of the whole village.'

The inspector asked in an odd voice: 'Can you be sure that others felt as you do about this, Mrs Sim?'

'Of course not. They may have been taking the longer and rougher road merely for the exercise.'

'If she did delve into the life of the village she would no doubt know a great deal about it?'

'She was a clever woman, Inspector, and as I said interested in our affairs.'

'She could easily have known something that somebody else might wish not made public.'

Mrs Sim laughed. 'I am quite sure, Inspector, that if Angela had not known something like that about at least one of us she would have considered her life empty and misspent. It would be wiser to assume that she knew some such thing about most of us.'

'If most of you were in some way or another in her power, that is not going to make life any easier for me, Mrs Sim.'

Again she laughed. 'No. I had thought of that. But you do see, don't you, that I can't alter Angela Pewsey's character, even to suit the convenience of Scotland Yard.'

'I do, madam.' He added grimly: 'And I don't think that you would do so even if you could. I am wondering why, madam?'

'The reason, Inspector, is that the pain you will cause to so many of us will be out of all proportion to the good you do.'

'Perhaps,' answered Inspector Fowler. 'Perhaps what you say is true.' He straightened his shoulders. 'Against that, there will be one less murderer in the world.' There was a kind of hard pride in his voice. Celia, aware of it, felt that the room had turned colder. Firth found himself braced in his chair. But Mrs Sim gave no indication that she had noticed any challenge or change.

'Now, Inspector,' she said, 'will you tell me any other way in which we can be of help?'

'Beyond implicating your friends you mean, madam?'

'I am quite sure,' she answered, 'that you will be able to find out about our friends more easily from other sources.'

Inspector Fowler found himself wondering why he was beginning to like this woman who clearly was going to be of no help.

'You might recall anything either of you ladies may have seen during the day of the murder.'

'I'm afraid I can't help,' Celia said. 'I left early for town and came back late with Firth.'

'And you, madam?'

'It was much like any other day, Inspector. With one important exception, of course.'

'That it was the day of the murder, you mean?'

She nodded. 'Yes.'

'But there was nothing to suggest that to you . . . nothing unusual?'

'No. Most of the day I was out of doors. I had taken my gardening basket and gloves down to the far corner of the road. I had decided to try to get the rose arbour into some sort of shape. You know this house was taken over by the Government during the war. The garden was really left in a quite horrible mess.'

'And you could see over into the road?'

'Oh yes, quite easily. You see the land on our side of the wall is much higher than the road level. It's quite easy for us to look into the road, whereas the wall on its road side is more than six feet high.'

'And you saw people passing to and fro?'

'Yes, I'm sure I did.'

'Could you give me the names of any of those who passed?'

Mrs Sim laughed. 'Really, Inspector, you don't realize how stupid I am about these things!'

'You did not strike me as particularly stupid, madam.' He did not give the impression that he was being gallant either. He sounded grim.

'No, you don't understand. What I mean is that I know

99

my limitations only too well. So you see I try to concentrate on the matter in hand. That day it was the roses.'

'But somebody must have seen you.'

'Of course, I'm sure they did.'

'And if they saw you, no doubt they called out a greeting?'

'They certainly would have done, I think.'

'Then perhaps you will cast your mind back and tell who did attract your attention?'

'But, Inspector,' Mrs Sim said patiently, 'nothing really attracts my attention when I am concentrating on something else.'

'But just try to think, madam.'

'Very well, Inspector,' she said obediently . . . And waited.

'You were working on the rose arbour, somebody passed and called out a greeting. Who would it be?'

'It could have been the vicar, of course,' she said vaguely. 'He would be almost sure to pass at one time or another, perhaps several times, and I'm quite positive he'd say good morning. In fact, I think . . . Yes, I'm almost sure he did.'

'Anything else, madam?'

'Something rough,' Mrs Sim said suddenly.

'Something rough?'

'Rough, a rough sound, abrupt, barking. Of course, Major Torrens passed before lunch.'

'Who is Major Torrens, Mrs Sim?'

Celia answered, as if to give her mother a rest. 'Major Torrens is retired. He lives at Impy House, a little farther down. He's a bit of a bore, really; got a sort of passion for being bossy. Heavily gallant to the ladies, of course. Rather the bulging type, you know.'

'I know,' the inspector said dryly. He turned back to Mrs Sim. 'Now, madam, we are getting on quite well. Was there anyone else?'

She was looking dreamily at the fire. 'I have an impression that there was a stranger.'

The inspector looked at her. 'You are not suggesting that you saw a tramp, are you, Mrs Sim?'

'It might have been. It's difficult to remember.'

The inspector's tone was drier still. 'I'm quite sure it is.'

'I don't think it was a tramp, I remember something blue.'

'Blue!' He looked startled, but Mrs Sim seemed not to notice.

'There wouldn't be anything blue about a tramp, would there?'

'Not unless he was feeling that way or he had a blue aura. You aren't a spiritualist by any chance, Mrs Sim?'

'I've taken an interest in it. No, I'm not a spiritualist.'

'So all that you can tell me is that you have an impression of a stranger and something blue.'

Mrs Sim straightened and smiled at him. She shook her head. 'That's all. I've told you everything. I'm sure you've found me the most stupid person you've ever met, but I do assure you that that is no fault of my own.'

'I've had better witnesses, I'd not deny that,' said Inspector Fowler. He stood up. 'However, I'm glad you didn't insist that the stranger was a tramp. That would have been a reflexion on my intelligence, wouldn't it?'

She smiled and held out her hand. 'Yes. I realized that.'

'But you do think it would be a good idea for me to look for something blue?'

'That, of course, you must decide for yourself.' She smiled again, and Inspector Fowler had an uncomfortable feeling that little Mrs Sim was laughing at him. 'Do let us know when we can help again, won't you, Inspector?'

'Thank you, madam. When next I call, I hope the questions I have to put to you will be more direct.'

The inspector walked with Firth to the door. There he turned and looked curiously at his companion. 'I wonder what on earth made Mrs Sim think she might need your help?' he asked.

Firth grinned. 'Possibly she felt you might turn violent and that it would be nice to have a man about the house.'

'Something blue!' The inspector gave a disgusted grunt and turned away into the night.

10

JUST as Sergeant Porter had set off on his search for a tramp, so now Inspector Fowler embarked on his journey in search of motive and opportunity.

Firth saw little of him during the next two days, but everyone in the village was aware that he was about. His lanky, sombre figure became temporarily a part of the scene, crossing the churchyard with his long gangling strides, towering above the regulars in the public bar of the 'Merry Harriers', opening white cottage gates, knocking soberly at doors and then ducking cautiously as he disappeared inside. He made no pretence that he was anything but what he was. He made it quite clear to everyone he spoke to what he was looking for. He tried no short cuts. There was no laughing behind hands at Inspector Fowler. Village people recognize a craftsman when they see one, and they recognized a craftsman in Inspector Fowler.

They had no wish to help him to find out who killed Angela Mason Pewsey, but they made no active move to hinder him. Each time he came away from a chance meeting, each time he came out and carefully closed a cottage gate behind him, he left behind someone who felt that willingly or unwillingly they had told Inspector Fowler something that he wanted to know.

He found out that if there was something between Celia Sim and Firth Prentice, it must have happened very quickly, because he had learned of the understanding between Celia and Graham Ward. He learned of the vicar's passionate attachment to his church and for the village of Inching Round. He learned that the poacher Artie Evans had no love for Angela Pewsey and he knew the reason. Thanks to information passed on by Pewsey, Artie's wife had left him on account of an affair with a girl over at Budney. It had been no use him telling her that the affair had been brief and over long ago. Wounded and unforgiving, she had taken her baby and gone away to her parents. Savage and vindictive, Artie had told anyone who would listen that Angela Pewsey would pay the full price and all the interest. But at the time of the murder Artie Evans was or should have been at his work hedging and ditching two miles away.

Fowler met Eric Daw and began quietly following up his impression that the doctor had something on his mind. He remarked that the doctor needed a holiday and someone in the bar agreed with him, and said that except for a week-end in London some weeks ago he hadn't been able to take a holiday for years.

He telephoned to London and a few hours later he knew where Dr Daw had stayed, and that he had not been there alone.

From then on when he mentioned the doctor, and how strained he looked, he would say: 'What that man needs is a wife.'

It only needed a little time for someone to say carefully, 'Ah,' look wise and add: 'That's what he can't have, not till the husband drinks hisself to death at any rate.'

Perhaps Dr Daw thought that only Angela Pewsey had known. But in the life of a village most things are known. Some are talked about, some not. In some cases the knowledge seems almost to communicate itself.

In a number of hours then Inspector Fowler knew. It was not unreasonable to suppose, therefore, that Angela Pewsey also knew. And to a woman of her character what a tremendous sense of power that would give her. How would she use her knowledge? The cat-and-mouse game would be most likely to appeal to her. Hints first perhaps, then threats.

Dr Daw. Inspector Fowler sat thinking of it coldly, as a case. Heaven knew that here was motive enough. Opportunity? It would be easy for a doctor. He was in and about the village every day, as familiar and as accepted a figure as the postman. The weapon was not one that a doctor would be likely to use; the defence would take up that line. But it would not be such a good defence, because it would easily be the sort of weapon a doctor might use if he wanted to draw attention away from himself.

The sympathy of the court would be with him, of course. He might get off with a light sentence. Inspector Fowler's reasoning suddenly stopped; and he found himself visualizing what a trial and the lightest of sentences would mean to Dr Daw. He caught himself entertaining reflexions that might easily have been put into his head by Mrs Sim herself. Was ever there a time when a man was justified in stopping in time and going back to London and reporting no progress?

Inspector Fowler pulled himself together with a jerk. He felt with a sense of horror that this place must be bewitching him. He was outraged at the thoughts he had permitted to cross the threshold of his mind.

Not very long after this battle with his wayward self Inspector Fowler was walking across the churchyard in the direction of Angela Pewsey's cottage. It was familiar to him now, but he had formed the habit of going there at intervals of following up some new line of investigation. It seemed to him that the threads went out from the cottage like the threads of a spider's web, linking first one and then another to death at the centre.

Inspector Fowler saw two small boys peering at him furtively from the protection of a grey tombstone. He stopped and looked down at them from a great height.

'Am I,' he said, 'a curiosity?'

'No,' said Jackie Day. 'You're a detective, sir.'

'Ah.'

'A real one,' Alfie Spiers said. 'Not like Mr Prentice that's staying at Mrs Sim's place. He don't do nothing now that you've come along. My dad said Mr Prentice knows more than what he lets on.'

'And who, may I ask, is your dad?'

'Won't say.'

'Ah.'

'Alfie and me was helping Mr Prentice, but my dad told us not to poke our nose into what wasn't our business.'

'Quite right.'

'But we found the paper.'

'What paper?'

'The paper we give to Mr Prentice.'

'And what did Mr Prentice do with the paper?'

'He tried to give it to Mr Wilks. But Mr Wilks gave a nasty laugh and said he didn't want no help from nobody, specially from London.'

'May I take it that Mr Prentice was offering his services to Constable Wilks?'

'That's right, and Mr Wilks he didn't want none.'

Inspector Fowler bent sternly over them. 'How do you know?'

'We heard them. Alfie and me were detectin' behind the churchyard wall and we heard them. Then Mrs Sim come and took sides with Constable Wilks. We thought she was real cross with Mr Prentice, but when Mr Wilks had gone she took Mr Prentice's arm and told him she thought he was clever and wasn't cross with him at all. She was real pleased.'

Inspector Fowler put his hands behind his back and reflectively contemplated his shoes.

'If Mrs Sim said that the young man had done something clever, I have no doubt that he had. Not,' he said, suddenly aware of the little boys, 'not that that is any business of yours.'

But Alfie Spiers was ready with a defence. 'We know lots about Pewsey,' he said. 'More than anybody. More than Constable Wilks and more than Sergeant Porter even.'

'That's right,' Jackie supported him. 'We know lots of things. And when Mr Prentice read the piece of paper we gave him he looked real serious.'

'What piece of paper?' Against his better judgement Inspector Fowler was interested.

'The one we found that Miss Pewsey had been writing on.'

'How do you know it was her writing? Do you claim to know what her writing is like?'

'Of course we do. She used to write the notices about the folk dances at the village hall.'

'And you read the paper, no doubt?'

'No, it was quick writing with long words. And we can't read Pewsey's writing when it's quick. But Mr Prentice could.'

'And he showed this paper to Constable Wilks, you say?'

'No, but he said he would if Constable Wilks would let him help. But Constable Wilks gave a sort of sneer and said that he couldn't be bothered with bits of paper torn out of kids' exercise books.'

Inspector Fowler looked at the two little serious intelligent faces in front of him. 'So the idea was that you two were going to help Mr Prentice to solve this crime?'

'That's right, sir. We told him that all he had to do was to sit here in the churchyard and we'd come and tell him everything that was going on.'

The inspector smiled. That would be a nice type of criminal investigation, if you could get it . . . and if it got results. And then he saw too that it would have its advantages. A small boy may not know why things are happening in his vicinity, but he misses very little of the action.

'Have you got good memories?' Inspector Fowler asked.

'I can remember five times,' said Alfie Spiers. 'Five ones are five, five twos are ten, five threes are fifteen.' He got well into his stride and seemed quite downcast when Inspector Fowler held up a hand to stop him.

'I mean, can you remember what happens in the village?'

They seemed to regard that question as hardly worth a reply, but they did throw in a scornful 'Of course.'

'Can you remember the day of the murder?'

That seemed even sillier. The confirmation of that most important date in the history of the village (if not the world), merited no more than a nod. Of course they remembered.

'Where were you at half past three o'clock?' He shot the question at them.

'Playing in the churchyard. Miss Pewsey was cattawauling.'

'You mean singing,' said the inspector primly.

'That's right, singing. Alfie and me were sitting with our backs agin the wall tying bits of string together to fix on my kite. Then she stopped catta – I mean singing.'

'What did you think about that?'

'We thought she must have remembered about the kettle.'

'That's right. She stopped all of a sudden like mum does when she remembers that she left the kettle, or the iron on.'

'Ah, and what did you do then?'

'We finished the string for the kite.'

'You were sitting with your backs to the wall, you say?'

'Yes, that's right. It was nice and warm.'

Alfie said regretfully: 'An' all the time the blood was runnin' out of a hole in her head. We might have seen the murderer.'

'Perhaps you did,' the inspector said.

They looked wide-eyed.

'We never saw no one with blood on him.'

'Never mind the blood. How long were you in the churchyard?'

'Oh, for a long time. We came out straight after dinner, that was just after one, and we stayed out there till my mum come and told us to come indoors on account of the murder.'

'Now tell me who you did see.'

'We didn't see nobody but what lives round here, except Mr Graham Ward. We had to get up and look at him to see who it was.'

'What do you mean by that?'

'Well, we knew everybody else by the noise they make.'

'How do you mean by the noise they make?'

'Oh, that's easy, we do it for fun.'

The inspector looked at them in some doubt. 'Would you know me by the noise I make?'

Alfie Spiers giggled. 'Oh, you're easy.'

'How?'

Jackie Day said apologetically: 'We been practising on you. You take big long strides and your feet go flap, flap, flap on the ground.' And he added with a grin: 'Now an' then you click your tongue.'

'I do nothing of the kind,' the inspector said. But he suddenly realized that he did. The whole thing made him feel quite shaken. He, Inspector Fowler of Scotland Yard, advertised his peculiarities in such a way that he could be recognized by small boys in the dark. He said: 'Nonsense.' But he meant it more to reassure himself than to rebuke the small boys. 'Rubbish.'

The little boys were not impressed. They knew.

The inspector seemed about to pursue the subject of himself, changed his mind and cleared his throat instead. Then to his annoyance he clicked his tongue.

'Now,' he said. 'Let us begin with what you *saw*. You say you came out to play shortly after one?'

'That's right.'

'You say that you saw a Mr Graham Ward?'

'That's right.'

'What time?'

'Ten to two.'

'How do you know the exact time?'

'We had a bar of chocolate and we weren't going to start eating it till two o'clock, so we were watching the church clock.'

The inspector's admiration for these two was beginning to strike deep roots.

'So he passed at ten minutes to two?'

'First time, he did.'

'Did he pass again?'

'Course, he had to come back, didn't he?'

'You mean that he was paying a call?'

'That's right, only she wasn't there. We thought he'd come back straight away, only he didn't.'

'As you seem to know everything, perhaps you know where Mr Ward was going?'

Jackie seemed genuinely surprised at such a question.

'Why to see Miss Celia Sim. But she wasn't there. She went to London. Alfie and me carried her bag to the station. Only,' he admitted, 'she helped a bit.'

'And so you expected him to come straight back?'

'Yes, because Mrs Sim, she came down into the rose garden not long afterwards, and there wouldn't be anyone for him to talk to at the house.'

'What time did he come back?'

'Ten minutes to three.'

The inspector grunted at such precision. 'How do you know that?'

'Because I bet Alfie he couldn't make his chocolate bar last till Mr Ward came back. He made it last till a quarter to three by just licking, and it was just gone when Mr Ward come back.

'Alfie was wild because he had to make his chocolate last so long, because he had to take such little slow licks he couldn't taste nothing.'

'And that was the last you saw of Mr Ward?'

'Yes, I suppose he went and got his car from Firlie's garage?'

'Why should he leave his car at Firlie's garage?'

'He got a puncture mended. We asked.'

'Why did you ask?'

'Because we never see him without his car before. He got a new one to show to Miss Celia,' he added, reluctantly it seemed. 'Boy, can he drive it! He killed Jim Mason's dog. Jim said he'd break Mr Ward's neck, but he didn't tell Mr Ward.'

'Why should he buy a new car to impress Miss Sim?'

'My mum says she blows hot and cold over him.'

'I see. And was he a friend of Miss Pewsey's too?'

'He called to see her the day before she was killed,' Alfie said. 'And when he came out he banged her door and run down to his car. Old Pewsey was standing at the window laughing and waving, but he never see her and drove away. Then ole Pewsey, she blew a kiss and done a little dance.'

'You are making all that up,' the inspector said sternly.

'No we ain't,' Alfie said.

'You couldn't see in Miss Pewsey's window because of the net curtains.'

'You can if you are up Jackie's and my tree because the lace curtain goes only half-way up the window.'

'And were you up the tree?'

Jackie hesitated.

'Were you?'

'No, but if I had of been up the tree, I could have seen in.'

'He can't climb it,' Jackie said. 'He knows because I told him.'

'You mean you actually saw what he described?'

'Yes, she danced round the room. She was dancing and kissing a book.'

'Kissing a book?'

'Yeah, a black un. I suppose it was some sort of folk dance. They're all daft,' he ended contemptuously.

The inspector frowned thoughtfully down at his toes. Only just in time did he prevent himself from clicking his tongue.

'A black book . . . what sort of black book was it?'

'I couldn't see very clear. But I think it was one she wrote in. It was about as big as an exercise book only lots thicker.'

The inspector had had time to go through all the documents at the disposal of the police in the Pewsey case. There was no black book. Yet this story of the little boy who looked through the window left him in no doubt that there was a black book somewhere. That it had disappeared might be a sign of its importance. In the hands of the police it might hang a murderer. The two little boys exchanged glances and very nearly giggled when all unknowingly Inspector Fowler clicked his tongue.

'So you saw Mr Ward pass up the road and an hour later he came back again?'

'That's right.'

'Did you see him again?'

'No, sir.'

'Who else passed?'

'The vicar. He said hello, Dee and Dum. Sometimes he calls us Tweedle Dee and Tweedle Dum, but mostly Dee and Dum. We could see him, because he was inside the churchyard the same as we were. He come out of the church. Then he went down the road on a visit. Then he come back again along the road where we could see. When he came back in the churchyard he hurried past us and didn't say nothing at all, like as if he was late for something.'

'No doubt he was,' the inspector said. 'Who else came past?'

'The doctor, he came past a few times in his car, but he's always doing that.'

The inspector asked casually: 'Did he come along about three o'clock too?'

'That's right, just after the vicar passed we heard his car start up and he drove past. He always drives pretty fast.'

'Did you see the car?'

'Of course not, but we know it. The engine makes a funny noise in low gear.' They implied that it would be absurd to suggest that they did not know the doctor's car.

'Where was it when you heard it start?'

'Down the road a piece.'

'You mean near Miss Pewsey's cottage?'

'Yes, somewhere about there.' Neither of them were particularly interested in the doctor's car. 'He leaves it in different places and sometimes he goes to three or four different cottages before he comes back to it, specially when there's chicken-pox or something about.' To them the doctor's car was as much a part of the scenery as the trees.

But Inspector Fowler's attitude was not at all the same. It would excite little attention when a doctor walked up any path in the village, stayed a while and walked out again. The neighbours would remark that the occupier must be ill. But it was more than likely that a woman like Angela Pewsey would demand more than her share of the doctor's attention, whether she needed it or not.

'Did the doctor often go to Miss Pewsey's?'

'Of course he did, but my dad said that all that was wrong with her is what's wrong with a lot of other old maids. But I don't know what that is.'

No, it would excite no interest to see the doctor making a routine call on Miss Pewsey. Even if somebody remarked and remembered the time, he could simply say that he had knocked, had got no answer, and had come away again. The front door was screened by a cluster of shrubs, so it would be hard to contradict him.

'And then,' Jackie Day said. 'Major Torrens come past.'

'Major Torrens.' The inspector's voice was vague. His mind was still speculating on the movements of the doctor, but he added with half-hearted defence: 'How do you know if you didn't see him?'

'He walks heavy,' Jackie said. 'You show him, Alfie.'

Quite seriously Alfie stood up and paraded before the inspector, very stiff-backed and emphatic. His feet banged on the path, but now and then the right foot scraped the gravel in its stride.

'That's right,' Jackie said. 'Only he carries a stick and he bangs that on the ground too.'

The inspector had no doubt in his mind that it was right. You couldn't give that impression of a man of military bearing unless you knew the original.

'So you heard Major Torrens pass?'

'That's right, but we didn't let him see us.'

'Why not?'

'Oh, he's always calling us scallywags and telling us to be off.'

The inspector smiled. 'Be off where?'

'Oh, anywhere. If we're in the road he tells us to be off.

If we're in the churchyard he tells us to be off. He comes to the school the other day and told Mr Millings that we had no discipline.'

'I see, and what did Mr Millings say to that?'

'Mr Millings got red in the face and said that what might be good for the natives wasn't the way to treat children in an English village.' He added defensively: 'We do do what Mr Millings tells us though.'

'Yes, an' I do too,' said Alfie.

'Major Torrens he said he was going to report Mr Millings to the authorities for insolence. But my dad says Mr Millings has only got to say the word and he and some other men will throw Major Torrens in the duck pond.'

The inspector scowled heavily. 'And if your dad does anything of the kind he will find himself up before the magistrates. Which,' he added half to himself, 'would be a great pity.'

'We heard him go down the road and we heard him come back.'

'And was he away long?'

'No, only about ten minutes. He come back just before the doctor drove away.'

'Do you think it likely that the Major was calling on Miss Pewsey?' He said that because the very idea seemed to him ludicrous.

'We think maybe he called to get his papers back.'

Inspector Fowler straightened with a jerk. 'His what?'

'His papers that we see Miss Pewsey taking out of his house.'

'You mean she called on him and came away with some papers?'

'Yes, only when she called Major Torrens wasn't there.'

'What on earth do you mean by that?'

'There wasn't nobody in the house. Mr and Mrs Watson that works for Major Torrens, they was away too. Every second Wednesday they go to Tonbridge and stay the night, and Major Torrens he goes to London. It was on Thursday morning we see Miss Pewsey.'

'What time in the morning?'

'It was just before six.'

The inspector was incredulous. 'What on earth were you doing about at six o'clock in the morning?'

Alfie shuffled his feet. 'Well, we were just up.'

'Come on now, out with it, what were you up to?'

'Well, sir, it was a sort of a little snare, only we weren't trying to catch anything – it was only practice, see?'

'Ha, and where exactly had you set this sort of a little snare of yours?'

Jackie said meekly: 'In Major Torrens' ground, sir. They was all away an ...' his voice broke, and he stood there looking a very frightened little boy.

But Alfie came to his defence. 'But we didn't catch nothing, only a silly little old rabbit that wasn't no bigger than this.'

'Well,' said Inspector Fowler with heavy superiority, 'these petty crimes of yours are matters for the local police. No doubt as these tendencies of yours develop you will fall into their hands and go to such places as Maidstone, Wandsworth and other prisons for periods of ten, fifteen and twenty years, where they will feed you on bread and bad fish.'

'Oh, please, Mister, we didn't mean to do nothing. We won't any more.'

'In that case, I shall not proceed further with the matter.' He cleared his throat. 'And so at six o'clock in the morning, for reasons which we shall not go into now, you were in the grounds of Impy House?'

'That's right.'

'And at that unusual hour you say you saw Miss Pewsey?'

'That's right,' Jackie was all eagerness again. 'We see her come popping out of the side door.'

'Did she see you?'

'No, we were on the lookout because we didn't want no one to see us.' He looked guilty again and added quickly: 'We popped down behind some bushes.'

'You are sure, absolutely sure, it was Miss Pewsey?'

'Of course. Anyone could tell it was her, the way she bobbed and popped about. She looked terribly excited. Close to us she stopped and looked at the papers she had. Then she pressed them against her chest and done a funny little dance. Then she nipped down the drive and out the gate.'

There was something in the way this boy gave his information that made it almost impossible not to believe him.

The inspector could almost see it all with his own eyes: the grey dawn, the half-frightened, excited little boys, crouching like alert little wild animals in the bushes, the startling appearance of Angela Pewsey, her own unrepressed excitement, her gloating over her discovery – it was very real.

Her discovery of what? Something that must be in her own line. Inspector Fowler knew now that Angela Pewsey specialized in other peoples' past lives. Only evidence of some wrongdoings on the part of Major Torrens could have made her as pleased as she was that morning. Miss Pewsey had discovered something. Some information had come her way and she followed it up by going through Major Torrens' papers. She took a risk, so she must have felt that the risk would be worth while.

'Damn the woman.' He said this aloud and was immediately angry with himself.

'How long ago did all this happen?' he asked brusquely.

'I think it was about three weeks. Yes, it was three weeks, because it was the Thursday before Alfie's brother got the chicken-pox.'

'Have you by any chance been gossiping about what you saw?'

'Oh no, sir. We wasn't supposed to be there at all, so we couldn't tell no one. My dad would have the hide off me if he knew.'

'So would my dad,' said Alfie, not to be outdone. 'He'd skin me alive with a knife.'

Major Torrens would know, surely, if important papers had been stolen from his own house. He made a mental note to inquire of the local police if there had been any complaint from the Major.

'Very well,' he said to the little boys. 'You can go back to your games . . . unless of course anyone else passed at the time we are inquiring about.'

'Only some women,' Jackie said. 'I forget who they were. There was one we didn't know by listening to her walk. We looked over the wall, but she'd gone.'

'And the ones you did recognize?'

'Mrs Tedder and Mrs John were talking as they passed, and then old Mrs Hibbs come by, she's lame and that was all.'

The inspector looked up to see Firth standing beside him, smiling at the group.

'Hello, Inspector. It must be a great relief to these two to have a real detective to work with. I'm afraid I sadly disappointed them.'

'Is that so, Mr Prentice. I didn't know you'd been going into the case.'

'Oh yes, indeed. At one time I thought of solving it.'

'Don't tell me,' the inspector said heavily, 'that it turned out to be too much for you?'

'That perhaps. Or on the other hand I may have thought it would be better to leave it to the authorities. It's always best in the long run.'

'Hum, that's a bit of a change of point of view, isn't it?'

'No, no, not really. Any other views I may have expressed were not really genuine.'

'But they were quite different, let's say, from those you expressed to Constable Wilks?'

'Wilks, Inspector, was most annoying. He seemed so terribly convinced that I wouldn't be any use.' He grinned. 'I'm consoling myself with the thought that very likely he is thinking the same way about you. He doesn't approve of Londoners.'

Inspector Fowler frowned impressively at the witnesses to this statement.

'Now then, run along, you boys,' he said.

They interpreted 'run along' as moving a few yards and sitting on a tombstone, well within earshot. In the end it was Inspector Fowler and Firth who moved.

'By the way,' Firth said, 'if Constable Wilks told you that I had offered to help, I hope at the same time he told you he was very rude about it. I was quite definitely hurt.'

The inspector shook his head. 'Apart from everything else,' he said, 'you can't exactly hurt a solicitor. So now perhaps you'll tell me why exactly you made this offer of yours to Constable Wilks.'

'I was merely trying to help.'

'Very well, you shall help me.'

Firth shook his head. 'Oh no, one snub is quite enough, thank you.'

'You mean you refuse?'

'But certainly. I'm not accustomed to being treated as a half-wit.'

'Now, come now, Mr Prentice. You and I know what these local people are. They'd treat me in the same way if they dared.'

'Nothing doing.'

'I understand that you have a piece of paper in your possession?'

'Have I?'

'Oh, for heaven's sake, man, don't hedge. Those boys told me all about it. They gave it to you.'

'Constable Wilks knew all about that. It was a bit out of an old exercise book. He made me feel an awful fool when he explained what it was.'

'Where is it?'

'My dear chap, what did you expect me to do with it after that? Keep it as a souvenir of my rebuff?'

The inspector looked at him thoughtfully. Very clever,' he said, 'you manoeuvred yourself into a position where you could dispose of some valuable evidence with impunity. Very well then, who did you think you were protecting when you did that?'

'Valuable evidence? Really, Inspector, that was by no means what I was told when last the subject was discussed with the police. They refused absolutely to have anything to do with this valuable evidence as you call it. Why on earth shouldn't I destroy it?'

'You haven't told me who you thought you were protecting.'

Firth smiled. 'Was I going to?'

'It would be interesting to know. Then we might know the name of the murderer.'

'Really! You police are a funny lot. You refuse my help, ask for my help, accuse me of giving succour and comfort to murderers; one honestly wonders what you will think of next.'

'Tell me this, Mr Prentice: was there a name mentioned on the document you have so conveniently refused to produce?'

Firth shook his head. 'No name, Inspector.'

'Perhaps you can remember what was written on it?'

'No, I'm afraid I can't, beyond the fact that it gave expression to the writer's happiness.'

'Miss Pewsey's?'

'I'd be in a better position to answer that if I knew what Miss Pewsey's writing was like.'

'Yes, we must rectify that.'

'In what way, inspector?'

'Oh, it won't be difficult to show you a specimen of Angela Pewsey's handwriting. The local police collected a good deal of it when they went through her belongings.'

'I'm not a handwriting expert, you know.'

'Really now,' the inspector permitted himself a discreet smile, 'I should have thought that as an amateur detective one of the first things that would have interested you would have been handwriting.'

'Ah, but my interest in detection is only a few days old.'

'Never mind, you can just tell me what you think.'

Firth had an uncomfortable feeling that there were

difficulties ahead of him. The inspector's next remark seemed to bring them appreciably nearer.

'I understand that Dr Daw is a friend of yours.'

'Dr Daw, why no. Not at all.'

'He drove you back from the inquest, I'm told.'

'Yes, but quite often in the country you find a motorist giving a pedestrian a lift.'

'Hum. I was wondering what you thought of him.'

'He seemed a nice enough quiet sort of chap.'

'Bit on the nervy side though, don't you think?'

'I imagine this business of leaping from one confinement to another and being rung up at all hours of the night isn't exactly a soothing job. What he probably needs is a long week-end in bed.' He stopped short and found the inspector watching him curiously.

'That, I understand, is just what he did have.'

Firth laughed and hoped he made it sound natural.

'In that case he probably needs another one.'

'On the other hand, he may have something on his mind.'

'Possibly, most of us have these days, particularly doctors. I understand that they feel that they are being pushed round a little.'

'You heard him at that inquest, didn't you?'

'Yes.'

'How did he strike you then?'

'Amusing. Doctors giving evidence always make me laugh. The jury wants to hear the gory details and the doctor for the like of him can't understand why he should tell them. So he tries to make the whole thing as unintelligible as possible.'

'Quite. But you didn't form any impression as to his state of mind?'

'None at all. It wasn't my business, in fact.'

'Really.' The inspector was incredulous. 'But surely at that time you were planning to put your services at the disposal of the police. Wouldn't it have been natural to have made it your business?'

Firth sighed. 'I'm beginning to think Wilks was right

after all. It's best to leave these things to the professional.'

Inspector Fowler was not impressed. 'And you talked about the inquest afterwards, I suppose?'

'I suppose so, inspector.'

'What did the doctor have to say about it?'

'As far as I remember he thought that his talents could be better used at the disposal of the living. I gather that from a doctor's point of view when a man or woman is dead they are very dead.'

'I see.'

'Do you?'

'What else did you talk about?'

'The weather, no doubt, the crops perhaps. I understand these are useful topics in this part of the world.'

'And nothing at all about Angela Pewsey?'

'Look, Inspector, I can truthfully say that ever since I have been here everybody has been talking almost exclusively about Angela Pewsey. At the very mention of her name a gloom descends on me that no words can penetrate. If you ask me if Dr Daw talked about Pewsey, I can only tell you that I am certain he did. I was with him for half an hour, and if I'd been with anyone for half an hour without her name being mentioned I'd have written to tell someone in London about it.'

'I understand,' said the inspector doggedly, 'that he was her doctor.'

'No doubt, no doubt he was. In fact, I think he said so at the inquest. She probably contrived to be attended by every doctor for miles. One doctor would be no use to an inquiring mind like Angela's.'

'You speak as if you knew the lady personally, Mr Prentice.'

'Oh, but I do, Inspector. I never saw her alive, but dead I know her only too well. No doubt if I had come on the scene earlier I should have murdered her myself.'

'So you think that the motive for this murder lay in the character of the deceased?'

'How the blazes do I know what the motive was?' Firth was suddenly desperately angry with the whole business.

'Well, well, we won't help ourselves by taking on like that, will we?'

'Don't you see, old boy, that I am not trying to help anybody, not even myself. I don't know what the motive was, and, what's more, I don't care. Anybody would have murdered her and somebody did, and that's that.'

'I'd put it a different way, Mr Prentice. Somebody murdered her and somebody will be brought to trial, and that will be that.'

Yes, Firth thought angrily, this elongated bloodhound would go on sniffing and snuffling till he had unearthed the one overpowering motive and then he would go lumbering along the trail from the motive to the murderer. It was the law and the process of the law and he, Firth Prentice, who lived by the law had no right to complain. But the reasons for his anger were not as simple as that. He was angry because of the people who were involved, angry because Celia was involved, in a small way perhaps, but involved. And Graham Ward – what did one do in his case? He might get away safely into the woods if the inspector's trail led him somewhere else and led him there directly enough. But would it ... Or to put in a grimmer way, could it? Graham Ward was one of those involved whom he did not like, but it was a monstrous thought that Celia should be associated with a murderer. He had been in the vicinity at the time of the murder. He was hardboiled enough or even vain enough to lash out at anything that stood in his way or held him up to contempt. And there was no doubt that he was in love with Celia; almost as much, Firth thought spitefully, as he loved himself.

And then there was the black book, destroyed now, or hidden perhaps among Mrs Sim's possessions. He could insist on Mrs Sim giving it up to the police. But no matter how strongly he insisted he had an idea she would refuse. He could ask her to hand over the book to him. That she might do. He would have to read it then and he might find the motive and the name. He shook his head and looked up to see the inspector watching him shrewdly.

'You do know more about this than you've owned to, Mr Prentice. Of that I am certain.' He added: 'That might be playing a dangerous game.'

Firth smiled. 'I'll make you a promise, Inspector. If I come across anything I feel I would like you to know, I will tell you whether you like it or not.'

'I believe,' the inspector replied, 'you could have told me more about Dr Daw.'

'I suppose I should be flattered. The total time I have spent in company of Dr Daw would be just a little less than one hour.'

'I know that, but he's one of your kind.'

'One of my kind! He's a hard-working, serious-minded country doctor.'

'Maybe, but he's not above getting himself pretty involved in a certain matter that could ruin him.'

Firth's smile remained easily on his lips. The inspector could trace no change in his expression.

'Oh, so that's why he's one of my kind; because he's capable of getting himself into trouble. It would serve you right, my boy, if I took an action against you for slander. The trouble with you is that you are overwrought.'

'Do I look overwrought, Mr Prentice?'

'No, I must confess you don't. As a matter of fact, you look about as overwrought as a tortoise.'

'But I think you'd like to divert my attention from your friend.'

'Listen, Inspector, I don't want to harp on this, but Dr Daw is not my friend. The other day I saw him for the first time. I have seen him once since then. He did give me a ride back from the inquest in his car, but if you are suggesting that that would make me obliged to divert your attention from him, then you must be crazy.'

'All right, Mr Prentice, all right, sir. Now don't let us

excite ourselves. I never said that it was the car ride that put you under an obligation to Dr Daw.'

'I'm not under any obligation to Dr Daw. I am not interested in Dr Daw.'

'I am, very interested. Well, I may call on you again, Mr Prentice. Unless you'll walk to the "Merry Harriers" and have a drink with me I'll be getting along.' Then, without waiting for a reply, Inspector Fowler got into his stride like a starting train. Firth watched him go. There was something about his progress that was as resolute as the law itself.

I I

THE Reverend Henry Holland was coming out of the church door as Firth came strolling back along the path.

'My dear chap,' he called out, 'how nice to see you.'

He hurried forward to shake hands. 'You know I feel very remiss about you. I promised myself that I would invite you in for a meal, and now my housekeeper is in bed. I don't know if it's 'flu or too much excitement for the old body. Dr Daw tells me she has a temperature, so of course she must stay in bed.'

'It is disconcerting, isn't it? I hope you aren't enjoying too much chaos.'

'Oh no, no. Her daughter Millie is filling in the gap. Millie thinks she can cook, but she is quite mistaken of course. It means that I can't ask anyone else to share my distress.'

'Let's hope that the 'flu or excitement abate quickly.'

'Yes, indeed. The tragedy is that I myself am an excellent chef. But if I went into the kitchen I'm afraid that Millie would be deeply hurt. There is one thing I can offer you, however, and that is an extremely palatable sherry.'

'That sounds very agreeable.'

'Splendid, splendid. Come along this minute, my dear chap.'

He took Firth's arm and propelled him eagerly along the path.

The vicar's study faced the sunlight of the south. At this moment the room was full of it, pouring through the long french windows that gave on to the lawn.

Firth looked about him with satisfaction. 'I envy you the room,' he said.

'I have to thank Mrs Sim for that. She took me out of a place I was pleased to call my den. It was very dark and very stuffy and had rather unpleasant imitation leather chairs.'

He poured the sherry into two glasses and it shone like old gold in the sunlight.

'Do sit down, my boy, and we shall make ourselves comfortable.' He settled himself facing his guest and looked appreciatively at the liquid in his glass. 'This is the one hour of the day when I behave with deliberate conscious self-indulgence. Literally, I am outraged if anyone disturbs me.' He cocked his eye as Firth took a sip from his glass. 'Do you approve of it?'

'I should think I do. It's delicious.'

'Truthfully, one can taste the sun of the Spanish hillsides.'

'I shouldn't deprive you of this,' Firth said. 'In these days it's very hard to come by.'

'Ah no, you may not know, but in my own small way I am quite an authority on sherry. I have been called into consultation many, many times with shippers and connoisseurs who value my opinion. It is perhaps a strange hobby for a vicar, but I can assure you it is a most enjoyable one.'

Firth laughed. 'Yes, indeed, I'm sure it is.'

'The added advantage,' the vicar said, 'is that you can't call a man into consultation about a shipment of wine without letting him have a case, at least, to meditate upon. No, my boy, you have no need to fear that you will drink me dry. Now do let me fill up your glass, or would you prefer to try something a little different?'

'No, no. I'm sure nothing could be better than this.'

The vicar replenished their glasses. 'I'm inclined to agree with you. This is my own favourite, certainly.' He seated himself again with a little sigh of satisfaction.

They sat for a while without speaking, and when he did speak it seemed that the vicar did so with reluctance.

'I noticed a little while ago that you were in consultation with Inspector Fowler. He is a most determined man, I should judge.'

'Very. He's a particularly shrewd one too.'

'So I should imagine. Do you suppose he's approaching a solution?'

Firth shook his head. 'I don't know. He does seem to have his nose pretty confidently on the trail though.'

The vicar seemed to have forgotten his drink. He seemed to be looking into the future. 'I wonder,' he said slowly, 'where that trail will lead him. Perhaps we may still hope that it will lead to nowhere.'

Firth looked at him quickly. 'I didn't think you would subscribe to that.'

His host frowned. His voice too, when he spoke, had hardened. 'The time will come when the person who killed Angela Pewsey will go to his just punishment. I believe that there is a higher justice than that which Inspector Fowler serves. At this tribunal Angela Pewsey herself will state her case for vengeance. I believe that the climax of Inspector Fowler's work will be only to pile misery upon misery here in our own village.'

'You believe, too, that it was somebody whom you all know?'

The vicar looked at him in surprise. 'But don't you?'

'I am afraid so.'

'Angela Pewsey was a wicked woman in the true sense of the word.'

'You knew what she had been doing?'

'Yes.'

'There was nothing you could do to stop her?'

'When I approached her she denied the whole thing. She

laughed and said I was too absurd. She spoke of her work for the parish. She had the effrontery to speak of what our little church meant to her ... smug, smiling and with an undercurrent of malice. I know now that her greatest desire in life was to be feared.'

'Yes, but it isn't Inspector Fowler's business to sit in judgement. His sole interest is in finding the person who killed her and to produce evidence in court to prove it. In certain circumstances the sentence might not be a heavy one.'

'My dear boy, death is not necessarily the heaviest sentence that can be imposed on man. There are times when it can seem the lightest.'

Firth emptied his glass without being aware that he tasted it. He said after a pause: 'I wonder if I might make a telephone call?'

The vicar seemed glad to break the train of his thoughts. 'Why, of course, my boy. There is the instrument in the corner. If it is a local number you simply dial it, otherwise you must dial "O", or would you rather I did it for you?'

Firth answered diffidently: 'I hate to ask you, Vicar, but I wonder if you would very much mind if I made this call privately? I know I shouldn't ask, but I'd rather telephone from here than from Mrs Sim's house. Nobody would want to hear, of course, but they might by accident, and I don't want that to happen.'

'But of course, of course I understand.' The vicar hesitated and added: 'You will be quite private here. Millie is out shopping. Her mother is in bed on the other side of the house.' He smiled. 'I will go out through the french windows and you can watch me till I am out of range.' He moved towards the exit.

'I know this sounds all very melodramatic,' Firth said. 'But you see, someone else is involved and it really would be better for you not to know whom I'm ringing up.'

The vicar gave him a quick speculative look. 'It would never occur to me that you would act in this way without a very good reason. Do call me when you have finished, won't you?' He smiled, gave an odd little wave of his hand as he stepped out on to the lawn.

Firth looked for Dr Daw's number in the book by the telephone. He was glad to find that it was a local number and there was no need to go through the exchange.

The doctor's maid answered the telephone, but she said that he had just come in, and presently he heard the doctor's own voice.

'This is Prentice, Doctor, I'm staying with Mrs Sim, if you remember.'

'Of course I remember. How are you?' In spite of his deliberately casual tone Firth could detect the strain in his voice.

'Doctor, I felt that I should ring you up. I think before very long you may be having a visitor.'

'Oh.'

'I think you can guess whom I mean.'

There was a long pause and then the reply, 'Yes.'

'It may help you to know that the letter involved in all this is still in my posssession.'

Firth thought he heard a gasp of relief, but the voice was cautious. 'Oh, yes.'

'All the same I think you should know that the matter referred to in the letter is known to your visitor.'

This time there was almost a cry of protest. 'No . . . But how?'

'Doctor,' Firth said gently, 'you know village life better than I do. Things become known almost as if the knowledge was floating in the air. Nobody intends deliberately to tell tales, but any shrewd investigator senses these things and follows them up.'

'But all this gossip doesn't prove anything. Surely if I deny . . . '

'I wouldn't hasten to deny things, Doctor. It's awfully easy to inquire at London hotels.'

'My God . . . '

'I should think it all over very carefully. Remember that I still have the letter. Be frank as far as you can be and explain what your position would be if it became known. Most people are human beings.'

There was another long pause. 'You are going to keep the letter?'

Firth snapped out a reply. 'I'll keep it till it becomes too dangerous. I've been thinking of your career. There might come a time when I've got to think of my own.'

'Yes, I see that. You mustn't take risks on my account.'

'For God's sake, Doctor, don't be so damned good. Don't say anything foolish and don't do anything foolish and then we may all get out of this infernal mess.'

'I didn't kill Angela Pewsey.'

'I didn't say you did. The point is that the police think that you could have done it. But if it's any comfort to you so could several others.'

He put up the receiver and strolled down into the garden to find the vicar. He found him sitting on a stone seat that overlooked a quiet pond.

'I've finished, thank you very much, Vicar. I hope you'll forgive me for disturbing your rest hour.'

The little man shook his head. 'I'm afraid my rest hour has not had the same quality during the last few days. It is almost incredible that the effects of one swift act could be so far-reaching.'

'I don't think, you know, that they are necessarily the effects of one act. What you are experiencing now had its beginnings in Angela Pewsey's character.'

'Perhaps. But I know now that the living must take their share of the responsibilities. It was a great mistake to think otherwise.'

'You speak as if the person most concerned were known to you.'

He half smiled. 'Did I give you that impression?'

'Well, it wouldn't be so unexpected. It is a small community and the place of the priest is rather a special one.'

'Yes, there are circumstances under which he has a special knowledge; and obligations.'

'And also, one supposes, occasions when he feels himself bound to secrecy.'

The vicar stood in the bright light by the window. His face was white, leaving a spot of high colour on each of his cheek-bones. His head was raised, his eyes gleamed. His voice vibrated with his emotion.

'All around us here in this village you see the enduring life, the work, the habits, the ways of life that have been handed down to us across the centuries. Old World is how we are described, and that is right. We in this little community can reach back and touch the hands of our ancestors. We can work as they worked. We can think as they thought. We can see visions as they saw them. We can hate as they hated.

'In that field you see from this window a witch was burned. She was denounced from the pulpit of my church. And now, Mr Prentice, in this same village another witch has been struck down. For in the true sense of the word that woman, Angela Pewsey, was a witch. She dealt in evil, she sought it in the hearts of others. She carried her venom in her heart and tongue and mind.' His voice rose. 'I should have denounced her as my predecessor denounced that other witch. Now I pray that God will shelter the one who struck her down.'

There was silence between them. The vicar was standing rigid, gazing out the window. Firth could think of nothing adequate to say.

Presently the little man turned back to face him and when he spoke again his voice had regained its old diffident charm.

'Well, Mr Prentice, unless you will have another glass of my sherry I'm afraid I'll have to prepare myself for the ordeal of one of Millie's execrable feasts.'

'Of course; I'm keeping you. Perhaps you'll let me have the sherry another time?'

'But of course. Any time between the hours of twelve and one I'm to be found alone and pining for companionship.'

He walked with Firth to the gate and waved as he walked away.

Sherry taster and man of God – Firth smiled affectionately as he thought of the little man he had left behind, who seemed to live wisely and so well.

12

INSPECTOR FOWLER did not go at once to visit Dr Daw. Twenty years' experience had taught him not to rush things. He had decided in the morning to have another look through the material that the police had taken possession of from the Pewsey cottage, Rooks Roost. He decided not to alter his plans.

Sergeant Porter he discovered was a tidy man. The Pewsey exhibits were assorted into neat lots: circulars, bills, personal letters, greeting cards, business letters, postcards and such odds and ends as might come under the heading of souvenirs.

Inspector Fowler went slowly and unemotionally through the personal letters. By and large they seemed to be from people whom Miss Pewsey had met on a holiday, or a cruise. Sadly none of them indicated a friendship of long standing or deep structure. Dogs and cats occupied much space in the emotional experiences referred to. In the main they were the letters of lonely women glad even of a trifling memory to keep green. There were no letters from anyone whom he had met since he came to the village; no familiar names except that of the vicar, who signed a scribbled note about some church meeting, the sort that is thrust through a letterbox when the occupier is out. That was all.

Inspector Fowler wound the tape round the bundle he had finished reading and turned to the next in order. This was an accumulation of bills; all but a few of the most recent were receipted. Obviously the dead spinster was most carefully honest with her tradespeople. He could have learned this from the first few that he opened. But the inspector went steadily through the whole collection. Near the end he opened an envelope and there dropped out a fragment torn from a letterhead. For a long time he sat holding this in his hand. One might have supposed from his expression and the way he was holding it that he was trying to guess its weight.

It was not until the inspector had completed the last document available that he turned back to the scrap of paper he had set aside. Then he took up the telephone and put a call through to London and asked for Sergeant Piggott.

'I've got something here, Sergeant, that may or may not mean something. But I want you to follow it up carefully. This is the name, "The Lynx Detective Service." They are in Fetter Lane. Do you know anyone there? You do? Good; well, I want you to go to them and find out if they are in any way connected with this case. Ask about the woman first, of course, Angela Mason Pewsey. You've got a picture of her there. You'd better take it along in case she was acting under an assumed name. Now I want you to make a note of this list of names.'

Slowly and carefully he read out the names of all those whom he had cause to associate even remotely with his case. He included Firth Prentice and here explained that Firth was a solicitor acting for the Sims. It might be possible that in that capacity he had employed the Lynx Agency.

'They may not want to talk, but if they try any rubbish about their business being confidential, tell them that this is a question of murder, and if we want them to talk we can make them talk.' Inspector Fowler expressed a mental wish that he could say the same of the people down here.

'If and when you find any connexion with this affair ring me up at once, will you, Sergeant? It may be very important. When will I be back? I thought when I came here I'd be back in a couple of days, now I don't know. They're all sticking together like glue. Before I get the one I want it looks as if I'll have to melt some of them down. Never try to be a gentleman in a case like this, Piggott, it's a waste of time. From now on I'm going to be a policeman.'

Sergeant Piggott grinned as he hung up the telephone. Old Long Tom was getting peeved.

When Inspector Fowler went to call on Dr Daw he was out. There was nothing unusual in that – country doctors spend a big percentage of their time away from home – but there was something cautious about the way the doctor's receptionist received him. In his usual painstaking way the inspector had found out about the doctor's household before he called. It consisted of an elderly housekeeper, who lived out. She was a motherly old creature who had years ago despaired of ever serving the doctor a meal on time, or if she did that he would ever finish it without being interrupted.

Ethel Carey, his receptionist, did not live in the house but boarded out in the village. She was plumpish, grave, and looked almost severely calm.

She offered the inspector a chair, but preferred to remain standing herself. The waiting-room was cool and rather drab and smelled faintly of drugs and of the procession of frightened or self-indulgent humanity who passed through it.

Ethel Carey held her hands clasped in front of her. She stood straight and still. Her grey eyes were steady and attractive. They were in contrast to her olive skin and shining dark hair. There was a suggestion of strength about her without hardness. It was surely foolish of Inspector Fowler to think at that moment that Dr Daw was a lucky man, because Dr Daw was in danger of losing his career and possibly his life.

He made the usual apologies for being troublesome and asked if he might see the doctor.

'He is out, I'm afraid.'

'Ah, I'm sorry to hear that, but of course I should have made an appointment. Should I wait, do you think?'

She was doubtful. 'I'm afraid I can't tell you when he'll be in.'

'He is out on his rounds, I suppose?'

'He has to be out a great deal.'

'What is his usual time of returning, Miss Carey?'

'It's difficult to say. Between morning and afternoon surgery all his appointments are taken up with calls.'

'I was wondering if it would help if you looked at his appointments book.'

She shook her head. 'I'm afraid I can't do that, he takes it with him on his rounds.'

'And you don't know where he is?'

She shook her head. 'Not to-day, I'm afraid.'

'That will be unfortunate surely if there is an urgent call for him?'

Her manner changed defensively. 'The doctor does not neglect his duty to his patients.'

'My dear young lady, I'm sure he doesn't. But it occurs to me that there must be some way of getting in touch with him urgently if need be.'

'He rings up at intervals to ask if there is an urgent call.'

'And if necessary he would come back?'

She hesitated and said: 'Yes, if it was a matter of life and death.'

He smiled grimly. 'But not to waste his time over a policeman, is that it?'

She raised her eyebrows slightly. 'Would you want him to?'

'No, no, of course not. No, Miss Carey, my business can wait. You see, I'm not going to die ... not before I've seen Dr Daw, at any rate.'

'If you'll leave your number, Inspector, I'll ask him to telephone. You realize, of course, that he's pretty tired at the end of a day. And people do get ill at night.'

'Yes, Miss Carey, I understand all that. But if something has to be done it's often better to do it quickly.'

Ethel Carey stood a while without speaking, and then she

said with an odd appeal in her voice: 'I suppose you insist on this interview, Inspector? I should have thought he'd done all he could to help. He attended when they found the body and gave evidence at the inquest. It upsets him if time is taken from his work.'

He answered in a matter of fact voice. 'I must insist, I'm afraid. You see, I've had to insist on seeing dozens of people since I came here. Perhaps I could have left some of them out if I'd known them better, but you see I'm a stranger and can only make up my mind when I've heard what they have to say.'

'But surely you know all about Dr Daw?' She spoke almost as if she were referring to a celebrity.

'Do you know all about him, Miss Carey?'

She coloured and for a brief moment seemed confused.

'I don't know what you mean.'

'I was wondering how well you knew him.'

'Of course, I know him. I've worked here for two years.'

'You don't necessarily know the people you work with.' He seemed to think the conversation was becoming personal, or suggestive of a significance he didn't intend, because he smiled and added: 'The trouble with detectives is that they suspect everybody.'

But with a note of dismay in her voice she said: 'You don't suspect Dr Daw?'

He laughed waggishly. 'Aha, you don't know me. Why, for all you know I may suspect even you.'

She might have scoffed at that, but instead she said with startling intensity: 'She was a horrible woman . . . Horrible. She . . . '

Miss Carey paused and the inspector prompted her insistently.

'Yes, Miss Carey, tell me what Miss Pewsey did to you?'

Again the colour flared up in her cheeks. 'She said . . . she suggested there was something between Dr Daw and me. I was furious . . . so furious that I was going to beat her with my hands. But she backed away and gave that dreadful laugh of hers and said that it was only her little joke.' She calmed down and added in a smouldering voice: 'But you can be quite sure that she went about telling everybody she met what my reactions were to her "little joke"!'

'You sound as if you really hated her, Miss Carey.'

'Yes, I hated her.'

The inspector thought he knew why. If she loved Dr Daw and not even the doctor himself knew it, it would be sacrilege when Miss Pewsey turned it into village gossip.

He wondered if Ethel Carey knew about the other woman in Eric Daw's life. If she did, would that have made her hate Angela Pewsey less, or more? More perhaps because she would have added ridicule to the rest.

'I suppose you were here when Miss Pewsey was killed, Miss Carey?' He found himself looking at her strong hands, folded quietly in front of her.

'It was my afternoon off.'

'Oh. Did you spend it at home?'

'I went for a long walk through Brecon Wood. I often do that.'

'I see. Did you meet anyone?'

'No, it's lonely up there.'

'Could you think of any way to prove that you were not near Miss Pewsey's cottage?' He remembered suddenly what the little boys had said about the woman's footsteps which they had not recognized.

'I didn't meet anyone in the woods, but someone may have seen me.'

'Did you kill Miss Pewsey?'

There was no reply. Even the calm expression showed no change.

'I asked you a question, Miss.'

She half smiled. 'How do you expect me to answer it?'

'You could answer simply "yes", or "no".'

'No.' Again the half smile. 'You didn't really expect me to say yes, did you, Inspector?'

'I expected you to tell the truth,' he said prosily, but only because he had a sudden feeling of frustration. He had come here to deal with one suspect and now he had another on his hands. The idea made him angry. He stood and reached for his hat.

'You realize that I will have to make further inquiries into this, I suppose?'

'Yes, I suppose so.'

'And also, Miss Carey, I must ask you to hold yourself in readiness for further questioning.'

'Yes, Inspector. Shall I tell the doctor that you called or shall I ask him to ring you?'

'Tell him I expect him to ring me as soon as he comes in.'

He strode away angrily and, at the same time, with the incredible feeling that somehow or other Ethel Carey had got the better of him. For the life of him he couldn't see how. She had put herself in a tight spot, so where the devil was the triumph in that?

She loved Dr Daw, he was sure of that. She loved him, and so ... His great shambling strides lengthened and he clicked his tongue as reasons and explanations came and went.

13

DAN EVERARD lived in one of the most attractive houses in the district. But he had neither the capacity nor the wish to appreciate it. Joyce Everard managed the place and saw that the orderly charm of it was maintained. He left it to her to take care of the details, but that did not prevent him from resenting her position. At regular intervals he made a row and accused her of going behind his back, of trying to lower him in the estimation of the servants. Perhaps he knew that the servants had made their own estimate of him long ago. If he did it only made him more resentful. He bestirred himself now and then to quarrel with everybody, to countermand perfectly reasonable instructions as to the garden or the farm, just to show who was boss. The workmen simply answered, 'Yes, very good, sir,' and left off doing the job they were engaged on. Then they kept out of his way till his rage blew over.

It was not so easy for Joyce. She, of course, had to live with him. She wondered often enough however she could have thought she loved him. She couldn't even remember now what he was like a few years ago. Yet it was only a few years ago, and then there had been a kind of ruthless arrogant charm about him that most women had found captivating. He was an athlete who dominated most of the local activities, cricket, rugby, cross-country riding, but his trouble was that he hadn't learned to do anything else. He hadn't even learned how to take a hiding. Rather than lose he wouldn't play. Resentfully he let himself go to seed. He kept on riding for a while because with that you could always blame the horse, but his nerve went and he had to be half full of whisky before he would start. Notable errors in judgement brought him two spells in hospital and gave him the excuse for giving that up too.

When Inspector Fowler called on him he was sitting in an after-lunch daze in his study. He pulled himself together, and when the inspector was shown in he was in frowning concentration before some papers on his desk. The inspector noticed that several of them were upside down. Everard got up heartily enough and shook hands.

'Ah, Inspector, so you're the sleuth from Scotland Yard?'

'That's one way of putting it, sir. I'm sorry to disturb you in the middle of your work.'

'It can't be helped, I suppose. As a matter of fact a farmer in these days is nothing but a bloody office boy. Forms, forms, look at them.' He picked up a grocer's bill and waved it indignantly. 'I wonder these Whitehall Johnnies don't move in on us and have done with it. Red tape ... have a drink, won't you?'

'No thank you, sir, it's the wrong time in the afternoon for me.'

But Dan Everard was not going to let that curb his activities. With his back to the inspector he went to the drink cabinet and poured out a drink the size of which he presumably preferred not to be seen. He put a dash of soda in the glass and took a good drink before he turned round again. 'Sorry you won't join me. I always feel unsociable talking without a drink.'

'I'm sorry. I suppose mine isn't a very sociable job, if you follow me.'

'No, I suppose you do feel a bit of a twerp most of the time.' The thought seemed to turn him sour. 'Well, what can I do for you?'

'I'm just making a few routine inquiries, sir.'

'Oh, yes, about the old bitch over at Inching Round. I can't think why you worry. She should have been put to sleep long ago: nosey old trout.'

'Just the same, when a murder is committed we have to find out who did it.' Inspector Fowler wondered irritably how many more times he would have to make that obvious explanation in this case.

'Well, I didn't kill her, if that's what you're getting at.'

'Nobody said you did, sir.'

'No? Well, take my tip and don't start now. If you don't think I had anything to do with it why come and see me at all?'

'There are certain routine inquiries that have ...'

'Routine inquiries ... They tell me that you fellows start making inquiries when you can't think of anything else.'

Inspector Fowler smiled. He was not the least put out. 'I have known it happen that way sometimes. Quite often we can't think of anything else, and it does seem to get results.'

'You mean someone gets clapped into the jug. Damned nearly was myself once. accused of being drunk in charge of a car ... never more sober in my life.'

'What was your suggestion? That the police had a grudge against you?'

'No, somebody just told them to get busy and earn their livings, so they hopped on the first motorist that came along. They were looking for something, and it's easier to catch a motorist than a thief, that's all.'

'Possibly, sir. If that is so, it must be because there are more motorists committing crimes. They kill a lot more innocent people than criminals do, you know.'

Everard was heavily contemptuous. 'So we're to have a little homily on the duties and responsibilities of the motorist, are we? Not me.' He got up and poured himself out another drink. 'If you've got anything important to say to me, say it. But get it into your head that I don't like being lectured by Scotland Yard or anyone else.' His eyes were smouldering resentfully. Inspector Fowler knew the type. In another minute he was just as likely to be laughing uproariously. It had nothing to do with what was happening or what was said. It was nothing but the seething uncertainty of his brain. Things happened that he did not understand, so some reaction was called for, some expression of his ego. He brought his eyes slowly into focus and fixed them on the inspector. 'I don't like your manners,' he said. 'Is that clear?'

'Quite clear, sir. I haven't had the advantage of your upbringing.'

For some reason that seemed to have a pleasing effect. 'You are quite right. You can't make a silk purse out of a sow's etcetera can you. I say, that's good, a sow's etcetera!' He laughed and took a drink. 'Forgive my unseemly mirth, won't you, Sergeant. Now tell me what can I do you for, old boy?'

'Well sir, it's just a general check up. I'd like to hear anything you think might be of interest.'

'You want to know if I've got an alibi?'

'Well, it would mean one less to worry about, wouldn't it?'

'Well, you can set your mind at rest. I've got a cast iron open-and-shut alibi.'

'Good, what was it?'

'I was in a nursing home ... stomach trouble. If you don't believe me ask the wife, or, better still, you can ask that little squirt Daw. Not even he can deny that I've got an alibi.'

'Good,' the inspector managed a sigh of relief. 'I'll check up with Dr Daw. He'll be envious of you.'

Everard looked at him suspiciously. 'What do you mean envious of me?'

'Well, an alibi is a very useful thing.'

'You mean that he hasn't got one?'

'Oh, well, you know dozens of innocent people can't produce an alibi when they want one. I imagine that it never occurred to the doctor that he might want one.'

'Why shouldn't it occur to him? I suppose all this means that you've made up your mind that he's a little saint.'

'No, no. He struck me as a hard-working, conscientious sort of chap.'

'Oh, he did, did he?'

'I see you have other views, sir.'

'You do, do you? So I've got other views, have I? Maybe I know something. Maybe I could just lift a finger and put him on the scrap heap, where he belongs. Wouldn't you like to know how, Inspector?'

'Not particularly, sir. I'm investigating a murder. When that is cleared up I'll go away and leave you all in peace.'

'I see, you don't want to hear anything that doesn't suit your book?'

The inspector looked at him soberly. 'Do you think what you could tell me would have any bearing on this case, Mr Everard?'

Dan Everard's eyes narrowed as he endeavoured to concentrate.

'It might. If that nosey old bitch had dug out something that she couldn't keep to herself.' He started up violently. 'By God, I won't have my name bandied about by the riffraff of this village. I'm going to deal with this, Mr

Scotland Yard, and when I do deal with it it will be in my own way!'

'Well now, you sound quite enraged, Mr Everard.'

'No man is going to make a fool of me; you understand?'

'I thought you were afraid a woman was going to make a fool of you?'

'You keep my wife out of this!'

Inspector Fowler raised his eyebrows. 'But I thought it was Miss Pewsey who was making a fool of you.'

Dan Everard shook his head in a kind of dark confusion. 'Leave her out, I said, leave her out.'

'Naturally you want to protect your wife.'

'Protect her . . . protect her after what she's done to me?' He got up and went to the drink cabinet again. 'She thinks she knows me. Listen, why do you think I drink like this?'

'I suppose,' said Inspector Fowler, 'the reason is that you want to get drunk.'

'I never get drunk, but they think so, like you. They thought I didn't know what was happening.' A note of self-pity crept into his voice. 'Why shouldn't I drink, they've ruined my life, haven't they? They've set the whole village sniggering behind my back, haven't they?'

'I suppose you are referring to your wife and Dr Daw.'

'So you know too, do you?'

'It is my business to know things, Mr Everard.'

'All right, you know, so why ask me why I drink?'

'I didn't ask you, sir.'

'I can see what's in your mind though by the way you've been watching me.'

'You and your wife have known Dr Daw for three years, haven't you?'

'Yes, it's just three years too long. Three broken years . . .'

Inspector Fowler was unimpressed. He found himself disliking Mr Everard actively.

'Three years,' he said. 'But you were taken up for being drunk in charge of a car much more than three years ago.

141

I think actually it was six. It's rather difficult to blame Dr Daw for that.'

'Very smart, oh very clever, Mr Inspector! But I've reminded you already that I wasn't drunk.'

'No, of course; you explained that that was a mistake.'

'I've told you the truth.' He added as if his tongue mumbled on on its own account: 'The truth the whole truth and nothing but the truth, so help me God.' Then he laughed. 'That's the drill, isn't it?'

'Is your wife away, Mr Everard?'

'She went to Lewes, some dressmaker or other. Anyway, that's what she told me. Have to take a lady's word for these things.'

Inspector Fowler got up. 'In that case I won't wait. I have learned never to wait when a lady has gone to a dressmaker.'

'That's right, Inspector. That's quite right, even when she only says she has been to the dressmaker.' He added suddenly in quite a normal voice: 'I say, do have a drink before you go, won't you?' He gave the inspector a smile that was quite attractive. 'You must think I'm an awful soak, drinking alone like this.'

The inspector refused reluctantly. It was against his established principles to drink in the afternoon, but he went away wishing that he could have accepted. Nobody was to blame for the condition that Everard had got himself into but Everard himself. Just the same it was a tragedy that to all intents and purposes a life should come to an end below forty. If things had been different and Everard had died in the war, he would be remembered now as a hero and a dashing young sportsman. But he was destined to outlive his welcome. The odds were that it would take him years to kill himself.

These villagers – the inspector shook his head irritably as he trudged down the drive. He didn't want to know about their intimate lives. He wanted to know who killed Angela Mason Pewsey, and then he wanted to get back to London where the public at large wanted their criminals brought to justice and were ready to assist to that end.

14

FIRTH was propelling himself indolently to and fro on the swing seat on the lawn. Mrs Sim reclined in a deck chair reading. Celia was lying on her stomach on a rug plucking idly at blades of grass. The sight of her long shapely legs in very short shorts was to Firth satisfying and disturbing.

Without looking up she said to Firth: 'So you've been boozing with the vicar?'

'On the contrary, I've been sampling some of the best wine in the country.'

'Bad,' she answered. 'Very bad. No young man should cultivate a taste that he cannot afford to gratify.'

'I will be able to if I cultivate the vicar. He's got plenty of wine.'

'Sponger.'

'That's right. Undignified, I agree, but look at the money I'll save.'

'The vicar sees nothing but good in everyone, but I imagine in due course he'll make an exception in your case. Why don't you go to work?'

'I prefer this.'

'Naturally. Replete as you are with our food and the vicar's wine.'

'Celia dear,' Mrs Sim put down her book. 'I do wish you wouldn't denounce people so violently, even in fun.'

'Don't mind me, Mrs Sim,' Firth said. 'It has become part of the country, like wasps.'

'Besides, Celia, he has been working.'

Firth looked surprised, Celia stopped plucking at the grass.

'Working? I can't believe it.'

143

'He was making up his mind about the vicar for one thing.'

'Ah no, I wasn't. I was talking to him about sherry.'

'And telephoning, of course.'

Firth looked at her in astonishment and she laughed.

'Firth dear, I saw the vicar walk purposefully down to the pond, quite obviously to leave you alone in his study. What other reason could he have for doing that? Of course you could just as easily have telephoned Dr Daw from here, but it was nice of you not to want us to be involved.'

Firth's breath escaped slowly. It was rather like a balloon going down. But he did finally manage a show of protest.

'Why on earth should I telephone Dr Daw?'

Mrs Sim gave a patient little sigh. 'Presumably, dear, to tell him that it was quite likely that Inspector Fowler would call. Naturally you wouldn't want him to be taken by surprise.'

Firth's pleasant after-lunch indolence had deserted him.

'There was nothing natural about it,' he said. 'Since what I did is public property, the thing has become insane.'

'But it isn't public property, you foolish boy. Apart from Celia and myself and the vicar, nobody knows.'

'The vicar, does he know too?' This seemed to Firth to be the end.

'But, Firth, of course he knows. Who else would you be likely to ring up?'

'Oh, any one of a thousand people.'

'But not in such a furtive manner, dear boy. It could only be somebody we all know, couldn't it? And of course, somebody in trouble, otherwise you wouldn't trespass on his hospitality in that way. Of course you couldn't go to the public call box because you'd have to ask for the number there and the girl might be listening.'

'I don't believe the vicar knew what number I rang, and as for you, Mrs Sim, I think you are guessing.'

'He still thinks we're half wits,' Celia said.

'I don't think anything of the kind. If you're as clever as

144

I'm beginning to think you are, I can't think why you want any help from me. The only person to be sorry for that I can discover is Inspector Fowler.'

Mrs Sim spoke patiently, as to a child. 'No, dear, you are really being most helpful. If you hadn't rung up Eric Daw I should have had to ring him myself.'

'Whatever for?'

'Why, of course, we couldn't have him thinking that that dreadful letter had been handed over to the police, and you know if the police had called unexpectedly that is just what he would have thought.' She rose from the chair and gathered up her cushion and book and smiled down at her guest. 'I was going to ask you what you thought of the vicar, but I'm afraid you are too cross with us to give me an unbiased opinion.'

'Since I have been here,' Firth said, 'I have given up having unbiased opinions. I have decided that it will be time enough to fight my way back to reason when we are all in gaol. It will take my mind off the disgrace.'

'I sometimes wonder if it would be a help,' Mrs Sim said, 'if I told you who the murderer really was.'

Firth sat up with a start. 'No, no really, Mrs Sim! I can't have you making these statements. I won't. For heaven's sake leave this business to the police.'

'Very well, dear. I am sure that if your uncle could see you now he would approve of you very much.' She smiled vaguely and turned and strolled away towards the house.

Firth lowered himself slowly back into his chair. 'I don't know, Celia,' he said. 'I'm damned if I know.'

'Know what?'

'Nothing, nothing at all. I just don't know, that's all. I'm a child of five . . . No, let's be on the safe side and say three.'

Celia wriggled over on her back and put her hands under her head. 'Just the same,' she said, 'it was pretty nice of you to ring up Eric Daw.'

'Nice maybe, but stark, staring, raving mad . . . If I did it.'

The end of the sentence brought a little smile to her lips. 'Listen, chum,' she said, 'if mother said you did it, you did it. I know, she brought me up.'

'Yes, but how did she know?'

'You've seen her methods, Watson.'

'Celia, do you honestly think that your mother knows who killed Angela Pewsey?'

'Yes . . . Yes, I think she does.'

'Has she told you?'

'No, of course not.'

'If she does know,' he said angrily. 'Why, in heaven's name, doesn't she let the law get on with it? She must know that when there is provocation enough to turn a decent man or woman into a murderer, the law is not brutal to them.'

'Perhaps not, but in a place like this it doesn't begin and end with the law.'

He made no reply to that, but lay back watching the shadows from the leaves above playing on her face. As if he had not troubles enough already, Celia Sim was turning into another one. Like the goof that he knew himself to be he heard himself saying:

'You look very sweet.'

'Do I?'

'Very.'

There was a long pause, which for some reason he found oddly satisfying. She was not looking at him, but lay very still, her eyes looking through the leaves above her head, and then in dismay he saw that she was crying. Her lips were still, but as if she were unaware of them, tears filled her eyes and were running on her cheeks.

'Celia.' He jumped from his chair and dropped down beside her. 'Celia, what's the matter?'

She turned over on her face and wrapped her head in her arms.

'I'm sorry, but . . . Everything's a bit bloody, that's all.'

'I upset you.'

'I think I'd rather you were horrid like you were yesterday

than nice like you were just now. I imagine I just can't take it.'

'But why?' He ran a hand gently over her hair. 'What can't you take?'

'You being nice to me, I imagine.'

'But I'm always nice to you.'

'I . . . You've disguised it better up to now.'

'But don't you want me to be nice to you?'

'I suppose so.'

'In that case, what are you crying for?'

Her body shook, half laughing, half crying. 'That's a ridiculous question. Anyway, I've stopped crying.'

'No, you haven't.'

'Well, I've stopped wanting to cry.'

'Celia, you're crazy.'

'I know, isn't it fun?'

'But I like you that way.'

'You aren't being nice to me again, are you?'

'No, no, no. Nothing like that. I'm just sitting here gloating over your distress. I'm loving it, you great cry-baby. Is that better?'

'It sounds more like you, I must say.'

'All right, now suppose you tell me what you were crying for?'

'I can't . . . Just nothing.'

'You don't cry for nothing.'

'All right, I'm crying because the little boy next door took away my hoop. The reason was childish, that's the main thing.' She groped for her handbag and without looking up began repairing her face.

Firth relaxed on his back on the rug beside her, looking up at the sky.

'Celia.'

'Yes.' She was sitting up beside him now.

'It's about Graham Ward, isn't it?'

'I suppose so.'

'He's been keeping away.'

147

'I suppose he thinks he should while this rotten business is going on.'

'You might try telephoning him?'

'I did.'

'And so?'

'He said he thought it would be better for all concerned if he kept out of the way. He said he was going up to town.'

'That wasn't very clever of him, Celia.'

She was defensive at once. 'Why shouldn't he go if he wants to?'

'Just that I think you can carry this out-of-sight, out-of-mind business too far.'

Defensively she said: 'I don't know what you mean.'

'Sometimes, darling, going away can look like running away.'

She leaned over and looked down at him angrily. 'Don't call me darling and then immediately afterwards say something horrid.'

'Sorry.' There was a pause, and then he said: 'Celia, do you know what it was that Angela Pewsey was holding over Graham Ward?'

'No, no idea at all.'

'Didn't you both think it would be a good idea to take those letters to the police?'

'I did, but Graham was upset at the idea. He said anything was better than having everything made public.'

'Yes, but what did he mean by everything? In your case you hadn't much to worry about.'

'That's what I thought, but he said it would be made to look like something awful, and you know what villages are like. Mother would have had to go about putting on a brave face. Personally, I don't think she'd have given a damn what people said, but Graham said there was no need to let it happen. After all, it hadn't come to blackmail.'

'Not for cash, certainly. But I'm interested in his own piece of scandal.'

'Why? I'm not.'

'Don't stick your head in the sand, Celia.'

'I'm not. I simply tell you I'm not interested.'

'You may not want to be. But if there were something in this that gave him a strong motive for murder, you'd have to be interested.'

'I don't know how you can say such a thing.'

'Celia dear, it really doesn't help not to be honest with yourself. The police are going to investigate everybody who had even the remotest connexion with this business. Sooner or later they'll get round to Graham Ward. Can't you think of anything that she might have got hold of which she might have confronted him with? Something did make him hate her pretty ardently: even you must admit that.'

'No more than a lot of other people must have hated her.' She added impatiently: 'I told you as soon as I saw what the letter was leading up to I threw it in the fire. I read one page only, that was enough.' She shivered.

'There was nothing definite in what you read?'

'No, it was a sort of peroration, bits about how I would be well advised to think before it was too late. There was something I should know now unless I wished to live with it in shame for the rest of my days. The man I thought of marrying might look handsome and gallant, but could one always judge by looks; that sort of drivel. It made me furious.'

'So furious that the first page was enough; you chucked it in the fire.'

'You know I did.'

'That's right, then you asked me to come and find out who had written it,' he laughed. 'Well, now you know.'

'Graham had nothing to do with it.'

'Just the same, I wish he hadn't gone away.'

Listlessly Celia ran a hand through her hair. 'So do I.' Her admission came reluctantly, spoken, it seemed, against her will.

15

DR ERIC DAW permitted himself one half day a week away from his practice, and this was the day. He walked to the station and caught the train to Lewes. He leaned back in the carriage and closed his eyes. The weariness he was feeling to-day was something that seemed to him like a permanent burden. It weighed too heavily on his shoulders, and lay too heavily on his mind. There would have to be an end to it, and his state of mind was such that the end, any end, would be a welcome one.

He lay back conscious only of this weariness and of a smouldering dull resentment that he had to feel like this. He had not asked much of life and he had been ready enough to put back into life what he took from it. There hadn't been much even in his days as a student, but that had been fun, and of course his ambition then had been terrific. With only himself to think of he might have gone some way along the road. But his father died and there was his mother left dependent on him, and a young brother who, at least, could claim some help from him. That had been the signal for drudgery, no prospect of specializing now, not much opportunity for pleasure, intellectual contacts become brief and rare. He had got himself a practice, and of course he had had to get in on borrowed capital.

The idea of marriage had not entered his head, but it hadn't entered his head either that when love entered into his life it would bring with it so much distress. The flower-strewn path . . . and at the end of it cackling and triumphant Angela Pewsey.

There had been many such journeys as this one in the past, so he supposed it was foolish to have expected that nobody would know about them. Foolish paradise . . . but it hadn't been paradise, not at any time; at best an un-bearable pleasure.

Yet it had all been so inevitable. Looking wearily back now he could see no point at which he could have foreseen anything or changed anything. Joyce had been as inevitable as everything else; inevitable that he should have been called in when Dan Everard had that accident, inevitable that he would see how things were in the household.

At first they had kept their feelings secret from each other. They had known from the first time the best they could look forward to was the sort of hole and corner association that could bring no real happiness to either of them. But in spite of all that nothing else in their lives had seemed to be of any consequence.

He left the train at Lewes and then from the High Street turned into a narrow lane. They usually met in the little tea-shop about half-way up the lane, mainly because it was unlikely that they would meet anyone they knew. Nothing had changed since they had known it. The same two old ladies always served the same homely-looking home-made scones and butter, and jam in the same little round glass pots, one pot for each person. Then there was the communal plate that contained two slices of swiss roll, one slice of chocolate cake and one slice of sponge sandwich, neatly arranged on a white paper napkin.

The cakes were on the table when he arrived, the scones and butter and jam would come in with the tea. He ex-changed a word with the two old ladies about the weather. He always did that. He explained that he would not have tea yet as he was waiting for someone. He always did that too, just as if the two old ladies did not know.

Joyce came in only a few minutes after he did, and as always at that moment, his heart stood still.

But no stranger would have noticed anything unusual in the way they greeted each other. They shook hands. Joyce said she hoped he hadn't been waiting long and he replied that he had only just arrived.

Joyce Everard was twenty-nine years old. She was tall and loose-limbed, like the dozens of other country girls you see at the local point-to-points, or the hunter trials. They look their best out of doors. They come up to town for the day, and generally only on special occasions stay longer and generally are glad to get back. There is a self-assurance about them that comes of living the kind of life they prefer.

Joyce's eyes were grey and direct under straight wide brows. Her nose was small and her mouth rather wide and full. For the most part her expression was immobile. When she was interested she gave her whole attention, when she laughed there was a swift lightening of her whole countenance. When she was serious she was completely serious, almost with an expression of heaviness.

She was serious now. The elder of the two old ladies brought the tea and scones, turned the handle of the teapot towards Joyce with a gnarled hand, removed the sugar, the jam, the milk, the butter, and the scones from the tray, told them not to forget to ask for more hot water if they wanted it, and then she went off through the curtained doorway at the other end of the dim little room and left them.

To-day they were alone in the café, but their behaviour remained that of two ordinary people meeting casually over tea. When the doctor had emptied his cup she asked for it, put in the milk as he liked it and refilled the cup. The old lady toddled in again and asked if they had everything they wanted, and they thanked her and told her that they had. She remarked that it was quiet to-day, and said that she was glad in a way because they had had such a busy week-end, and it made the work so much harder when everything was crowded and there wasn't room to move. She smiled at them and went away again.

It was only then that anything personal was said. Joyce touched his hand almost shyly and said: 'Eric, have you been working very hard?'

'No more than usual, darling, why?'

'I don't know, I feel worried when you look like you do now, all sort of drawn and tired.'

'It isn't work I'm afraid of, Joyce. I don't mind work.'

'Eric, it isn't something about us, is it?'

'I'm afraid so, dear.'

'Dan ... Is he, did he ...?'

He shook his head and said bitterly: 'Somebody forestalled him. It looks as if he is going to be cheated of his little triumph after all.'

'But if it wasn't Dan, who else would want to interfere?'

'Can't you guess?'

'No. How could I guess?'

'Angela Pewsey.'

She gasped. 'But, Eric, she's dead!'

'Yes,' he said wearily, 'she's dead, but her capacity to cause suffering is not, Joyce. She can influence our lives from beyond the grave. Sometimes at night, I have a feeling that she is still here, spying, watching, not dead at all.'

'Eric dear, no; you are just tired. I said you must be, and you're imagining things.'

He laughed shortly. 'I wish to God I was! I didn't tell you, because I hoped that somehow I would find a way out of it all, even if it meant ... even if it meant paying her,' he finished quickly.

'But, dear, what could she know about us that could do us any harm? If we were afraid, we were afraid of Dan, not Angela Pewsey.'

'That, it seems, is where we were wrong. She turned out to be much the more deadly of the two.'

The colour had gone from her cheeks. 'Eric, she didn't know ... She couldn't!'

'She did, darling, and could. I don't know how. She knew we went away together and where we stayed.'

Joyce said quickly, insistently: 'But she can't hurt us now, Eric, she's dead ... Eric,' her eyes widened with fear as she looked at him. 'Why did you say she – seemed to be still alive?'

'The evidence was not destroyed with Angela Pewsey. She wrote me a letter telling me what she knew. It was full of threats. She kept a diary. You can't imagine her leaving such a juicy piece of drama as ours out of it, can you?'

She shook her head as if she were incapable of speech.

'The diary will be found, and then . . . '

'But you have the letter?'

He shook his head. 'No.'

Almost hopefully she asked: 'You destroyed it?'

'No, Joyce. It would have been destroying evidence. The police would have said it was a guilty action.'

'The police, Eric, what do you mean?'

'The police, Joyce, are trying to find out who killed her.'

Her body stiffened and her voice took on an angry edge.

'But how could they suspect you . . . you of having anything to do with it?'

He shrugged hopelessly. 'Why not? Surely I had as good a reason as anyone for killing her.'

'How dare they!'

'Joyce,' he said patiently, 'even you, loyal as you are, must see that I seemed to have everything to gain by her death.'

'No, no, you mustn't say it! You mustn't even think it, Eric!'

'The police think it,' he said slowly.

'You are being ridiculous; you know you are. How can they know, even about us?'

'They do know.'

'They haven't the letter, have they?'

He shook his head. 'Not yet.'

Then he told her how he had given the letter to Firth Prentice.

Even in her agitated state she was able to listen carefully and give all her attention to what he said and when he finished she tried to reassure him.

'He seems to have been nice about it. I can't see from

what you said how he could turn against you and give the letter to the police.'

'He may have to, darling. He can't be expected to risk his professional career for someone he scarcely knows. I, of all people, should know better than to ask him.'

'You don't think he has given them the letter, do you?'

'I know he hasn't.'

'Why then, in that case you'll most likely hear nothing more about it.'

He shook his head. 'But I am going to hear more about it. That inspector, the man from London, Fowler, has called, has been asking for me at the surgery, and yesterday Prentice rang up to tell me that the police know pretty well all there is to know about you and me, dear. Of course, Fowler will see that if Pewsey had found out too and threatened to use her knowledge . . . well, there's the motive they've been looking for.'

'You mustn't talk like that, Eric, you mustn't!'

'What else is there to talk about? Don't you see that there is nothing? We went into this because our feelings were stronger than we were. Nothing else seemed to matter then. And now,' he gave a little shrug, 'now, well, nothing matters.'

'But, Eric, you didn't kill Angela Pewsey.' She paused and added in a still voice, 'Even if you had . . . '

'Yes, Joyce?'

The little café seemed deathly still, listening for the things that had been hidden remotely in their hearts.

'Even so, Eric, even that couldn't make any difference now. She had destroyed us, hadn't she?'

He shook his head. 'Not entirely. Her purpose was to give a picture of us to the world. A picture of us by Angela Pewsey would have been unbearable. But the material for the picture was provided by us. That is what makes it unbearable, Joyce.'

He picked up the bill from the table and waited for her to stand up. Their old lady appeared from behind her curtain and smiled at them as they went out. Two of her regular customers ... Such a nice couple. Ah yes, there was his sixpence peeping discreetly from under the plate. Not a tip, of course – more like flowers to the hostess, or a note of thanks. How well-bred they were.

'You enjoyed your tea ... How nice ... Do come again quite soon ...' She had no means of knowing that they were not coming again; but they knew, of course.

16

ERIC DAW switched on the light and came into the waiting-room and stood looking round him. He seemed to find it strange that everything was the same, the oddly assorted pictures on the walls, the dog-eared periodicals, the hard chairs, the faint smell of ether. Beyond through the door he could see his surgery. In there were the tools of his trade, not much more expensive than those in any other well-equipped workshop. He would never have believed that he would regret leaving this behind. But now he had the un-bearable realization that this was his life. His knowledge and compassion had matured in these two rooms. His personal ambitions were buried here and had been replaced by the demands of others. Here necessity had made a better man of him than his own ambitions could have done.

These two drab little rooms: who would have believed that they could hold so much and mean so much?

A light pressure on his arm told him that Joyce was there. He touched her hand and guided her to the stairway that led to his flat above. He could not have told her what instinct had made him come through the surgery instead of the more direct way through the front door of the house. Perhaps he needed her support.

He had not asked her to come back with him, but they both felt appearances were no longer involved. It didn't matter now what was said or thought. On that score there was nothing to add.

On the stairs he paused and said curiously: 'There is a light on. It's funny that I should have left it. But I couldn't have done, I left in daylight . . . That's funny.' He quickened his steps a little and opened the door. Joyce stood a little back. There was a light burning in the sitting-room but no sound.

The doctor went quickly into the room. Mrs Sim was sitting in his favourite easy chair, reading one of his books.

She looked up and smiled vague, but welcoming greeting.

'Oh, there you are, Eric. You are quite late.'

He stammered a little.'. . . I, well, I didn't know you were expecting me. Nobody is ill, I hope?'

'Oh no. We are all flourishing, thank you. But don't keep poor Joyce standing out there on the landing.' She raised her voice. 'Joyce dear, do come in.'

Joyce came and stood wonderingly by the doctor's side. 'We . . . That is I didn't expect to meet you here,' she said.

'Of course not, my dear. People are always meeting people they didn't expect to meet. I hope you don't mind, but I felt you should have a chaperon.' She smiled. 'Not, of course, in the old-fashioned way. Celia and that dear boy from London with the strange father are quite alone at this moment, quite abandonedly, no doubt, except that your people nowadays are so very straight-laced. I meant, of course, in case you had another caller.'

The doctor hesitated and then excused himself to bring them drinks. Joyce walked slowly to a chair and sat down.

'You think there will be a caller?' she asked.

'One never knows in times of crisis what may happen. Also, you know, Joyce, I am going to take you home.'

Eric Daw had returned and was standing with a tray in the doorway. He walked quietly and put it on the table.

'I think we ought to tell you, Mrs Sim, Joyce is not going back there again.' His voice was quiet, but quite decided. 'We realize that what is left to us is nothing but the remnants of a future. Whatever it is, and for however long, we have decided to spend it together.'

Mrs Sim shook her head. 'Events can alter decisions, Eric.'

But Joyce interrupted. 'I don't think you understand that nothing matters to us. You see we . . . we've given up.' The whole tragedy of a wretched relationship was in the words.

Mrs Sims ignored it. 'There is a good reason for going home, Joyce. Dan went riding this afternoon. He had a fall and was killed.'

For a moment the room was quite silent. It was the doctor who spoke at last.

'That has its moments of irony, too, hasn't it?'

Joyce seemed to drag herself back from her reflexions.

'How did it happen?'

'Well, dear, I'm afraid you could guess as well as I can explain. Hinchcliffe, your foreman, was telephoning round trying to locate you. He asked me if I would come over. You know Dan. He took one of the young horses out. It was not properly schooled, I understand. Well, he rushed it at a stone wall along Downlands Lane and it fell. Inspector Fowler tells me that Dan was drunk this afternoon.'

'Inspector Fowler.' The doctor said the name as if its connexion with tragedy was inevitable.

'Yes, he was there this afternoon . . . making routine inquiries, he told me.'

'I suppose,' Joyce said, 'he will somehow or other discover that I'm responsible for Dan's death.'

'Joyce.' The doctor's voice was sharp with protest.

But she went on, speaking wearily, as if she hadn't noticed the interruption. 'I am responsible really, I suppose. I was schooling Randolph – that's the horse that killed him. Last week he came out and watched me. He was in one of those moods of his. He said I was spoiling the horse. He kept on and on till I couldn't bear it. I went up in the air and told him that I wouldn't be doing it at all only he was too much of a coward to do it himself. I . . . thought he was going to do something violent then, and I was frightened; but he got himself in hand and walked away. You see, for some reason he really was afraid of the horse and Randolph was just as nervous of him. Since then he has scarcely spoken a word to me.' She sat looking down at her hands and presently turned to Mrs Sim. 'Is he . . . Is he at home?'

'No, dear. They got him off to the hospital. But there was nothing to be done. I think they are waiting now to hear from you.'

'I'll attend to that, Joyce. I'm his doctor, even now, I suppose.'

Joyce turned to Mrs Sim again. 'You want me to go home?'

'I think it would be better if you came with me, dear. We can go back to the house and you can put some things in a suitcase and then you can come home with me.'

Eric Daw asked: 'Is it really necessary, Mrs Sim? You see, Joyce and I have given up caring what people think.'

'Nonsense.' There was nothing vague about Mrs Sim at this moment. 'I know quite well what your feelings are, but I certainly will not permit you to make a public display of yourselves.'

'I think that is going to be done for us.'

'Now listen to me, Eric. You may have decided to let yourself down in this matter. I think at least you might consider your friends.'

'Friends,' he said bitterly. 'Have I any friends?' Then he said quickly. 'No, no, I didn't mean that. But if I have friends I'd rather they weren't dragged into something of my own making.'

'Oh Lord,' said Mrs Sim. 'I might have known that was coming. Let me tell you, Eric, there is nothing makes my hackles rise so much as this wishy-washy self-denunciation. I have only the slightest idea what you've done, something any other reasonable man would have done much sooner and with more discretion. I've not the slightest doubt that if Inching Round still had stocks on the village green you and

Joyce would have been in voluntary occupation long ago. As for Joyce staying here, that is quite ridiculous.'

'I see no reason why it should be. There isn't going to be much left for us, and I don't quite see why we should be deprived of each other.'

'Deprived of each other! My dear boy, if you really want to be deprived of each other, you are bringing it about in the quickest possible way.'

Joyce said flatly: 'If Eric wants me to stay here, I don't really think there is any more to be said. You see, I can't pretend any longer.'

'You realize, both of you, that there will be an inquest. If the police have to come here to make their inquiries that is going to look peculiar for a start. You spoke about your friends. I tell you both there could be no surer way of turning them against you. There are formalities in the life of a village that make demands on all of us. There are occasions when you owe something to the community, and this is one of them.' She paused and added: 'There may come a time, Eric, when the goodwill of the people of this district will mean more to you than you think.'

'You mean when I am tried for the murder of Angela Pewsey?'

'Eric!' Joyce's exclamation was like a cry of pain.

But Mrs Sim's voice was sharp only with anger. 'I know perfectly well that you did not murder Angela Pewsey.'

Joyce was looking at her, wide-eyed. 'You know? You are sure of that?'

'Of course,' Mrs Sim seemed surprised at the question. 'Aren't you, Joyce?'

'Yes, I hoped, yes, I know I was sure.'

Eric Daw said mildly: 'You said it wouldn't make any difference.'

'More heroics.' Mrs Sim shook her head impatiently. 'If there were fewer of these between the pair of you and a little more practical self-preservation there would be some hope for you. Now will you please be good enough to listen to me.

I am going to tell you this, that if Joyce stays here with you in this house, Eric, you may quite easily hang for the murder of Angela Pewsey. People can sympathize with human short-comings up to a point, but when these are flaunted in front of them they turn into outraged moralists. Believe me, I know these villagers better than you do.'

Joyce protested. 'But Eric is innocent, Mrs Sim. You said so yourself!'

'Yes, dear, I know, and Eric knows, and you, at least, are beginning to think so. But what about everybody else? What has happened? Angela Pewsey has been murdered and she is known to have knowledge that could have ruined Dr Daw, absolutely and finally. Angela is murdered; Dr Daw and Joyce Everard are in love, but this husband stands horribly in the way. Then what happens? Most conveniently he is killed in an accident as direct result of a charge of cowardice by his wife.'

'Don't, oh don't!' Joyce clasped her head in her hands. 'That wasn't what I intended! I swear it wasn't!'

Eric Daw jumped to his feet. 'I won't have you saying that, Mrs Sim. This is too much.'

Mrs Sim answered mildly: 'My dear children, of course it's too much. The only thing to add is that immediately after the accident Mrs Everard came to take up open residence with Dr Daw.'

Joyce was looking at her in angry despair. 'How can you say such things, Mrs Sim? You know Eric and me and call yourself our friend. How can you say them?'

'I am saying them, my dear,' she said mildly. 'Because you both propose to offer an open invitation for them to be said.' She sighed and added: 'They will be said, you know. Angela Pewsey is dead, but she was not the only gossip in Inching Round. She was the worst, of course, but gossip is just as inherent in the life of a village as prejudice. We can no more help gossiping than we can help breathing.' She paused and added impatiently: 'The best thing you can do in your own defence, Eric Daw, is to appear at your morning surgery as usual and behave like a useful member of society.'

'But why should he do anything in his own defence?' Joyce repeated. 'You said yourself he was not guilty.'

'Of course, he's not guilty.'

The doctor said with weary irony: 'Then perhaps you know who is guilty?'

'Perhaps.'

'Then wouldn't it help if you told the police?'

'The police have not asked for my help.' She smiled reflectively. 'At least they have not asked me who committed the murder.'

'I should have thought,' Joyce said, 'that if you were as eager to help Eric as you seem to be that that would be the best way to help?'

Mrs Sim answered gently: 'I know, dear, that it may appear to you and Eric that there are only two people in the world, but there are others in spite of what you may think. Eric may be in trouble, but so far the trouble is largely anticipation of what might happen. And you know I am old-fashioned enough to believe that a little wholesome fear of retribution never hurt anyone.' She stood up and picked up her gloves. 'There, I've said what I think, but of course you will decide for yourselves.' She smiled a little. 'At worst I can go home with a virtuous feeling that I have done my duty . . . nauseating, isn't it?'

Joyce hesitated. 'I think if you don't mind, I'd like to go with you, Mrs Sim. That is if Eric . . .'

Dr Daw said quickly: 'Yes, Joyce.'

'I'll be waiting in the car.' Mrs Sim walked purposefully out of the room and downstairs without looking back.

She wanted to leave them for a little while alone. Another reason was that she had a shocked feeling that she was going to cry.

Joyce and Eric stood facing each other.

'I wonder,' he said slowly, 'If it is too much to hope . . .'

She put a hand on his arm. 'No, darling, no, don't say it, please. Perhaps if we had a few days without thinking, without feeling anything.' Then suddenly, desperately, she flung herself into his arms. 'I'm afraid, more afraid than before. I thought we had lost everything and I could bear it, but now . . . now . . . Oh Eric darling, how much more can we stand?'

He held her tightly in his arms. 'Anything, darling. Everything if that has to be.'

17

FIRTH PRENTICE was no less fed up with what he was doing because he was acting on a decision of his own. Nobody had asked him to set out on this pilgrimage. He knew that if he had asked the advice of anyone with any sense they would have told him to mind his own business.

For two days he had been haring about the country like an amateur sleuth, lacking only the false moustache. He had been so mysterious about it that Celia had described his behaviour as nothing short of furtive.

'But what is it all about?' she asked him. 'What's cooking?'

'I don't like to say this, darling,' he answered. 'But I feel I must be out and about. I find all this female cosseting a little cloying.'

'I'm sorry we bore you.'

'No, no, it isn't that, but a man of my temperament and habits must be ever on the move.'

'On the move? How far do you move each day in London, may I ask?'

'Oh, you'd be surprised, what with hiding from clients, dodging work, eating, drinking, courting and so on, my whole days are spent in darting hither and yon.' He grinned and added: 'If you would be content to let me lie in the shade all day I wouldn't mind so much.'

'I thought you were supposed to be here on business? Anyway, why be so mysterious?'

'Because, my dear, on the few occasions when you have known of my activities, you have criticized them whole-heartedly.'

'Ha, so this is something that even you are ashamed of? I suppose, if the truth were known, you are chasing some landgirl from rick to rick? You can confide in me, you know. I won't be jealous.' She did sound a little jealous, none the less. He put that down to the possessive instinct that every woman has and repudiates.

'No,' he said, 'there is no particular landgirl, but of course, if one comes within the orbit of my inquiries, well naturally, I inquire.'

'Inquire *what?*'

'Oh, the usual thing. Has she seen a dark sinister stranger? Because if not, she is seeing one now.'

'And what snappy comeback do they make to that flower of wit?'

' "Funny aincher." And with that they flounce off on their tractors. At least some of them do. Others, public schoolgirls and the like, begin thinking of their hours of loneliness.'

'Drivel.'

'Yes, isn't it. It's my blunt way of telling you to mind your own business.'

In point of fact, Firth was acting on the theory that what Angela Pewsey could find out he could find out also. But lacking that lady's years of experience and knowledge of the emotional terrain, he found that progress was slow and difficult. But progress there was.

Firth rang at a door on the fifth floor of a block of flats in Knightsbridge. There was no reply. He kept on ringing because he couldn't decide what to do next. When at last and without the slightest warning the door was flung wide open he found himself staring rather foolishly at Graham Ward. The first thing he was aware of was that the man facing him was frightened. The next thing was that Graham had been expecting someone else, and now the fear was giving way to anger.

'Well . . . so it's you?'

'Don't tell me you were expecting someone else?'

'What's it to do with you?'

'Because if you were,' Firth said mildly, 'it took you an awfully long time to open the door, or was I being impatient?'

'I neither know, nor care what you were being, except interfering.'

'Sorry, I was only trying to help.' Firth turned away as if to go back to the lift.

Graham hesitated and said: 'I don't know that I need your help.'

'Really. I thought once upon a time that you asked for it. However, we'll forget about that.'

Again Graham paused doubtfully. 'Well, since you have come here, I suppose there is no harm in listening to what you have to say. I haven't much time, but you'd better come inside.' He added angrily: 'Or would you prefer to stand here shouting in the corridors?'

'No, no, I've no preferences whatever.' Firth walked ahead into a fairly luxuriously but quite impersonally furnished flat. It was one of those modern places where hundreds of brief tenants can come and go without leaving a trace or a memory. 'Nice place you have here; nice and clean, I mean.'

'It suits me.'

'Staying long?'

'Is that important to you?'

'No, just social chitter chatter; talk about the weather if you prefer it, or the cricket, or Monet, or Burne-Jones. I don't mind. I like to talk, that's all; nervous habit of mine, or maybe it's a frivolous mind; I wouldn't know.' He found an easy chair and stretched out his legs luxuriously.

Graham planted himself in front of him. 'Well, what have you got to say?'

'So now you want me to talk, that makes a nice change, I must say.'

'You know perfectly well what I mean, and I told you I haven't much time.'

Firth looked mildly surprised. 'Why not, the aircraft doesn't leave till six, does it?'

Graham stood looking down at him in stunned silence.

'You know about that?'

'Of course, my dear chap, the most natural thing in the world.'

'What is the most natural thing in the world; prying into other people's affairs?'

'No, no – running away. People have been doing it ever since the beginning of time . . . ever since the first guilty conscience, in fact.'

'Who said I had a guilty conscience? You'd better be careful, Prentice.'

'What, of slander? No witnesses, old boy.'

'You accused me of having a guilty conscience.'

'Oh no, I indicated that it was a primary cause for flight – that and, of course, fear.'

Graham's face was turning white. 'Nobody accuses me of cowardice, Prentice.'

'Don't they?' He paused and deliberately lighted a cigarette. 'What do they accuse you of?'

Graham pulled himself together, but it meant an effort. His voice when he spoke again was half pleading. 'I thought your idea in coming here was to offer your help.'

'No, I reminded you that you had asked for my help.'

'Oh, why quibble about it? What did you come here for?'

'To find out why you ran away, for one thing.'

'I tell you I did not run away. Am I entitled to come up to town or not?'

'It might have been an idea to have left your address, don't you think?'

'With Celia, you mean? It wasn't worth it. I was only here for a few days.'

'I know.' Firth waited.

'Since you seem to know it already, I might as well tell you that I'm on my way to the continent.'

'Why?'

'Damn it, because I feel that I want a holiday.'

'Yes, you look a bit washed up.' Firth looked at him reflectively. 'What causes that? The suspense?'

'What do you mean?'

'I mean waiting for the inspector to arrive.'

'Why should I worry about that? Why should I be affected by this nincompoop from Scotland Yard?'

'Oh, he can be quite formidable. Very careful, but very persistent. People generally tell him what he wants to know.'

'Perhaps you can tell me what he would want to know from me?'

'I expect in the first place he would want to know what made Angela Pewsey such a menace to you; what she knew about you, in fact.'

'She knew nothing.'

'In that case, why run away?'

'I've told you already, I'm going for a holiday.'

'Yes, yes. But will anyone believe you, that's the point.'

'I don't give a damn whether they believe me or not.'

'On the whole, I think if I were you I'd put off this little jaunt of yours and go back.'

'No.'

'You'll feel an awful fool if they send a large police sergeant after you to bring you back. There'll be a nice photograph of the pair of you coming down the gangway.'

'You're not working for the police by any chance, are you?'

'Oh no.'

'Then why not mind your own business?'

'It is my business in a way.'

'I see, so Celia sent you hopping up here after me? Or would it be more likely to be her mother?'

'No, it was my own idea and I didn't come hopping. I came by train and a most tedious journey it was too.'

167

Graham sneered: 'But the main idea was to protect the family, eh?'

'Basically, that was the idea.'

'Well, it may interest you to know that my idea is the same. I'm going away to avoid a lot of unsavoury publicity.'

'There won't be any publicity . . . unless you are brought back and charged with murder of course. My advice to you is to go back, stay there till the police have come to question you and then go where you please.'

'I tell you I won't have them questioning me. I tell you I can't stand their questioning.' He put a match to his cigarette and Firth saw that his hand was shaking.

Firth waited deliberately and then said: 'I don't think the questioning will be as bad as last time, you know.'

Graham held the lighted match till it burned his fingers.

'I don't know what you are talking about.'

'No? Angela Pewsey could have told you. In fact, she did tell you, didn't she?'

Graham was like a man at bay. His voice shook so as to be almost inarticulate. 'That woman . . . that woman. Why are they hunting whoever was good enough to kill her? And you; why are you prying into this? You saw . . . saw what happened to her. She couldn't mind her own business either.'

'Oh, I'm not prying. I'm telling you that it would be better to tell your own story to the police than have them find it out from someone else. They might question Bert Repton, for instance.'

Graham sat staring at him. 'How did you know . . . I . . . I don't know what you're talking about.'

'I'll just tell you how I know and let it go at that. I wanted to know what made you run away, so naturally I inquired. I knew that Angela Pewsey had found out something about you, that was obvious, and just as obviously it was something that scared you. You've lived in the district for the best part of your life and everybody knows you. Not everybody likes you, but that's neither here nor . there.

Anyway, not even those who disliked you could think of any particular villainy that could be brought home to you.

'But then there was the time you were away at the war; so I found out what regiment you were in and I scouted round to find if any of the locals had been in the same unit. I found one . . . Bert Repton. He didn't want to talk about it, but his wife did. She came to see me after he had gone to work. Bert's wife is one of those who do not like you.'

Graham answered with almost pathetic eagerness. 'Bert wouldn't say anything. I took care of him, I looked after him. He didn't say anything when our people picked us up, did he, after the Japs had been cleared out?'

'No, but he told his wife.'

'The dirty little tike . . . My God, after all I'd done for him!'

'Perhaps he thought he'd paid you off for that by not talking to the military authorities. But his wife; well I suppose naturally he had to tell her how he came to lose all his fingernails.'

'He'd have lost his life, if it hadn't been for me.'

'Perhaps. He must have been a gallant little chap. They pulled off one fingernail at a time, but he didn't tell them where the airstrip was, did he? He must have felt that that was a bit of a waste, when you told them immediately afterwards. His wife feels that way, certainly.'

Graham was pressed back in his chair, staring wide-eyed before him. He seemed unable to speak.

Firth went on: 'I suppose they tackled Bert first because he was only a little runt of a private, and you, of course, were an officer. Naturally they would think that Bert would be more likely to talk.'

Graham found his voice. He was almost shouting. 'You weren't there. You wouldn't understand. They caught us there in the jungle. We were at their mercy and they knew it. You talk about Bert Repton and his heroics. All right, what did it really matter to him if they knocked him about, broke his bones. He's a misshapen little creature, anyway. But look at me.' He jumped from his chair and stood before Firth magnificently. 'They threatened me with all sorts of foul things. Tell me, how would I have felt if I'd come home with a twisted, misshapen body?' He held out his hands dramatically. 'How would these look with the nails torn from my fingers?'

Firth shook his head. 'I can't answer that. It seems possible though that you would have felt better than you do at this moment.'

'That's not true. How would I have felt if people had had to make an effort to shake hands with me?'

'I don't know. People are rather proud to shake hands with Bert Repton, it seems to me.'

'But I have told you; these things don't matter so much to people like Bert Repton. His hands are gnarled and misshapen in any case. They don't suffer as we do. Their feelings aren't the same. I know, I tell you I saw him stand there while they had their way with him and he never said a word. To me, even watching it was agony.' He paused for breath and went on: 'Suppose I did tell them where the airstrip was? A precious lot of good it did them. Things got so hot for them they had to run away and leave us. As for Bert Repton, I fixed up his wounds, but he wasn't fit to walk, so I carried him; literally carried him fifteen miles to our own lines.' He drew himself up again.

Firth looked at him reflectively. 'I advised you before and I can only say again that I think it would be better for you if you went to the police and told this story yourself. You might also be advised to tell it a little more modestly than you have told me.'

'Tell the police! Do you think for a moment those dunderheads would understand? Tell me this one thing: would they, or would they not see in it a motive for murdering Angela Pewsey?'

'A very good motive, I should think. Against that would be the fact that you yourself had come to them openly and voluntarily.'

'I know quite well what is the best thing to do and I am doing it, and let me tell you I am doing it as much for Celia's sake as my own. I am going out of the country to an unknown address and I will stay there under an assumed name till someone else is hanged for murdering Angela Pewsey. I'd like you to tell Celia that too, if you really want to help.'

'On the other hand, I can stop you from leaving.'

Graham laughed. 'What will you do? Hang on to my coat?'

'Oh no. It would be simpler than that. I would telephone a man I know at Scotland Yard and he would telephone someone else and an unimaginative but stubborn man would be waiting at the airport to take your passport away from you.'

Just as days before in the seaside hotel Firth had seen the other gripped by ungovernable rage, so he saw it happen again now. But that was almost the last thing he did see. The very last was a powerful and beautifully shaped hand snatch up a heavy vase from the table by his side.

When next he saw the light of day it was through a swirl of scarlet spots and there was a lump on his head the size of a turkey's egg. There was a little broken delf at his feet and he was quite alone.

When he got back to Inching Round, Firth was in no mood for idle banter. Celia told him he was behaving like a bear with a sore head, which was so apt that he went to bed without answering her.

Firth had a lot to think about, but he was hardly in a condition to think. There was the problem of what to do about Graham Ward. It seemed fairly clear that had there been a more formidable weapon to Graham's hand than a vase he, Firth, might have been the second victim in the Pewsey murder case. He reflected morosely that there is a lot to be said for minding one's own business. One thing he was convinced of, and that was that Graham Ward would not be a nice husband for Celia to have about the house. A family tiff might have disastrous results.

He could warn Celia, of course, but in his own peculiar position the idea did not attract him. He could go to the police. He realized that he should go to them, but the suppression of evidence had become almost a habit with him. Inspector Fowler would almost certainly take a poor view of his trip to London and its sequel.

He consoled himself with the thought that when the police wanted Graham Ward they would find him with the greatest of ease.

Then he tried to go to sleep, which was even more difficult than trying to think.

18

INSPECTOR FOWLER went loping across the churchyard once more. He had gone back and forth so often that he was heartily sick of it. What irritated him was that the place was so small. So small, and yet here, right under his long nose, there was a murderer. The whole damned case should have been cleared up in the first day and it wasn't. The piddling little place seemed to be defying him. Whisperings, hints, evasions everywhere, and everywhere a sort of tacit conspiracy to keep him on the outside. To hell with these villagers! They had a murderer in their midst and as far as he could see they were determined to keep him there; or her there.

'How the blazes many murders do you have to commit in a place like this before you begin to make yourself unpopular?' He posed the question to himself but he could not answer it.

And now this latest piece of doings. He had just had a telephone call from Mrs Sim. Dr Daw and Mrs Everard, it appeared, would like to have a chat with him, if he could make it convenient to look in. Chat with him! He wondered what jiggery-pokery was behind this particular call. There must be something, he decided, or Mrs Sim would not be mixed up in it. He had promoted Mrs Sim to the top of the list of obstructionists.

When he arrived they were all sitting on the lawn in the shade of a great beech tree. All very pleasant and informal, he thought. Uncomfortably as he approached he felt more like a victim than an investigator.

Mrs Sim came forward to meet him, smiling quite graciously. 'Ah, there you are, Inspector. It was so nice of you to come.'

'Not at all, Mrs Sim. You wouldn't have asked me, I'm sure, if you hadn't felt that it would help me in my investigations.'

'Of course not. And I'm sure that if you must investigate it's so much nicer to do it sitting in the shade. Do come along and sit down.'

Mrs Sim introduced him to Joyce and directed him to a deck chair. There is only one way to sit in a deck chair and that is to lean back in it. Inspector Fowler could not see himself conducting an official interrogation and at the same time reclining at his ease, so he sat upright with his legs wide apart and the chair protruding between them; and he was definitely not at his ease.

'There, now we can talk in comfort,' Mrs Sim said. 'Inspector, did you ever know such weather? I can't recall when last it was so gloriously fine.'

'We are having a very fine spell,' agreed Inspector Fowler reluctantly, and waited.

Firth came out of the house with a tray of drinks and the Inspector admitted to himself with sour respect that they certainly knew how to get on the right side of a man. But could he drink while on duty? But was he on duty? Of course, he wasn't contemplating arresting his hostess for anything, at least not yet, so he supposed there was no harm in taking a drink with her. Added to which he felt that he would like a drink.

He found himself looking at Joyce Everard. She was not quite what he had expected. He had expected something a little more flighty, a bit on the fluffy side. This one looked like a lady, but you couldn't judge by appearances. And the doctor, sitting there in his neat quiet way – well, come to that, he didn't look much of a goer either. Neither, he consoled himself, had Doctor Crippen. Dr Crippen was a great standby when you began to get the idea that people looked respectable.

After he had observed the social customs for what he considered a decent interval, Inspector Fowler cleared his throat and said: 'And now I understand there are certain matters that this lady and gentleman wish to discuss with me?'

'That's true,' Firth said. 'I more or less bullied them into telling you their story, Inspector. The doctor was a bit reluctant because, you see, Mrs Everard is involved and it's a thoroughly wretched position to be in altogether.'

'Yes, it often happens like that. But you know, Dr Daw, these things are bound to come out sooner or later. So perhaps if the others will excuse us you and I and Mrs Everard will get down to business.'

'If you don't mind,' Joyce said, 'I'd rather they stayed. They know all about us. If we allowed them to go away it would seem that we were ashamed.' Her voice rose a little. 'And I, that is we, want you to understand, Inspector Fowler, that we are not.'

Inspector Fowler thought privately that if they were not they should be, but he contented himself with saying doubtfully: 'Just as you wish, Mrs Everard.'

Looking back on it afterwards, Inspector Fowler thought how odd it would have sounded to a stranger looking at this scene and listening to this quiet country doctor telling of an affair with the wife of one of his patients, and of their trip to London, of their brief meetings in woods and lanes, and of their behaviour in the presence of a husband now a few hours dead. It was fantastic to himself that Inspector Fowler could have listened with an air of understanding and sympathy. When it came to the letter from Angela Pewsey the Inspector to his horror began to feel a kind of sympathy for her murderer.

Dr Daw gave a full account of the whole thing, beginning at the beginning and speaking without pause to the end. He made no excuses either for himself or Joyce; then at the end he handed over the letter. He said nothing about having handed it over to Firth, and the Inspector assumed it had never left his possession. He unfolded it and read it through carefully to the end.

'You realize, Doctor, I shall have to keep this? It may have to be used as evidence?'

'I quite understand.'

Inspector Fowler folded the letter carefully and put it away. Then after a pause he said: 'I can make no promises, but if this letter is not necessary to my case I will not produce it. I only hope that I can return it to you and forget its contents.'

Mrs Sim smiled at Joyce. Celia, like the fool she felt herself to be, wanted to cry.

Dr Daw nodded, 'Yes, I would appreciate that if it is possible.'

Inspector Fowler got up from his chair and stood looking down at them. He felt more sure now of his authority.

'I must warn you, of course, that what you have told me must lead to a number of inquiries.'

'Yes, I see that.'

'I will have to ask you to give me a detailed account of your movements on the day of the murder.'

'Yes, I'll try to do that.'

'And further, Dr Daw, and you, Mrs Everard, I must ask you not to leave the neighbourhood without first informing me about your movements.'

Eric Daw said sharply: 'But Mrs Everard has nothing to do with this!'

'With what, sir?' When there was a delay in the doctor's reply, Inspector Fowler felt that he had scored a point.

'With everything . . . with the death of Angela Pewsey.'

'And had *you*, sir?'

'Really, Inspector,' Firth spoke, protesting ruefully. 'You know if you start asking questions like that I'll have to advise my client not to answer them.'

Inspector Fowler looked annoyed. 'I didn't know that Dr Daw was your client.'

Firth laughed. 'Neither did he till this moment.'

'Why not represent the whole village and have done with it?'

'Thanks for the suggestion, I'll think it over.'

Dr Daw broke in on them. 'Thanks for the offer, Prentice, I'll accept it. Just the same I see no harm in answering his question.' He turned to Inspector Fowler. 'I had nothing to do with the death of Angela Pewsey.'

'But you'll admit that on what you have told me this morning you had a good reason for wishing her out of the way?'

Firth sighed. 'One thing leads to another, doesn't it? No, no, Inspector; I might have a good reason for wishing you out of the way, but that doesn't make me want to murder you.'

'I wish I could honestly return the compliment, sir,' Inspector Fowler said grimly. He seemed about to say something to Dr Daw, but changed his mind and turned back to Prentice. 'I shall look to you to produce your client when I need him, Mr Prentice.' He raised his hat to Mrs Sim, wished them all a comprehensive good morning, and strode away down the drive.

He was frowning as he turned back across the churchyard. 'He may not have murdered that old vulture,' he muttered. 'But if he didn't do it, I can't think why.' And at least three of the little group in the garden who had listened to Dr Daw telling his story were thinking along much the same lines.

19

WHEN Inspector Fowler got back to the local police station he found Constable Wilks waiting for him at the door. They were holding the line for him with an urgent call from London.

Sergeant Piggott was calling from London to report.

'I think I've got something at this end,' he said.

'All right,' the Inspector answered morosely. 'Go ahead and tell me what it is and don't sound so self-satisfied.'

'The Lynx Detective Service turns out to be Willie Black. I don't know if you remember, he used to be at Bow Street, retired at his own request. He was a very good man.'

'All right, all right. I know Willie Black better than you do. I didn't send you over to take up his references.'

'No, I mentioned it so that you'd know what he said was reliable.'

'Yes, but what did he say?'

'Well, he picked out one of your names right away.'

'Who was it?'

'Major George Torrens.'

'Ah . . . Well, go on. What did he want from Willie Black?'

'He didn't want to tell me at first. I had to tell him this was a murder matter.'

'Listen Piggott. I know you are not paying for this call, but there may be some citizen who wants to use the line. If you are going to take a couple of hours over this you'd better warn the exchange there'll be a two hours' delay. Now then . . .'

Sergeant Piggott noted without undue rancour that so far most of the talking had been done by Inspector Fowler. It was easy to guess that Inspector Fowler was feeling that he had been too polite to too many people for too long.

'Yes, sir. Well, what Willie Black has been doing for years is watching Major George Torrens' wife.'

There was a pause at the other end of the line that told Sergeant Piggott that he had scored a definite hit.

'Major Torrens' wife . . . he hasn't got a wife.'

'That's what you think,' Sergeant Piggott amended that hastily. 'I mean, sir, he may be a bachelor down there, but he's married all right, all signed and sealed and tied up in red tape. I've seen it.'

'Are you sure, Piggott?'

'Certain.'

'But what does he have his wife watched for like this? There's no talk of another woman down here. He can't be thinking of getting married again, or they'd know it down here.' He added grimly: 'They know everything.'

'They didn't know about Mrs Torrens, it seems.'

'No, they didn't know about her . . . at least . . .' He guessed that there could have been one exception.

He snapped into the telephone: 'What about this Mrs Torrens? What is she? Where does she live?'

'She lives in Bristol, and she's a cook.'

'A cook. You did say *a cook?*'

'Yes. Not a very good cook either. At least that's what Willie Black says, and he's eaten some of the stuff she dishes out. For the last couple of years she's been working in a third-rate boarding-house in the city . . . small, commercial travellers and the like. Willie gave out that he was a commercial traveller when he used to go there to check up.'

'But it's ridiculous! I'll bet if Willie Black told the truth he'd admit he was taking money under false pretences. Did Major Torrens tell Black that this woman was his wife?'

'Oh no. He gave the impression that she was a disreputable sort of relative, whom he naturally didn't want to have crossing his path.'

'But what was his idea in having her watched?'

'He simply wanted to know where she was. She had a habit of taking different jobs in different seaside towns. If he knew which town she was in all he had to do was not go there. The only reports he wanted from Willie were something like this: "Maud Emily Torrens, still in Scarborough." "Maud Emily Torrens – moved to Southend," and so on.'

Inspector Fowler interrupted. 'Most likely the man was telling the truth and she was just someone out of the family cupboard that he didn't want to meet.'

'No, she was his wife all right.'

'But damn it man, it doesn't make sense. This Major Torrens is a man of substance. He has one of the best houses in the neighbourhood. He's this, that and the other in local affairs. He keeps a couple of servants and a gardener. His wife a cook in a cheap boarding-house . . . Bosh!'

Piggott answered with more than a hint of smugness in his voice. 'Yes, there's a story behind that too.' It seemed to the irate Fowler at the other end of the line that Piggott's smugness was almost patronizing.

'God damn it, man,' he shouted. 'To listen to you you'd think you were telling this story to give a lot of kids the creeps. You're a policeman making a report. Get on with it.'

Piggott held the receiver a more comfortable distance from his ear, and smiled as he listened. Damn if the old boy wasn't jealous.

'Well, as time went by Willie Black began to get curious about this client of his.'

'As time went by, eh? So now we get back to the life story of Willie Black.'

'Yes. He says that in his business it's never a bad idea to find out a bit about the man who's employing you.'

'Gems from the philosophy of Willie Black . . . So that's what we are wasting our time on now, is it? . . . Well, get on with it.'

'Willie decided that it was time he had a chat with the cook.'

'Ha, the blasted plot thickens, I take it.'

'Yes, he took her for a drive on her afternoon off and

179

pumped her about her past. She told him she was a widow.'

'By God, Piggott, don't you realize yet that the man you claim is the poor widow's husband is alive? He walks about, I've talked to him.'

'Yes, but she doesn't know that.'

Inspector Fowler said with a kind of desperate patience: 'Go on Piggott, go on. We've still got the whole afternoon ahead of us.'

'She told him she was a widow,' Piggott began again. 'The last she heard of him was in 1917 when he was reported missing, presumed dead. That was the last she heard.'

'Why was it the last she heard? If he turned up anywhere the authorities would have let her know.'

'I told you; she moved about. If the authorities presumed him dead there was no reason to presume he was alive; not in those days. The thing that interested her most was that he had said that he had a chance of coming into a bit of cash. But even that she took with a grain of salt. He was always giving himself funny airs, and pretending that he was something that he was not.'

'All right, what was he, this so-called husband of hers?'

'A batman.'

'A what?'

'A batman.'

'Look here, Piggott.' Inspector Fowler seemed to be searching for words. 'I'm not here to stop you from wasting the Yard's time, and I can't help Willie Black wasting his own, but I will not have you wasting mine . . . A batman, my God! And a dead batman!'

'There's more to come,' said Sergeant Piggott pleasantly.

'I suppose I'll have to listen to you, Piggott, if it's only for the sake of the report I'll have to make recommending that you are put back into uniform again, so go on.'

Sergeant Piggott had heard all this before. He didn't mind in the least, specially not on the telephone.

'Well, while they were talking, she dug down into her bag, and produced a faded snapshot, and sure enough it was

Blackie's employer. This chap in the picture was thin and his hair, of course, was different and he was clean-shaven. But Willie Black had no doubt it was the same.'

This time there was no outburst from Inspector Fowler. He was remembering suddenly that at identification there had been no equal to Willie Black in the service. If he really was convinced that these wildly unlikely men were one and the same man he was very possibly right.

In a surprisingly mild voice he said: 'Go on, Piggott.'

'Well, once he got hold of the picture, he forgot to give it back. I got it from him and I'm putting it in the post with my report. You'll be able to see for yourself.'

Inspector Fowler grunted and waited for Piggott to go on.

'Willie wanted to know more after that. He says he was getting interested in the story for its own sake, so he asked her if she knew who this Torrens was batman to. She knew that because of her husband's boasting about him. He was Major Christian Seymour, v.c. He was killed, you remember, at the end of 'seventeen.'

'I remember, we took it like a national disaster. Go on, Piggott.'

'When Willie Black came back to London he couldn't get the queer business out of his head. This story of a legacy he saw might have something in it after all, and he reasoned that when a batman got a legacy it more often than not came from the man employing him. He fossicked round till he found the name of Major Seymour's solicitors. And as often happens with Willie he found he knew the head clerk. You know how it is. I know most of these fellows myself.'

Inspector Fowler nodded, forgetting that the other man was sixty miles away.

'The head clerk saw no harm in telling him the story. The Major was dead long ago, and there was nothing to hide, anyway. The story was that, on his last leave before he was killed, Seymour called at the office, more to see how everyone was than anything else. He was fond of the old head of the firm, and rather for whim than anything else he drafted his will.

You see, Major Seymour had no money to leave to anyone beyond a few hundred pounds and none of his friends really needed that. He decided to leave it to his batman, whom he described with amusement as the world's greatest snob, but also a good batman and a good soldier. But the irony of it is that a week before Seymour was killed his aunt died and left him a fortune of fifty thousand pounds. Everyone had always thought she'd barely enough to live on. Torrens, of course, was with the Major when he died and Seymour gave him the name of the solicitors and told him to look them up. But Seymour never knew about the fortune he'd inherited. The next day Torrens was taken prisoner, at least that is what he told the solicitors when he identified himself. There were hundreds of others with him, and when the list was made out presumably the Jerries left his name out. But he could easily prove who he was. When they handed over the money to him the head clerk remembers the old man asking him if he was married, or single, and Torrens hesitated a bit and said single. They were all ready to bet afterwards that he was lying, but they decided that they may have been prejudiced because he had made a bad impression on them. Domineering and arrogant the minute he was sure of the money; practising for the future. But anyway, whether he was married or single was none of their business. The old man had already declined to handle the account.'

Inspector Fowler pondered. 'And this woman; this so-called wife of his: do you mean to tell me he left her to fend for herself?'

'I don't suppose for years he knew where she was. I suppose he was too busy building himself up into a gentleman. I bet it was a shock to him when he saw her again.'

'You mean to say they met again?'

'Not met exactly. He saw her, but she didn't see him. I don't know that she'd have recognized him in the street if she had. But he didn't dare risk it. He managed to find out where she worked; followed her home, I suppose, and then came running to Willie Black with this scheme of his. Willie says he was so blustering that he very nearly turned down the job.'

'All right, Piggott, for the time being I'll accept this cock and bull story of yours.' Inspector Fowler was only mildly grumbling now. 'Get hold of the woman now, I'll want to talk to her.'

'I've tried to get hold of her, but she's gone.'

'She's gone?'

'A week ago Torrens rang up to tell Willie he was calling the whole thing off.'

'Ha!' Inspector Fowler's anger flared up again. 'Ha, so now that you haven't got Willie Black to do all the work for you you're stuck. Where has the woman gone to?'

'I don't know. I got through to Bristol and they sent a man round to look for her. All he could find out was that she had packed up and gone and hadn't left an address.'

'Well, damn it man, put out a call for her, find her. Send out her picture.'

'There isn't any picture.'

'But surely, Torrens gave Willie Black a picture of some kind so that he could recognize her in the first place?'

'No, he told Willie her name and where she worked and he didn't need anything else.'

'But you presumably, with the whole police force to help you, do. All right, Piggott, send down your report and the picture and get to work finding that woman.' He replaced the receiver. He was not displeased that his subordinate had to admit at least one small failure, specially in view of his own record here in Inching Round.

20

INSPECTOR FOWLER sat before the telephone thinking over what he had been told. In spite of what he had told Piggott he believed the story was almost certain to be true.

There couldn't be much doubt either that Angela Pewsey had got hold of it. That must have been what she found so deliciously entertaining when she raided Major Torrens' house.

If she had found out, the chances were that she had written to Mrs Torrens, telling her that something to her interest might be found in Inching Round. That would explain why the cook had disappeared. Inspector Fowler knew only too well the horror that people like that have of 'being mixed up in a murder case'. That she would have read about it was certain. The papers had been full of it. Mrs Torrens could change her name and disappear into the basement kitchen of some other nondescript boarding-house, just another unremarkable middle-aged female. Yes, that wasn't going to be easy.

And this Major Torrens. He'd come across him several times and of course seen him striding about the village generally chucking his weight about. He was accepted obviously for what he had seemed to be, the peppery army man retired; one of the older school, ready to pounce at once on anyone or anything that did not measure up to what he conceived to be County standards. His favourite words were 'outsider' and 'upstart' . . . amusing when you thought of it. But he had lived in the district for ten years and so having served his probation was more or less accepted. He did the right things, wore the right clothes (he could) and did his best to cultivate the right people. Everything in his past he had tucked away and had quite under control. Not for years and years had it been necessary for him to pretend that he was something that he was not. He was, in fact, a country gentleman, independent and secure, a figure in the life of the county.

Then had come Angela Pewsey's discovery, giving her the means to smash the whole proud edifice that he had built so carefully. He could hope for nothing unless Angela Pewsey were silenced. He would know that there was only one way to do that.

Inspector Fowler's reflexions were disturbed by voices. Constable Wilks put his head through the door to say that

Miss Carey was waiting to see him and she didn't seem to be in too good a mood.

'All right Wilks, fetch her in.'

Ethel Carey looked calm enough, but he thought her face looked drawn; the skin was white over her cheekbones.

'Sit down please, Miss Carey.'

Dr Daw's nurse sat and folded her hands in her lap. He noticed again how controlled and capable they were. Most people he remembered gave themselves away with their hands. But hers were disciplined. She waited without speaking.

'Well, you didn't come here to pay me a social call, I'm sure of that.'

Her voice when she spoke was quite flat. 'You've been to see Dr Daw, haven't you?'

'Well, you know, I can't talk about these things to you, Miss Carey, even if I wanted to.'

'You don't have to tell me if you don't want to. I know.'

'Well now, you sound as if you objected.'

'I do object. Dr Daw is not to be worried.'

'Oh, but my dear young lady, murder is a very worrying business. I'm sure you'll be glad when it is all cleared up.'

'Dr Daw had nothing to do with it.'

'Don't you think,' he said mildly, 'that Dr Daw is quite capable of taking care of himself?'

'No, I don't.'

'Why not, Miss Carey?'

'Because he is always trying to protect someone else.'

'I see. He didn't necessarily give me that impression.'

She leaped on that. 'So you *have* been to see him?'

'I'll tell you this, if it eases your mind. If I did go to see Dr Daw, it was at his own invitation.'

Her voice shook. 'You drove him to it, waiting, watching, spying, preying on everyone's nerves. You didn't go to him direct, oh no. You talked to me, you talked to Dan Everard, to anyone who would drop the least hint to you. And you knew all the time that all this would get back to him and he would feel that you were closing a net round him, closing the gaps, coming nearer all the time, with the whole village whispering and watching you stalking him. You are persecuting him.'

Inspector Fowler said patiently: 'Miss Carey, if anyone is being persecuted in this case they are being persecuted by their own conscience.'

'How can you say that when you know that Dr Daw is innocent?'

'But do I know?'

'Well, if you don't know, I do.'

'It would be a great help if you would tell me how you know Miss Carey.'

'I know Dr Daw.'

'I see. After years filled with surprises, Miss, I have long ago given up believing that I know anyone.'

'I tell you I know he is not guilty.' Even her carefully-schooled hands were losing some of their discipline. They were clasped so tightly that the nails were biting into her palms.

'For any other reason than that you know him, Miss Carey?'

There was a long pause, and then Ethel Carey said in a voice quite without emotion: 'Yes.'

Inspector Fowler was startled out of his calm.

'You are serious about that? You have some evidence that clears Dr Daw?'

'Yes.'

'What is it?'

'I know who is guilty.'

'That is a very serious statement to make, Miss Carey.'

She half smiled. 'Yes, isn't it?'

He drew a writing-pad towards him. 'Who murdered Angela Pewsey?'

'I did.'

There was a long pause. His mind flew back to the last meeting he had with her. He remembered how she had impressed him then. He remembered his anger at having added to, rather than eliminated from, his list of suspects.

He looked at her. Now that she had said what she had obviously come to say she was quite calm. Her hands once more lay passively, one above the other in her lap. Her features had relaxed into their normal immobility.

'You realize, Miss Carey, the seriousness of what you have said?'

'Yes.'

'And you are prepared to make a statement, knowing that it may be written down and used as evidence.'

'Yes. You can write it down. I killed her.'

She waited and she said a little impatiently: 'Aren't you going to write it down?'

'Not yet. It might help you if we went over the details first. Last time I spoke to you you told me that you walked in the wood at the back of the village.'

'Yes, that was true. I went there afterwards.'

'Afterwards, I see.'

'I went to her cottage first.'

'What time was that?'

'I'm not sure, not within half an hour. I – you see I was upset. I walked about trying to think. I think it may have been a little after three o'clock.'

'Did you meet anyone as you walked about?'

'I don't know. I may have done, but I wouldn't have noticed in the state I was in.'

'If you were upset to that extent you would have drawn attention to yourself, wouldn't you?'

'I don't know. Outwardly I may have looked calm enough. I don't show my feelings a great deal.'

'No, I've noticed that. You think you arrived at the cottage at about three?'

'Some time after, but I can't be sure how long.'

'And the dead woman let you in?'

'I walked in.'

'And she was surprised to see you?'

'No, no. I suppose she half expected me.'

'What makes you think that?'

'She knows that when I have something to say, I say it to the person concerned.'

'Go on.'

'I told her that if she didn't stop spreading her horrible insinuations about Dr Daw and me, I would find a way of stopping her.'

'What did she say to that?'

'She laughed. She gave that high-pitched laugh of hers. I . . . snatched up the first thing that came to my hand and hit her with it.'

'I see. And she fell to the floor?'

Ethel Carey nodded without speaking.

'But when the body was found it was on a chair, slumped over the spinning wheel.'

'Yes, I lifted her up and put her there.'

'Why? She was dead, wasn't she?'

'Yes.' She paused and added: 'I thought if anyone looked through the window and saw her there they might think she was alive.'

'Was she singing while you were there, Miss Carey?'

She looked surprised. 'Singing? No.'

'That's funny, we have evidence that she was singing when she was killed.'

'She may have been. After she had laughed at me she may have begun to sing too.'

'It must have been quite a gay little party.'

'I've told you what happened.'

'Were you at the inquest, Miss Carey?'

'No, of course not.'

'Did you read the account of the murder in the papers?'

'I couldn't bear to read, talk, or even think about it.'

'That's a pity, because according to the evidence at the inquest the blow that killed Miss Pewsey was struck from behind and from above while she was sitting in a chair.'

'Does it matter what was said at the inquest? I've told you I killed her, Inspector Fowler. I'm quite ready to take the consequences.'

Inspector Fowler put the tips of his fingers together and looked at her across the desk. 'Miss Carey, if you had not been desperately afraid for Dr Daw's sake, would you have come here with this story of yours?'

Her self-control flew from her. 'I came here to tell the truth. You've got to believe me. You've got to believe me. You pretend not to because you won't give up torturing Dr Daw. Do you think I would come here and confess to a murder if I hadn't done it? Do you think I want to die?'

'Since you ask me, Miss Carey, I believe that if you thought it would help your employer, you would die willingly.'

'No, no. It isn't true. I'm guilty, I tell you. I'm ready to take my punishment.'

'Well now, let us think a moment. Supposing for the sake of argument Dr Daw is the guilty one. Do you think, for a moment, he would stand by and let you be hanged?'

Without answering she dropped her head in her hands.

He stood up and looked down at her bowed figure with something like compassion. 'You know, Miss Carey, I believe I have a higher opinion of Dr Daw than you have. I don't believe that he would let you do this to save his reputation, or even his life.'

She lifted a stricken face to look at him. 'If you have a high opinion of him, how can you think he is guilty?'

'Miss Carey, I have not said that I think he is guilty.'

'But you do think so?'

'Dr Daw has loyal friends, Miss Carey, but if he or anyone else is guilty of this murder they will have to take the consequences. Now please do not try to help him by diverting me from my duty. I have not said that I think he is guilty. If I had evidence that he was, he would be under lock and key. Let me tell you that and also that your own story will be investigated.' He stressed his words. 'The discrepancies in your story could easily be the device of a very clever woman to make it appear that she was ready to sacrifice herself for someone else. In my view, Miss Carey, you may possibly be a very clever woman, or alternatively a very foolish one.' He opened the door pointedly. 'One way or another, you will be hearing from me in due course.' He waited without speaking while she walked slowly through the door.

These women; on one hand an almost passionate desire to destroy themselves and on the other a desire to hold men and enslave them. He walked back to his desk thinking of Ethel Carey and escaped into the conclusion that she should be married and have children of her own. But her potentialities for childbearing did not alter the fact that her story bothered him. She said that she had murdered Angela Pewsey and he had no doubt in his mind that if the motive were strong enough, she would do it. Dr Daw could easily be a strong enough motive. The kind of love she felt for him was secret and precious.

Yes, she had motive enough, most likely. Motive, Inspector Fowler gritted his teeth. They all had motive enough. There was too much motive everywhere. Everyone he came across seemed to have a reasonable motive for murdering Angela Pewsey . . . if there was such a thing as a reasonable motive for murder. Motive, means, opportunity, there was so much of everything he decided that the murder might just as well have been a community affair, like the village fête or gathering the hay in the churchyard.

But it was Jackie Day and Alfie Spiers who produced the piece of evidence that to the Inspector's mind was worth more than all the confessions and theories and motives that had bothered and frustrated him since he came to Inching Round . . . Jackie and Alfie and, of course, their dog.

The dog ran into Major Torrens' grounds. That would have been a disaster, but fortunately for them this was the day when the house was unattended. They followed the dog and as usual, they found him with his eager rear end sticking out of a rabbit burrow. From between his legs there flowed a stream of loose earth. As they reached the burrow there was a convulsive heave and a piece of old sacking flew out. This was followed immediately by what had once been a clean linen handkerchief.

Jackie without ceremony took the dog by the tail and hauled him out of the burrow. They secured the dog with a piece of string and then stood toeing the material from the burrow.

'That's a nice-looking handkerchief,' Jackie said.

'Yes, I bet it's a real smart 'un if it were washed out.'

'Why don't you take it home and give it to your dad?'

'My dad would tell me to take it back where I found it. No matter what you give to 'im it's always someone else's 'e ses.'

'So do mine, but he says there's no harm in takin' what the Lord sends.' He picked up the handkerchief and they speculated on its merits as they walked. They were so absorbed in building up its character that they almost collided with Inspector Fowler as he came through the gate.

Guiltily Jackie tried to pocket the handkerchief, but the long hand of Inspector Fowler reached out for it and got it.

'Ha, up to the old tricks again, eh? I find you on private property in possession of a valuable piece of household linen ... very grave.'

'But we never took it, sir. The dog run in an' we run after the dog. And the dog dug the handkerchief out of a rabbit burrow.'

'Out of a rabbit burrow? A likely story that is ... ha ha ... ha.' But suddenly the laughter died on Inspector Fowler's lips. He was turning the stained but delicate handkerchief over in his hands. 'In a rabbit burrow, you said? Where?'

'Over here, sir.' They were so eager to prove their innocence that they ran ahead of him.

Inspector Fowler stood staring at the newly scratched earth and at the piece of grease-stained sacking and at the handkerchief. 'Which came out of the burrow first?'

'The sackin', sir.'

Inspector Fowler bent himself like a folding yard measure and peered into the hole. Then he thrust in a long arm and pulled out a tyre lever. That was all. But that was enough.

That night as he came off the London train Major George Torrens was met by Inspector Fowler and Sergeant Porter and taken to the police station. Later he was charged with the murder of Angela Mason Pewsey.

21

GEORGE TORRENS was tried at Lewes before Mr Justice George and a jury of twelve. Mr Miles Radlett, K.C., appeared for the Crown, and Torrens was defended by Sir William Rubens. The public was served by as many star reporters as could be jammed into the limited space. They referred to it variously as 'The Spinning Wheel Murder Case', 'The Batman Squire Case', 'The Singing Spinster Case', and 'The Poison Pen Case'.

Mr Miles Radlett for the Crown told the jury in a waspish voice that it was their duty to decide on the evidence that would be placed before them by the Crown whether the prisoner was guilty or not guilty. That was their business and their only business. He implied that they were to listen, keep awake and keep quiet, and that his opinion of them as a group was not high.

The Crown prosecutor then hitched his gown a little more securely on his shoulders, glanced at his brief, pushed it aside and got down to this business in hand. He intended to make his points now, knowing that never again during the trial would the jury be as wide awake.

First he dealt with the murdered woman Angela Mason Pewsey. Here was a woman, fortunately rare in any community in the land, who made it a hobby, a lifework almost, to pry and ferret into the lives of others and having got the information she needed to use it to torture. Evidence would show one of her victims was the prisoner at the bar; no doubt there were others.

'When you have heard what she had discovered in the

past of this man, and when it has been shown to you how she confronted and threatened him with this knowledge, you may say that here indeed is a powerful motive for murder.

'Now let us consider the position of the prisoner; it is imperative that we should do this.

'George Torrens, who was known until recently as Major George Torrens, is thought of in the district where he lived – for want of a better description – as "one of the gentry". He is a man of undoubted means and is accepted for what he says he is, a retired officer of the regular army. Torrens has been in the regular army, but not as he suggests with the rank of major, but as a batman.

'For ten years he lives in this country village, maintaining the position he has assumed, taking a more and more influential part in local affairs and no doubt feeling more and more confident that his past is buried.

'But there is something else in his past. As Major George Torrens he posed as a bachelor, but in fact he has a wife, and in order to ensure that she will never cross his path he employs a detective agency to have her watched. The evidence will show that this woman made no effort to locate her husband for the good reason that she believed him dead, killed in the nineteen-fourteen-eighteen war. She wanders about from place to place, earning her living as a cook. She has no idea that he is alive, no idea either that he has inherited a considerable fortune from the officer who employed him. Knowing where she was and what she was doing, George Torrens made no effort to rejoin his wife, or to contribute to her support. In fact, as you will see from the evidence, he did exactly the reverse.

'But he had reckoned without the prying eyes and the sinister motives of Angela Pewsey. You will be shown in the evidence how this woman pried into the affairs of George Torrens. She was seen to leave his house which she had entered in his absence and come away carrying papers. She was found to have in her possession a document bearing the heading "The Lynx Detective Service". It will be shown that the only person in the district who employed that Agency was George Torrens, and that he employed them to watch his wife.

'You will have read to you a letter found in Torrens' possession in which the dead woman tells him that she knows of the existence of the wife and threatens to write to her telling how Major George Torrens is living in luxury in Inching Round.

'Now as to the murder itself . . .' Here the Crown Prosecutor outlined the evidence he would produce as to the time and cause of the death, and then he came to the discovery made by the two small boys and their dog; the handkerchief which was the undisputed property of the Major, the tyre lever which came from his garage, and the soiled piece of sacking which also came from his garage.

There could be no dispute that the case which Inspector Fowler had assembled for the Crown prosecutor was a complete one. The public analyst was there to show that the linen handkerchief was stained with human blood and that it was not of the same group as the prisoner's, but was the same as that of Angela Pewsey. There was human blood of the same group on the tyre lever and a strand of human hair.

Pewsey's letter to the prisoner was produced and the handwriting was identified as hers. Willie Black gave evidence of his employment by Torrens and of his conversations with his wife. The marriage certificate was produced and a copy of the will under which he inherited his fortune in which he was referred to as a batman.

Inspector Fowler gave evidence covering his inquiries and the arrest.

Sir William Rubens, for the defence, rose and confronted the Inspector with a bland confidence that he was far from feeling.

'Inspector, is it not a fact that from first to last Torrens has protested his innocence in this matter?'

'Yes, sir.' Inspector Fowler's air was one of giving a

routine answer to a routine question. He had been through it all before.

'You met him at the station?'

'Yes.'

'In fact, his principal reaction was one of indignation?'

'Yes, he said it was preposterous.'

There was a murmur of laughter from those who knew Major George Torrens, but this died when Sir William looked into the body of the court and said contemptuously: 'A man here is on trial for his life.' He went on:

'He said it was preposterous. Then, I understand, Inspector, you took him to the police station and formally charged him with the murder of Angela Mason Pewsey?' Sir William had no special motive in asking these questions except to create a general impression that all might not be well.

'That is so, sir.'

'And he again protested?'

'He laughed.'

'He made no statement?'

'No, sir.'

'I see.' Sir William paused significantly, for no reason except that it was good technique.

'Now, Inspector, does it occur to you that there is one witness whose word would carry a great deal of weight in this trial?'

'I beg your pardon?'

'Oh come now, Inspector, there is a missing witness surely?'

'That is not for me to say, sir.'

'We have heard a great deal about a person who is said to be the prisoner's wife.' Sir William's voice cracked like a whip. 'Where is she?'

Inspector Fowler looked a little put out. 'She has not come forward.'

Sir William smiled. 'I see. She has not come forward. So you have been waiting for her to come forward, have you?'

'No, we have not.'

'You mean you have tried to find her?'

'Yes, sir.'

'With all the resources at your command?'

'We have circularized a description and put out a radio appeal.'

'Still nothing?'

'No.'

'Are you reluctant to testify on this matter, Inspector?'

'Not at all, sir.'

'In a case like this, Inspector, you could, if you wished, have the whole resources of the nation's police organization at your call, could you not?'

'Possibly.'

'Possibly, eh? In fact, Inspector, when you put out your description every policeman in the land was on the lookout for the so-called Mrs Torrens. Is that so?'

'That is so.'

'And you found her?'

'We were unable to locate her.'

Sir William waited. 'And yet, Inspector, we have been told that one private detective with no resources whatever was able to keep track of this woman for ten years.'

Inspector Fowler paused and said 'Yes.'

'In fact, the minute this so-called wife of the prisoner ceased to be a source of revenue to a private detective she to all events and purposes ceased to exist.'

'I would not say that.'

'No? What would you say?'

'We have failed to locate her.'

'How very interesting.' Sir William wrapped his gown about himself and sat down.

Firth Prentice had watched the proceedings with more than professional interest. In spite of Sir William he knew that the case for the prosecution was cast-iron. It is notorious that law clerks, solicitors and barristers can lay the odds to a point on the outcome of a trial. The further it went the more certain it became. There were the usual collection of handwriting experts and witnesses of remote association who came forward for Torrens. They were there to cloud the issue, to create the doubt from which the benefit might accrue, but the case against the prisoner, to anyone who knew, was like a rock. Then there was Torrens himself.

Firth had been wondering how he would behave. He went into the witness box as he had lived for ten years in Inching Round . . . as the man who had created the personality of Major George Torrens. You disliked the man, you were sorry for him, and you admired him. He was trapped but he was fighting for his life . . . for the life of Major George Torrens.

He admitted that he had been a batman and he countered that by asserting that he had held a commission earlier and because of a gambling debt and a scandal had joined the ranks. He had done this because he was at heart a soldier. He had married, yes, in a foolish moment of despair he had married. Yes, he had employed a firm of detectives because he could not bear this brief mad interlude in his life to intrude into his proper and natural position. Angela Pewsey, of course he had been furious with the interfering old busybody, who wouldn't? As for killing her, wasn't it perfectly obvious that he could have bought off this cook, this mistake at any time he cared to for a few hundred pounds? He had told the dead woman so when she challenged him. He had threatened her with the courts. What had she done? She had looked damned sick.

But when it came to explaining the tyre lever and the handkerchief Torrens was not so confident. Firth Prentice found himself leaning forward watching him. He did not explain them because he could not. It seemed as if they defied him, angered him, and somehow frustrated him. At this point he was no longer Major George Torrens, but Private Torrens, the batman, frightened at being found out in something deadly serious.

It was at this point that Firth left the court. Celia who was sitting beside him knew that he had gone only when she turned round to whisper to him. He went quickly because he was in a hurry.

Firth took the first train to London and the first from there to Bristol.

22

It would be wrong to say that Celia had been hanging on the end of the telephone; she had been doing nothing more than loitering about the house in case it rang. It was obvious and galling when she almost ran to answer the greengrocer and Firth's father and those who wanted social intercourse with the Sims, but she kept on answering because women, of course, have no pride.

The call when it did come gave her little satisfaction.

'Hello.'

'Yes.'

'Oh hello, is that you Celia?'

'Yes' (coldly).

'Sorry I had to rush away, but I had to . . . Listen.'

'Yes.'

'Is everything all right?'

'Yes, of course.'

'I didn't mean that, I meant has nobody done anything silly?'

'Of course not. Why should they?'

'I didn't mean you, I meant anyone connected with the case?'

'The case?'

'Yes. What was the verdict?'

'Oh, Firth. He's been convicted. I suppose it's a relief, but . . .'

'Listen, Celia, this is very important . . . Listen carefully . . . I want you to do something very important for me. Are you listening?'

'Yes, of course I'm listening.'

'I want you to ring everyone connected with this case, ring casually and just mention ordinary things and find out what they are doing.'

'But Firth, why?'

'Never mind why, please do it Celia. If anyone says anything odd (and do please listen carefully), if anyone says anything at all odd, tell them I want to see them, most urgently.'

'You're coming back?' Her voice was oddly relieved, but he failed to notice it.

'Of course, I'm coming back.'

'You said ring everybody. I can't ring Graham.'

His voice was cold. 'Can't you? . . . well, ring the others. Ring them again to-morrow.'

'Is that all?'

'No, listen. Is what's his name – Ted? – on duty at the railway station to-night?'

'I think so, he was there this afternoon when I came in from Lewes.'

'Good, tell him to stay there till I see him to-morrow afternoon.'

'You're coming back to-morrow afternoon?'

'Yes, but don't meet me.'

Indignant voice. 'Why ever should I . . . ?'

'And for heaven's sake, Celia, don't forget to do that telephoning. Is the verdict announced yet?'

'You mean in the papers? I haven't seen it; but I suppose everyone knows.'

'All right, Celia, start ringing now. I won't keep you.'

The phone went dead. Celia glared at it, rebelled, changed her mind and took up the telephone book.

Firth came off the train from London and the porter Ted was waiting for him.

'Evening, sir.'

'Hello, Ted. No luggage, I'm afraid.'

'No, sir. I heard you left rather smart like . . . Excuse me, sir.' He turned and waved the train away as if it were nothing.

'She said you wanted to see me like, Miss Celia did. It's properly my time off, but I stayed on curious-like.'

Firth waited and then said: 'Ted, I want you to think very seriously about something. Do you remember the day of the murder?'

'Remember.' Ted smiled. 'That were a red letter day as you might say.'

'There is a train before this one, isn't there?'

'Yes, the three forty-five.'

'Did anyone come off it?'

Ted scratched his head. 'That's askin' . . . now then she was on time!' He shook his head. 'Let me see: I looked at my watch and I ses to myself . . . No, that's askin', that is.'

'It would be a stranger.'

'A stranger.' With heavy intensity he tried to cast back his mind. But he was silent.

Then Firth showed him the photograph and he remembered . . .

Major Torrens' house had already that unlived-in appearance that a well-kept dwelling develops after even a few days of neglect. The servants had gone, the gardener had gone. The grass was growing fast, the windows were closed.

Firth hurried up the drive. He hardly looked at the house itself, but walked round to the garage at the back. He could work fast now because he knew where he was going and what he was looking for.

He wanted to see the garden in the vicinity of the garage. Between the garage and the kitchen there was a paved courtyard. Firth went carefully over the paving stones. Over one small group he went down on his knees and made a more careful examination. He was satisfied with what he saw and continued his hunt. At the back of the garage there was a pile of loose earth. That was all he wanted to see. He hurried away.

Celia was obviously waiting for him and obviously pretending that she was not.

'Oh hello,' she said. 'I thought you weren't coming.'

'No, you didn't, you were looking out for me through the window.'

'If I was,' she said, 'I was curious to see if you'd follow your ludicrous melodrama through to the end.'

'I have done. It's all over.'

'I see. So I've wasted my time with all that subtle telephoning I indulged in.'

He took her hands. 'I say, Celia darling, please don't be so utterly fed up with me. I'll soon be gone.'

'I'm not fed up with you. It . . . it's the way you behave.'

To her annoyance he switched away and said abruptly: 'So you did ring those people?'

'Of course. If you make an ass of yourself, why shouldn't I?'

'What did they say?'

'They behaved normally, thank God. Nurse Carey was at work, quite cheerful. Joyce Everard was going off to an appointment with her solicitor. The doctor was on his way to a baby case. He rang me from there. It's a boy. The vicar was packing to go to a conference . . . Why, what's the matter.'

He had been sitting down and now he leaped violently to his feet.

'Going away to a conference . . . Going where?'

'He didn't say. You never know with these conferences. They hold them anywhere and everywhere.' She looked at him in surprise as he made for the door. 'I say, don't tell me you're running out on us again?'

He turned and smiled at her. 'Yes, but I'll be back.'

'But you stay such a short time, wouldn't it be simpler if you just waved from the gate.' She found herself addressing the closed front door.

Mrs Sim came drifting downstairs.

'Are you alone, Celia dear? I thought I heard voices.'

Celia came back into the room. 'We had a visitor.'

'They couldn't have stayed long, dear. I was here myself five minutes ago.'

'It was Firth. He's gone again.'

'Oh dear, I wanted to talk to him.'

'He wouldn't let that stop him, mother . . . Talking I mean. I was talking to him when he dashed out of the door.'

'But where did he go?'

'Didn't say, all he said was that he'd be back, so I suppose he will. I never saw such a performance – just jumped up and charged out of the house.'

'But dear, something must have caused it.'

'If it didn't sound so crazy I'd say it was caused by my telling him that the vicar was going away on a conference.'

Mrs Sim surprised Celia by her sudden change of manner. She nodded slowly. 'Yes, that would have caused it.'

'Mother, what on earth do you mean?'

'Don't ask me, Celia. You see, it's something that I'm not permitted to talk about.' She put her arm about her daughter's shoulders. 'It involves someone else, Celia, someone I'm very fond of. If I told you you would wish that I had not. Do you mind?'

'No darling, I don't mind.' She smiled at her mother. 'You always do know so much more than you ever tell, don't you?'

'Much more.' She gave her head a sad little shake and walked across the hall and out through the front door.

23

WHEN Firth arrived the vicar of Inching Round was standing by his own gate. A suitcase was at his feet and a light overcoat was over his arm. He had discarded his clerical attire and was wearing an ordinary collar and tie and a grey flannel suit.

'Hello, Vicar,' Firth said casually. 'It looks as if I just got here in time, doesn't it?'

The vicar gave a little smile. 'A little too late, I'm afraid. I've only just time to catch my train.'

'I'm sorry to hear that.'

'I have to attend a conference.'

'I know.' Firth made no effort to move out of his way. 'The Conference is in Lewes, isn't it? That is what I came to talk about.'

The vicar hesitated, then resigned. 'There is a bus in an hour.' He sighed. 'I suppose one hour will not really matter very much.' He turned to lead the way back into the house. Firth picked up his suitcase and followed him.

The blinds in the study were drawn. Everything in the room was neatly arranged . . . so neatly, in fact, that it looked unoccupied.

The vicar stood looking about the room he must have only just left, but as he stood there he gave an odd impression that the room was unfamiliar to him.

'There is some sherry, I think.' He turned to Firth doubtfully. 'That is, of course, if you would care to take wine with . . . me.'

'I should like to very much.'

'May I also have a glass of sherry?'

They turned in surprise to face Mrs Sim, and she spoke to the vicar. 'I would not like to think you had gone without saying good-bye to an old friend.'

The vicar raised his eyes swiftly to meet her own.

'You knew?'

She nodded. 'Yes.' She hesitated and then said: 'I saw you at her gate only a few minutes after the singing stopped. I hoped and kept on hoping, but . . . you were carrying a black book.'

Without speaking the vicar put three glasses on the table and filled them with wine. Then he turned to Firth.

'And you? Did you know too?'

He shook his head. 'I had to wait till I found out who was proposing to go away. I knew that someone was almost certain to do that as soon as the verdict of guilty was returned.'

'I should have gone sooner,' the little man said. 'But as

that story of wickedness was unfolded I saw that it was right that that man should be punished as much as he has been. But that is enough. We will drink and then I will go.'

Firth said mildly: 'But is there any need to go?'

Mrs Sim looked at him in surprise. 'Firth, I don't understand you. You are surely not suggesting that he can possibly stand by and let this man be hanged.'

'Again, I don't see why not.'

The vicar interposed. 'I have committed a terrible sin. It would be a viler sin to let an innocent man be hanged for it.' He looked at Firth in angry reproach. 'You surely must think me far, far worse than I am.'

Again the stubborn young man shook his head.

'But you see the man you are talking about is not innocent. He was found guilty, and he is guilty. I tell you, vicar, if you go to the police as you propose to do they will laugh at you at first and then get angry with you, and finally dismiss you as one of those harmless lunatics who confess to murders they haven't done.'

'But they must believe me . . . they must. It's the truth.' The vicar's eyes were widening with dismay.

Mrs Sim, too, was uncontrollably distressed. 'Then I'll go with him and tell what I saw.'

'That won't help. You saw him at the gate, you say. You remember it only after he has gone to them with this story of his. Look, Mrs Sim, they will decide that he is slightly mad and that you are a sentimental lady with a vivid imagination. Listen, Vicar, while they are humouring you they will ask you why you did it. What will you say?'

The vicar drew himself up. 'I did it,' he said, 'because there are people in this parish whom I love. I discovered that that woman was planning to lay waste to their lives, to spread ruin and despair. I saw myself as men in the Old Testament saw themselves. I saw myself as the instrument of an avenging God. I know now the magnitude of my sin, but that is how I saw myself then. That is my motive for murdering that unhappy woman.'

Firth insisted mildly: 'They'll still say you are quite mad, you know. Instead of just an ordinary crank, they'll say you're a religious one.'

The vicar sat down and bowed his head into his hands. Mrs Sim turned to Firth in despair. 'Firth, you can't condemn us like this, I for withholding my knowledge, the vicar to a life of torment. What are we to do?'

'Nothing.'

She turned to the vicar. 'You must produce the diary.'

He answered wearily: 'I destroyed it. It was so vile.'

She cried to Firth: 'You know that what the vicar says is true. You said yourself you knew.'

'Yes,' he said gently, 'I know.'

'Then you must help us – don't you see – you must help us?'

He shook his head. 'I know, because you see I know the whole story. The reason Major George Torrens is going to be hanged for murder is because he committed one.'

They looked at him as if they thought him insane.

He walked over and leaned against the fireplace and turned to face them.

'Yes, it's quite true that I know that Torrens did not murder Angela Pewsey. He murdered his wife.'

'Firth.' Mrs Sim's word escaped her like a sigh.

'You see everything was right about the trial except that one thing. I guessed it when Sir William Rubens was baiting the police for not producing the wife. As a matter of fact, you know, she is not very far from here.'

Mrs Sim gasped. 'But you said she was dead.'

'She is dead. She is under the flagstones between Major Torrens' garage and the kitchen door. She arrived here on the day of the murder. Old Ted at the station verified that, but I was careful not to let him know what he was verifying. He recognized a photograph I found of her wearing the same hat and dress. I went to Bristol to get that and it took me hours. I'd almost given up when someone remembered that she had a woman friend on the outskirts of the city, probably the only friend she had in the world, and this woman, a retired nannie, had the picture in her album.

'The train arrived a few minutes after the murder. I'm only guessing now, but I think Major Torrens may have seen Pewsey's body; you remember how it was known that he walked past about the time she was killed. As I said, he may have seen her and decided that his motives for killing her were so good that he was better out of the vicinity. And then, just after he was safely home, along came the wife whom he had been told by Angela Pewsey to expect . . . Pewsey was dead, and only this one unknown woman was between him and absolute security. He killed her in his own house and that lovely moonlight night he buried her deep under the flagstones behind his house. I could show you the ones that have been moved. I could show you the earth behind the garage. They found the weapon, but that was sheer bad luck.' He paused to inhale from his cigarette.

'Major Torrens might have sold that house and moved somewhere else; on the other hand, it might have given him a certain satisfaction to have lived on so close to his wife. He was a cold-blooded brute.'

There was a pause and Firth said: 'His wife told her friend that she had heard something to her advantage and that she was going away to live like a lady for a change.'

Mrs Sim said softly: 'The poor thing, and what a beast.'

'Yes, you can imagine how he must have felt at the trial. He might have cleared himself of one murder, but only by producing evidence of another.'

The vicar said slowly: 'If you brought this to the notice of the police, then of course they would have to believe me, wouldn't they?'

Firth half-smiled. 'They don't like amateur detectives. They wouldn't be a bit grateful you know. No, I think they'd much rather have things their way, and if it comes to that, so would I.' He strolled over and finished his sherry at a gulp.

The vicar had risen and was standing in the centre of the

room. When he spoke all the emotion had gone from his voice.

'When I did what I did it seemed a simple stroke in the execution of the will of God. Now I see it as a terrible presumption. I forgot my responsibilities to my church and to its congregation. I could bear the thought of bringing shame and punishment on myself, but too late I saw that I would bring it upon them as well.' He paused.

'But there may be a way. Dr Daw knows that my heart is not sound. He has told me like the honest man he is that I may not have long to live. Perhaps if once again I make myself God's instrument, He may in His mercy forgive me.'

Each in turn they took his hand without speaking. He escorted them to the gate and then turned quickly back into the house.

Mrs Sim's hand as it rested on Firth's arm was trembling.

'What can one do . . . What can one do?'

'Nothing,' he said gently. 'But you know that, don't you?'

'Yes, I do know.'

Two holiday makers found the vicar's body at the foot of a chalk cliff on the downs. The only surprise expressed by Dr Daw was that he should have gone walking up so steep a slope. With the kind of heart he had, what had happened was obvious. He had had an attack of giddiness, stumbled and had fallen over the edge. Only Firth and Mrs Sim knew what was more likely to be the truth.

Celia and Firth were sitting in the buttery of the Berkeley Hotel. She was up for the day. The atmosphere of the place was good. The food had been good and the drinks good and everybody had seemed to be enjoying themselves . . . or nearly everybody.

Celia was studying the end of her cigarette.

'You haven't been to see us. Any reason?'

'No need. You haven't had any murders.'

'Do we have to have a murder to lure you down there?'

'Not to lure me, darling, to need me.'

'We must be popular with you. What do you expect us to do? Bring you down on the pretext that there is some business to do?'

'I wouldn't put it past you.'

Celia looked at him and looked away again. 'Well, I do need you in a sort of way . . . That's to say –' She seemed a bit nervous. 'As a matter of fact I've been using you a bit already.'

'Ha . . . So that's the cause of the visit. Come on! Out with it. What have you been up to this time?'

'Graham's back.'

'I see.'

'No, you don't.'

'I see, I don't see.'

'I told him I was engaged – well, not exactly engaged, but sort of.'

'I see.'

'But what you don't see is that I told him I was sort of engaged to you.'

He didn't look at Celia because he was afraid to. 'And are you? . . . I mean sort of?'

'Yes . . . No. Well, you see I thought that might be one of the things you might come and see us about.'

He jumped up. 'Well, come on, what are we waiting for?'

Then he sat down again. 'This wouldn't by any chance be a stratagem to make Master Graham jealous, would it?'

'Oh, Firth.' She did look at him then. 'Do you mean to tell me you haven't even noticed how much I love you.'

'I am noticing it . . . Now. Celia, you darling.'

She smiled. 'Mother said you might take some notice of me, if I asked you to. She refers to you now as that nice boy Henry.'

A CATALOGUE OF
SELECTED DOVER BOOKS
IN ALL FIELDS OF INTEREST

A CATALOG OF SELECTED DOVER
BOOKS IN ALL FIELDS OF INTEREST

LASERS AND HOLOGRAPHY, Winston E. Kock. Sound introduction to burgeoning field, expanded (1981) for second edition. 84 illustrations. 160pp. 5⅜ × 8¼. (EUK)   24041-X Pa. $3.50

FLORAL STAINED GLASS PATTERN BOOK, Ed Sibbett, Jr. 96 exquisite floral patterns—irises, poppie, lilies, tulips, geometrics, abstracts, etc.—adaptable to innumerable stained glass projects. 64pp. 8¼ × 11.   24259-5 Pa. $3.50

THE HISTORY OF THE LEWIS AND CLARK EXPEDITION, Meriwether Lewis and William Clark. Edited by Eliott Coues. Great classic edition of Lewis and Clark's day-by-day journals. Complete 1893 edition, edited by Eliott Coues from Biddle's authorized 1814 history. 1508pp. 5⅜ × 8½.
                              21268-8, 21269-6, 21270-X Pa. Three-vol. set $22.50

ORLEY FARM, Anthony Trollope. Three-dimensional tale of great criminal case. Original Millais illustrations illuminate marvelous panorama of Victorian society. Plot was author's favorite. 736pp. 5⅜ × 8½.   24181-5 Pa. $8.95

THE CLAVERINGS, Anthony Trollope. Major novel, chronicling aspects of British Victorian society, personalities. 16 plates by M. Edwards; first reprint of full text. 412pp. 5⅜ × 8½.   23464-9 Pa. $6.00

EINSTEIN'S THEORY OF RELATIVITY, Max Born. Finest semi-technical account; much explanation of ideas and math not readily available elsewhere on this level. 376pp. 5⅜ × 8½.   60769-0 Pa. $5.00

COMPUTABILITY AND UNSOLVABILITY, Martin Davis. Classic graduate-level introduction th theory of computability, usually referred to as theory of recurrent functions. New preface and appendix. 288pp. 5⅜ × 8½. 61471-9 Pa. $6.50

THE GODS OF THE EGYPTIANS, E.A. Wallis Budge. Never excelled for richness, fullness: all gods, goddesses, demons, mythical figures of Ancient Egypt; their legends, rites, incarnations, etc. Over 225 illustrations, plus 6 color plates. 988pp. 6⅛ × 9¼. (EBE)   22055-9, 22056-7 Pa., Two-vol. set $20.00

THE I CHING (THE BOOK OF CHANGES), translated by James Legge. Most penetrating divination manual ever prepared. Indispensable to study of early Oriental civilizations, to modern inquiring reader. 448pp. 5⅜ × 8½.
                                                             21062-6 Pa. $6.50

THE CRAFTSMAN'S HANDBOOK, Cennino Cennini. 15th-century handbook, school of Giotto, explains applying gold, silver leaf; gesso; fresco painting, grinding pigments, etc. 142pp. 6⅛ × 9¼.   20054-X Pa. $3.50

AN ATLAS OF ANATOMY FOR ARTISTS, Fritz Schider. Finest text, working book. Full text, plus anatomical illustrations; plates by great artists showing anatomy. 593 illustrations. 192pp. 7⅞ × 10¼.   20241-0 Pa. $6.00

EASY-TO-MAKE STAINED GLASS LIGHTCATCHERS, Ed Sibbett, Jr. 67 designs for most enjoyable ornaments: fruits, birds, teddy bears, trumpet, etc. Full size templates. 64pp. 8¼ × 11.   24081-9 Pa. $3.95

TRIAD OPTICAL ILLUSIONS AND HOW TO DESIGN THEM, Harry Turner. Triad explained in 32 pages of text, with 32 pages of Escher-like patterns on coloring stock. 92 figures. 32 plates. 64pp. 8¼ × 11.   23549-1 Pa. $2.50

SMOCKING: TECHNIQUE, PROJECTS, AND DESIGNS, Dianne Durand. Foremost smocking designer provides complete instructions on how to smock. Over 10 projects, over 100 illustrations. 56pp. 8¼ × 11. 23788-5 Pa. $2.00

AUDUBON'S BIRDS IN COLOR FOR DECOUPAGE, edited by Eleanor H. Rawlings. 24 sheets, 37 most decorative birds, full color, on one side of paper. Instructions, including work under glass. 56pp. 8¼ × 11. 23492-4 Pa. $3.50

THE COMPLETE BOOK OF SILK SCREEN PRINTING PRODUCTION, J.I. Biegeleisen. For commercial user, teacher in advanced classes, serious hobbyist. Most modern techniques, materials, equipment for optimal results. 124 illustrations. 253pp. 5⅜ × 8½. 21100-2 Pa. $4.50

A TREASURY OF ART NOUVEAU DESIGN AND ORNAMENT, edited by Carol Belanger Grafton. 577 designs for the practicing artist. Full-page, spots, borders, bookplates by Klimt, Bradley, others. 144pp. 8⅜ × 11¼. 24001-0 Pa. $5.00

ART NOUVEAU TYPOGRAPHIC ORNAMENTS, Dan X. Solo. Over 800 Art Nouveau florals, swirls, women, animals, borders, scrolls, wreaths, spots and dingbats, copyright-free. 100pp. 8⅛ × 11. 24366-4 Pa. $4.00

HAND SHADOWS TO BE THROWN UPON THE WALL, Henry Bursill. Wonderful Victorian novelty tells how to make flying birds, dog, goose, deer, and 14 others, each explained by a full-page illustration. 32pp. 6½ × 9¼. 21779-5 Pa. $1.50

AUDUBON'S BIRDS OF AMERICA COLORING BOOK, John James Audubon. Rendered for coloring by Paul Kennedy. 46 of Audubon's noted illustrations: red-winged black-bird, cardinal, etc. Original plates reproduced in full-color on the covers. Captions. 48pp. 8¼ × 11. 23049-X Pa. $2.25

SILK SCREEN TECHNIQUES, J.I. Biegeleisen, M.A. Cohn. Clear, practical, modern, economical. Minimal equipment (self-built), materials, easy methods. For amateur, hobbyist, 1st book. 141 illustrations. 185pp. 6⅛ × 9¼. 20433-2 Pa. $3.95

101 PATCHWORK PATTERNS, Ruby S. McKim. 101 beautiful, immediately useable patterns, full-size, modern and traditional. Also general information, estimating, quilt lore. 140 illustrations. 124pp. 7⅞ × 10¾. 20773-0 Pa. $3.50

READY-TO-USE FLORAL DESIGNS, Ed Sibbett, Jr. Over 100 floral designs (most in three sizes) of popular individual blossoms as well as bouquets, sprays, garlands. 64pp. 8¼ × 11. 23976-4 Pa. $2.95

AMERICAN WILD FLOWERS COLORING BOOK, Paul Kennedy. Planned coverage of 46 most important wildflowers, from Rickett's collection; instructive as well as entertaining. Color versions on covers. Captions. 48pp. 8¼ × 11. 20095-7 Pa. $2.25

CARVING DUCK DECOYS, Harry V. Shourds and Anthony Hillman. Detailed instructions and full-size templates for constructing 16 beautiful, marvelously practical decoys according to time-honored South Jersey method. 70pp. 9¼ × 12¼. 24083-5 Pa. $4.95

TRADITIONAL PATCHWORK PATTERNS, Carol Belanger Grafton. Cardboard cut-out pieces for use as templates to make 12 quilts: Buttercup, Ribbon Border, Tree of Paradise, nine more. Full instructions. 57pp. 8¼ × 11. 23015-5 Pa. $3.50

25 KITES THAT FLY, Leslie Hunt. Full, easy-to-follow instructions for kites made from inexpensive materials. Many novelties. 70 illustrations. 110pp. 5⅜ × 8½.
22550-X Pa. $1.95

PIANO TUNING, J. Cree Fischer. Clearest, best book for beginner, amateur. Simple repairs, raising dropped notes, tuning by easy method of flattened fifths. No previous skills needed. 4 illustrations. 201pp. 5⅜ × 8½.
23267-0 Pa. $3.50

EARLY AMERICAN IRON-ON TRANSFER PATTERNS, edited by Rita Weiss. 75 designs, borders, alphabets, from traditional American sources. 48pp. 8¼ × 11.
23162-3 Pa. $1.95

CROCHETING EDGINGS, edited by Rita Weiss. Over 100 of the best designs for these lovely trims for a host of household items. Complete instructions, illustrations. 48pp. 8¼ × 11.
24031-2 Pa. $2.00

FINGER PLAYS FOR NURSERY AND KINDERGARTEN, Emilie Poulsson. 18 finger plays with music (voice and piano); entertaining, instructive. Counting, nature lore, etc. Victorian classic. 53 illustrations. 80pp. 6½ × 9¼. 22588-7 Pa. $1.95

BOSTON THEN AND NOW, Peter Vanderwarker. Here in 59 side-by-side views are photographic documentations of the city's past and present. 119 photographs. Full captions. 122pp. 8¼ × 11.
24312-5 Pa. $6.95

CROCHETING BEDSPREADS, edited by Rita Weiss. 22 patterns, originally published in three instruction books 1939-41. 39 photos, 8 charts. Instructions. 48pp. 8¼ × 11.
23610-2 Pa. $2.00

HAWTHORNE ON PAINTING, Charles W. Hawthorne. Collected from notes taken by students at famous Cape Cod School; hundreds of direct, personal *apercus*, ideas, suggestions. 91pp. 5⅜ × 8½.
20653-X Pa. $2.50

THERMODYNAMICS, Enrico Fermi. A classic of modern science. Clear, organized treatment of systems, first and second laws, entropy, thermodynamic potentials, etc. Calculus required. 160pp. 5⅜ × 8½.
60361-X Pa. $4.00

TEN BOOKS ON ARCHITECTURE, Vitruvius. The most important book ever written on architecture. Early Roman aesthetics, technology, classical orders, site selection, all other aspects. Morgan translation. 331pp. 5⅜ × 8½. 20645-9 Pa. $5.50

THE CORNELL BREAD BOOK, Clive M. McCay and Jeanette B. McCay. Famed high-protein recipe incorporated into breads, rolls, buns, coffee cakes, pizza, pie crusts, more. Nearly 50 illustrations. 48pp. 8¼ × 11.
23995-0 Pa. $2.00

THE CRAFTSMAN'S HANDBOOK, Cennino Cennini. 15th-century handbook, school of Giotto, explains applying gold, silver leaf; gesso; fresco painting, grinding pigments, etc. 142pp. 6⅛ × 9¼.
20054-X Pa. $3.50

FRANK LLOYD WRIGHT'S FALLINGWATER, Donald Hoffmann. Full story of Wright's masterwork at Bear Run, Pa. 100 photographs of site, construction, and details of completed structure. 112pp. 9¼ × 10.
23671-4 Pa. $6.50

OVAL STAINED GLASS PATTERN BOOK, C. Eaton. 60 new designs framed in shape of an oval. Greater complexity, challenge with sinuous cats, birds, mandalas framed in antique shape. 64pp. 8¼ × 11.
24519-5 Pa. $3.50

JAPANESE DESIGN MOTIFS, Matsuya Co. Mon, or heraldic designs. Over 4000 typical, beautiful designs: birds, animals, flowers, swords, fans, geometrics; all beautifully stylized. 213pp. 11⅜ × 8¼. 22874-6 Pa. $6.95

THE TALE OF BENJAMIN BUNNY, Beatrix Potter. Peter Rabbit's cousin coaxes him back into Mr. McGregor's garden for a whole new set of adventures. All 27 full-color illustrations. 59pp. 4¼ × 5½. (Available in U.S. only) 21102-9 Pa. $1.50

THE TALE OF PETER RABBIT AND OTHER FAVORITE STORIES BOXED SET, Beatrix Potter. Seven of Beatrix Potter's best-loved tales including Peter Rabbit in a specially designed, durable boxed set. 4¼ × 5½. Total of 447pp. 158 color illustrations. (Available in U.S. only) 23903-9 Pa. $10.50

PRACTICAL MENTAL MAGIC, Theodore Annemann. Nearly 200 astonishing feats of mental magic revealed in step-by-step detail. Complete advice on staging, patter, etc. Illustrated. 320pp. 5⅜ × 8½. 24426-1 Pa. $5.95

CELEBRATED CASES OF JUDGE DEE (DEE GOONG AN), translated by Robert Van Gulik. Authentic 18th-century Chinese detective novel; Dee and associates solve three interlocked cases. Led to van Gulik's own stories with same characters. Extensive introduction. 9 illustrations. 237pp. 5⅜ × 8½.
23337-5 Pa. $4.50

CUT & FOLD EXTRATERRESTRIAL INVADERS THAT FLY, M. Grater. Stage your own lilliputian space battles. By following the step-by-step instructions and explanatory diagrams you can launch 22 full-color fliers into space. 36pp. 8¼ × 11. 24478-4 Pa. $2.95

CUT & ASSEMBLE VICTORIAN HOUSES, Edmund V. Gillon, Jr. Printed in full color on heavy cardboard stock, 4 authentic Victorian houses in H-O scale: Italian-style Villa, Octagon, Second Empire, Stick Style. 48pp. 9¼ × 12¼.
23849-0 Pa. $3.95

BEST SCIENCE FICTION STORIES OF H.G. WELLS, H.G. Wells. Full novel *The Invisible Man*, plus 17 short stories: "The Crystal Egg," "Aepyornis Island," "The Strange Orchid," etc. 303pp. 5⅜ × 8½. (Available in U.S. only)
21531-8 Pa. $3.95

TRADEMARK DESIGNS OF THE WORLD, Yusaku Kamekura. A lavish collection of nearly 700 trademarks, the work of Wright, Loewy, Klee, Binder, hundreds of others. 160pp. 8¾ × 8. (Available in U.S. only) 24191-2 Pa. $5.00

THE ARTIST'S AND CRAFTSMAN'S GUIDE TO REDUCING, ENLARGING AND TRANSFERRING DESIGNS, Rita Weiss. Discover, reduce, enlarge, transfer designs from any objects to any craft project. 12pp. plus 16 sheets special graph paper. 8¼ × 11. 24142-4 Pa. $3.25

TREASURY OF JAPANESE DESIGNS AND MOTIFS FOR ARTISTS AND CRAFTSMEN, edited by Carol Belanger Grafton. Indispensable collection of 360 traditional Japanese designs and motifs redrawn in clean, crisp black-and-white, copyright-free illustrations. 96pp. 8¼ × 11. 24435-0 Pa. $3.95

CHANCERY CURSIVE STROKE BY STROKE, Arthur Baker. Instructions and illustrations for each stroke of each letter (upper and lower case) and numerals. 54 full-page plates. 64pp. 8¼ × 11. 24278-1 Pa. $2.50

THE ENJOYMENT AND USE OF COLOR, Walter Sargent. Color relationships, values, intensities; complementary colors, illumination, similar topics. Color in nature and art. 7 color plates, 29 illustrations. 274pp. 5⅜ × 8½. 20944-X Pa. $4.50

SCULPTURE PRINCIPLES AND PRACTICE, Louis Slobodkin. Step-by-step approach to clay, plaster, metals, stone; classical and modern. 253 drawings, photos. 255pp. 8⅛ × 11. 22960-2 Pa. $7.00

VICTORIAN FASHION PAPER DOLLS FROM HARPER'S BAZAR, 1867-1898, Theodore Menten. Four female dolls with 28 elegant high fashion costumes, printed in full color. 32pp. 9¼ × 12¼. 23453-3 Pa. $3.50

FLOPSY, MOPSY AND COTTONTAIL: A Little Book of Paper Dolls in Full Color, Susan LaBelle. Three dolls and 21 costumes (7 for each doll) show Peter Rabbit's siblings dressed for holidays, gardening, hiking, etc. Charming borders, captions. 48pp. 4¼ × 5½. 24376-1 Pa. $2.00

NATIONAL LEAGUE BASEBALL CARD CLASSICS, Bert Randolph Sugar. 83 big-leaguers from 1909-69 on facsimile cards. Hubbell, Dean, Spahn, Brock plus advertising, info, no duplications. Perforated, detachable. 16pp. 8¼ × 11. 24308-7 Pa. $2.95

THE LOGICAL APPROACH TO CHESS, Dr. Max Euwe, et al. First-rate text of comprehensive strategy, tactics, theory for the amateur. No gambits to memorize, just a clear, logical approach. 224pp. 5⅜ × 8½. 24353-2 Pa. $4.50

MAGICK IN THEORY AND PRACTICE, Aleister Crowley. The summation of the thought and practice of the century's most famous necromancer, long hard to find. Crowley's best book. 436pp. 5⅜ × 8½. (Available in U.S. only) 23295-6 Pa. $6.50

THE HAUNTED HOTEL, Wilkie Collins. Collins' last great tale; doom and destiny in a Venetian palace. Praised by T.S. Eliot. 127pp. 5⅜ × 8½. 24333-8 Pa. $3.00

ART DECO DISPLAY ALPHABETS, Dan X. Solo. Wide variety of bold yet elegant lettering in handsome Art Deco styles. 100 complete fonts, with numerals, punctuation, more. 104pp. 8⅛ × 11. 24372-9 Pa. $4.00

CALLIGRAPHIC ALPHABETS, Arthur Baker. Nearly 150 complete alphabets by outstanding contemporary. Stimulating ideas; useful source for unique effects. 154 plates. 157pp. 8⅜ × 11¼. 21045-6 Pa. $4.95

ARTHUR BAKER'S HISTORIC CALLIGRAPHIC ALPHABETS, Arthur Baker. From monumental capitals of first-century Rome to humanistic cursive of 16th century, 33 alphabets in fresh interpretations. 88 plates. 96pp. 9 × 12. 24054-1 Pa. $3.95

LETTIE LANE PAPER DOLLS, Sheila Young. Genteel turn-of-the-century family very popular then and now. 24 paper dolls. 16 plates in full color. 32pp. 9¼ × 12¼. 24089-4 Pa. $3.50

TWENTY-FOUR ART NOUVEAU POSTCARDS IN FULL COLOR FROM CLASSIC POSTERS, Hayward and Blanche Cirker. Ready-to-mail postcards reproduced from rare set of poster art. Works by Toulouse-Lautrec, Parrish, Steinlen, Mucha, Cheret, others. 12pp. 8¼× 11. 24389-3 Pa. $2.95

READY-TO-USE ART NOUVEAU BOOKMARKS IN FULL COLOR, Carol Belanger Grafton. 30 elegant bookmarks featuring graceful, flowing lines, foliate motifs, sensuous women characteristic of Art Nouveau. Perforated for easy detaching. 16pp. 8¼ × 11. 24305-2 Pa. $2.95

FRUIT KEY AND TWIG KEY TO TREES AND SHRUBS, William M. Harlow. Fruit key covers 120 deciduous and evergreen species; twig key covers 160 deciduous species. Easily used. Over 300 photographs. 126pp. 5⅜ × 8½. 20511-8 Pa. $2.25

LEONARDO DRAWINGS, Leonardo da Vinci. Plants, landscapes, human face and figure, etc., plus studies for Sforza monument, *Last Supper*, more. 60 illustrations. 64pp. 8¼ × 11⅛. 23951-9 Pa. $2.75

CLASSIC BASEBALL CARDS, edited by Bert R. Sugar. 98 classic cards on heavy stock, full color, perforated for detaching. Ruth, Cobb, Durocher, DiMaggio, H. Wagner, 99 others. Rare originals cost hundreds. 16pp. 8¼ × 11. 23498-3 Pa. $2.95

TREES OF THE EASTERN AND CENTRAL UNITED STATES AND CANADA, William M. Harlow. Best one-volume guide to 140 trees. Full descriptions, woodlore, range, etc. Over 600 illustrations. Handy size. 288pp. 4½ × 6⅜. 20395-6 Pa. $3.50

JUDY GARLAND PAPER DOLLS IN FULL COLOR, Tom Tierney. 3 Judy Garland paper dolls (teenager, grown-up, and mature woman) and 30 gorgeous costumes highlighting memorable career. Captions. 32pp. 9¼ × 12¼. 24404-0 Pa. $3.50

GREAT FASHION DESIGNS OF THE BELLE EPOQUE PAPER DOLLS IN FULL COLOR, Tom Tierney. Two dolls and 30 costumes meticulously rendered. Haute couture by Worth, Lanvin, Paquin, other greats late Victorian to WWI. 32pp. 9¼ × 12¼. 24425-3 Pa. $3.50

FASHION PAPER DOLLS FROM GODEY'S LADY'S BOOK, 1840-1854, Susan Johnston. In full color: 7 female fashion dolls with 50 costumes. Little girl's, bridal, riding, bathing, wedding, evening, everyday, etc. 32pp. 9¼ × 12¼. 23511-4 Pa. $3.50

THE BOOK OF THE SACRED MAGIC OF ABRAMELIN THE MAGE, translated by S. MacGregor Mathers. Medieval manuscript of ceremonial magic. Basic document in Aleister Crowley, Golden Dawn groups. 268pp. 5⅜ × 8½. 23211-5 Pa. $5.00

PETER RABBIT POSTCARDS IN FULL COLOR: 24 Ready-to-Mail Cards, Susan Whited LaBelle. Bunnies ice-skating, coloring Easter eggs, making valentines, many other charming scenes. 24 perforated full-color postcards, each measuring 4¼ × 6, on coated stock. 12pp. 9 × 12. 24617-5 Pa. $2.95

CELTIC HAND STROKE BY STROKE, A. Baker. Complete guide creating each letter of the alphabet in distinctive Celtic manner. Covers hand position, strokes, pens, inks, paper, more. Illustrated. 48pp. 8¼ × 11. 24336-2 Pa. $2.50

KEYBOARD WORKS FOR SOLO INSTRUMENTS, G.F. Handel. 35 neglected works from Handel's vast oeuvre, originally jotted down as improvisations. Includes Eight Great Suites, others. New sequence. 174pp. 9⅜ × 12¼.

24338-9 Pa. $7.50

AMERICAN LEAGUE BASEBALL CARD CLASSICS, Bert Randolph Sugar. 82 stars from 1900s to 60s on facsimile cards. Ruth, Cobb, Mantle, Williams, plus advertising, info, no duplications. Perforated, detachable. 16pp. 8¼ × 11.

24286-2 Pa. $2.95

A TREASURY OF CHARTED DESIGNS FOR NEEDLEWORKERS, Georgia Gorham and Jeanne Warth. 141 charted designs: owl, cat with yarn, tulips, piano, spinning wheel, covered bridge, Victorian house and many others. 48pp. 8¼ × 11.

23558-0 Pa. $1.95

DANISH FLORAL CHARTED DESIGNS, Gerda Bengtsson. Exquisite collection of over 40 different florals: anemone, Iceland poppy, wild fruit, pansies, many others. 45 illustrations. 48pp. 8¼ × 11. 23957-8 Pa. $1.75

OLD PHILADELPHIA IN EARLY PHOTOGRAPHS 1839-1914, Robert F. Looney. 215 photographs: panoramas, street scenes, landmarks, President-elect Lincoln's visit, 1876 Centennial Exposition, much more. 230pp. 8⅜ × 11¾.

23345-6 Pa. $9.95

PRELUDE TO MATHEMATICS, W.W. Sawyer. Noted mathematician's lively, stimulating account of non-Euclidean geometry, matrices, determinants, group theory, other topics. Emphasis on novel, striking aspects. 224pp. 5⅜ × 8½.

24401-6 Pa. $4.50

ADVENTURES WITH A MICROSCOPE, Richard Headstrom. 59 adventures with clothing fibers, protozoa, ferns and lichens, roots and leaves, much more. 142 illustrations. 232pp. 5⅜ × 8½. 23471-1 Pa. $3.50

IDENTIFYING ANIMAL TRACKS: MAMMALS, BIRDS, AND OTHER ANIMALS OF THE EASTERN UNITED STATES, Richard Headstrom. For hunters, naturalists, scouts, nature-lovers. Diagrams of tracks, tips on identification. 128pp. 5⅜ × 8. 24442-3 Pa. $3.50

VICTORIAN FASHIONS AND COSTUMES FROM HARPER'S BAZAR, 1867-1898, edited by Stella Blum. Day costumes, evening wear, sports clothes, shoes, hats, other accessories in over 1,000 detailed engravings. 320pp. 9⅜ × 12¼.

22990-4 Pa. $9.95

EVERYDAY FASHIONS OF THE TWENTIES AS PICTURED IN SEARS AND OTHER CATALOGS, edited by Stella Blum. Actual dress of the Roaring Twenties, with text by Stella Blum. Over 750 illustrations, captions. 156pp. 9 × 12.

24134-3 Pa. $7.95

HALL OF FAME BASEBALL CARDS, edited by Bert Randolph Sugar. Cy Young, Ted Williams, Lou Gehrig, and many other Hall of Fame greats on 92 full-color, detachable reprints of early baseball cards. No duplication of cards with *Classic Baseball Cards.* 16pp. 8¼ × 11. 23624-2 Pa. $2.95

THE ART OF HAND LETTERING, Helm Wotzkow. Course in hand lettering, Roman, Gothic, Italic, Block, Script. Tools, proportions, optical aspects, individual variation. Very quality conscious. Hundreds of specimens. 320pp. 5⅜ × 8½.

21797-3 Pa. $4.95

HOW THE OTHER HALF LIVES, Jacob A. Riis. Journalistic record of filth, degradation, upward drive in New York immigrant slums, shops, around 1900. New edition includes 100 original Riis photos, monuments of early photography. 233pp. 10 × 7⅞. 22012-5 Pa. $7.95

CHINA AND ITS PEOPLE IN EARLY PHOTOGRAPHS, John Thomson. In 200 black-and-white photographs of exceptional quality photographic pioneer Thomson captures the mountains, dwellings, monuments and people of 19th-century China. 272pp. 9⅜ × 12¼. 24393-1 Pa. $12.95

GODEY COSTUME PLATES IN COLOR FOR DECOUPAGE AND FRAMING, edited by Eleanor Hasbrouk Rawlings. 24 full-color engravings depicting 19th-century Parisian haute couture. Printed on one side only. 56pp. 8¼ × 11. 23879-2 Pa. $3.95

ART NOUVEAU STAINED GLASS PATTERN BOOK, Ed Sibbett, Jr. 104 projects using well-known themes of Art Nouveau: swirling forms, florals, peacocks, and sensuous women. 60pp. 8¼ × 11. 23577-7 Pa. $3.00

QUICK AND EASY PATCHWORK ON THE SEWING MACHINE: Susan Aylsworth Murwin and Suzzy Payne. Instructions, diagrams show exactly how to machine sew 12 quilts. 48pp. of templates. 50 figures. 80pp. 8¼ × 11. 23770-2 Pa. $3.50

THE STANDARD BOOK OF QUILT MAKING AND COLLECTING, Marguerite Ickis. Full information, full-sized patterns for making 46 traditional quilts, also 150 other patterns. 483 illustrations. 273pp. 6⅞ × 9⅝. 20582-7 Pa. $5.95

LETTERING AND ALPHABETS, J. Albert Cavanagh. 85 complete alphabets lettered in various styles; instructions for spacing, roughs, brushwork. 121pp. 8¾ × 8. 20053-1 Pa. $3.75

LETTER FORMS: 110 COMPLETE ALPHABETS, Frederick Lambert. 110 sets of capital letters; 16 lower case alphabets; 70 sets of numbers and other symbols. 110pp. 8⅛ × 11. 22872-X Pa. $4.50

ORCHIDS AS HOUSE PLANTS, Rebecca Tyson Northen. Grow cattleyas and many other kinds of orchids—in a window, in a case, or under artificial light. 63 illustrations. 148pp. 5⅜ × 8½. 23261-1 Pa. $2.95

THE MUSHROOM HANDBOOK, Louis C.C. Krieger. Still the best popular handbook. Full descriptions of 259 species, extremely thorough text, poisons, folklore, etc. 32 color plates; 126 other illustrations. 560pp. 5⅜ × 8½. 21861-9 Pa. $8.50

THE DORÉ BIBLE ILLUSTRATIONS, Gustave Doré. All wonderful, detailed plates: Adam and Eve, Flood, Babylon, life of Jesus, etc. Brief King James text with each plate. 241 plates. 241pp. 9 × 12. 23004-X Pa. $6.95

THE BOOK OF KELLS: Selected Plates in Full Color, edited by Blanche Cirker. 32 full-page plates from greatest manuscript-icon of early Middle Ages. Fantastic, mysterious. Publisher's Note. Captions. 32pp. 9¾ × 12¼. 24345-1 Pa. $4.50

THE PERFECT WAGNERITE, George Bernard Shaw. Brilliant criticism of the Ring Cycle, with provocative interpretation of politics, economic theories behind the Ring. 136pp. 5⅜ × 8½. (Available in U.S. only) 21707-8 Pa. $3.00

CATALOG OF DOVER BOOKS

THE RIME OF THE ANCIENT MARINER, Gustave Doré, S.T. Coleridge. Doré's finest work, 34 plates capture moods, subtleties of poem. Full text. 77pp. 9¼ × 12. 22305-1 Pa. $4.95

SONGS OF INNOCENCE, William Blake. The first and most popular of Blake's famous "Illuminated Books," in a facsimile edition reproducing all 31 brightly colored plates. Additional printed text of each poem. 64pp. 5¼ × 7. 22764-2 Pa. $3.00

AN INTRODUCTION TO INFORMATION THEORY, J.R. Pierce. Second (1980) edition of most impressive non-technical account available. Encoding, entropy, noisy channel, related areas, etc. 320pp. 5⅜ × 8½. 24061-4 Pa. $4.95

THE DIVINE PROPORTION: A STUDY IN MATHEMATICAL BEAUTY, H.E. Huntley. "Divine proportion" or "golden ratio"in poetry, Pascal's triangle, philosophy, psychology, music, mathematical figures, etc. Excellent bridge between science and art. 58 figures. 185pp. 5⅜ × 8½. 22254-3 Pa. $3.95

THE DOVER NEW YORK WALKING GUIDE: From the Battery to Wall Street, Mary J. Shapiro. Superb inexpensive guide to historic buildings and locales in lower Manhattan: Trinity Church, Bowling Green, more. Complete Text; maps. 36 illustrations. 48pp. 3⅞ × 9¼. 24225-0 Pa. $1.75

NEW YORK THEN AND NOW, Edward B. Watson, Edmund V. Gillon, Jr. 83 important Manhattan sites: on facing pages early photographs (1875-1925) and 1976 photos by Gillon. 172 illustrations. 171pp. 9¼ × 10. 23361-8 Pa. $7.95

HISTORIC COSTUME IN PICTURES, Braun & Schneider. Over 1450 costumed figures from dawn of civilization to end of 19th century. English captions. 125 plates. 256pp. 8⅜ × 11¼. 23150-X Pa. $7.50

VICTORIAN AND EDWARDIAN FASHION: A Photographic Survey, Alison Gernsheim. First fashion history completely illustrated by contemporary photographs. Full text plus 235 photos, 1840-1914, in which many celebrities appear. 240pp. 6½ × 9¼. 24205-6 Pa. $6.00

CHARTED CHRISTMAS DESIGNS FOR COUNTED CROSS-STITCH AND OTHER NEEDLECRAFTS, Lindberg Press. Charted designs for 45 beautiful needlecraft projects with many yuletide and wintertime motifs. 48pp. 8¼ × 11. 24356-7 Pa. $1.95

101 FOLK DESIGNS FOR COUNTED CROSS-STITCH AND OTHER NEEDLE-CRAFTS, Carter Houck. 101 authentic charted folk designs in a wide array of lovely representations with many suggestions for effective use. 48pp. 8¼ × 11. 24369-9 Pa. $1.95

FIVE ACRES AND INDEPENDENCE, Maurice G. Kains. Great back-to-the-land classic explains basics of self-sufficient farming. The one book to get. 95 illustrations. 397pp. 5⅜ × 8½. 20974-1 Pa. $4.95

A MODERN HERBAL, Margaret Grieve. Much the fullest, most exact, most useful compilation of herbal material. Gigantic alphabetical encyclopedia, from aconite to zedoary, gives botanical information, medical properties, folklore, economic uses, and much else. Indispensable to serious reader. 161 illustrations. 888pp. 6½ × 9¼. (Available in U.S. only) 22798-7, 22799-5 Pa., Two-vol. set $16.45

DECORATIVE NAPKIN FOLDING FOR BEGINNERS, Lillian Oppenheimer and Natalie Epstein. 22 different napkin folds in the shape of a heart, clown's hat, love knot, etc. 63 drawings. 48pp. 8¼ × 11. 23797-4 Pa. $1.95

DECORATIVE LABELS FOR HOME CANNING, PRESERVING, AND OTHER HOUSEHOLD AND GIFT USES, Theodore Menten. 128 gummed, perforated labels, beautifully printed in 2 colors. 12 versions. Adhere to metal, glass, wood, ceramics. 24pp. 8¼ × 11. 23219-0 Pa. $2.95

EARLY AMERICAN STENCILS ON WALLS AND FURNITURE, Janet Waring. Thorough coverage of 19th-century folk art: techniques, artifacts, surviving specimens. 166 illustrations, 7 in color. 147pp. of text. 7⅞ × 10¾. 21906-2 Pa. $8.95

AMERICAN ANTIQUE WEATHERVANES, A.B. & W.T. Westervelt. Extensively illustrated 1883 catalog exhibiting over 550 copper weathervanes and finials. Excellent primary source by one of the principal manufacturers. 104pp. 6⅛ × 9¼. 24396-6 Pa. $3.95

ART STUDENTS' ANATOMY, Edmond J. Farris. Long favorite in art schools. Basic elements, common positions, actions. Full text, 158 illustrations. 159pp. 5⅜ × 8½. 20744-7 Pa. $3.50

BRIDGMAN'S LIFE DRAWING, George B. Bridgman. More than 500 drawings and text teach you to abstract the body into its major masses. Also specific areas of anatomy. 192pp. 6½ × 9¼. (EA) 22710-3 Pa. $4.50

COMPLETE PRELUDES AND ETUDES FOR SOLO PIANO, Frederic Chopin. All 26 Preludes, all 27 Etudes by greatest composer of piano music. Authoritative Paderewski edition. 224pp. 9 × 12. (Available in U.S. only) 24052-5 Pa. $6.95

PIANO MUSIC 1888-1905, Claude Debussy. Deux Arabesques, Suite Bergamesque, Masques, 1st series of Images, etc. 9 others, in corrected editions. 175pp. 9⅜ × 12¼. (ECE) 22771-5 Pa. $5.95

TEDDY BEAR IRON-ON TRANSFER PATTERNS, Ted Menten. 80 iron-on transfer patterns of male and female Teddys in a wide variety of activities, poses, sizes. 48pp. 8¼ × 11. 24596-9 Pa. $2.00

A PICTURE HISTORY OF THE BROOKLYN BRIDGE, M.J. Shapiro. Profusely illustrated account of greatest engineering achievement of 19th century. 167 rare photos & engravings recall construction, human drama. Extensive, detailed text. 122pp. 8¼ × 11. 24403-2 Pa. $7.95

NEW YORK IN THE THIRTIES, Berenice Abbott. Noted photographer's fascinating study shows new buildings that have become famous and old sights that have disappeared forever. 97 photographs. 97pp. 11⅜ × 10. 22967-X Pa. $6.50

MATHEMATICAL TABLES AND FORMULAS, Robert D. Carmichael and Edwin R. Smith. Logarithms, sines, tangents, trig functions, powers, roots, reciprocals, exponential and hyperbolic functions, formulas and theorems. 269pp. 5⅜ × 8½. 60111-0 Pa. $3.75

HANDBOOK OF MATHEMATICAL FUNCTIONS WITH FORMULAS, GRAPHS, AND MATHEMATICAL TABLES, edited by Milton Abramowitz and Irene A. Stegun. Vast compendium: 29 sets of tables, some to as high as 20 places. 1,046pp. 8 × 10½. 61272-4 Pa. $19.95

REASON IN ART, George Santayana. Renowned philosopher's provocative, seminal treatment of basis of art in instinct and experience. Volume Four of *The Life of Reason*. 230pp. 5⅜ × 8.   24358-3 Pa. $4.50

LANGUAGE, TRUTH AND LOGIC, Alfred J. Ayer. Famous, clear introduction to Vienna, Cambridge schools of Logical Positivism. Role of philosophy, elimination of metaphysics, nature of analysis, etc. 160pp. 5⅜ × 8½. (USCO)
20010-8 Pa. $2.75

BASIC ELECTRONICS, U.S. Bureau of Naval Personnel. Electron tubes, circuits, antennas, AM, FM, and CW transmission and receiving, etc. 560 illustrations. 567pp. 6½ × 9¼.   21076-6 Pa. $8.95

THE ART DECO STYLE, edited by Theodore Menten. Furniture, jewelry, metalwork, ceramics, fabrics, lighting fixtures, interior decors, exteriors, graphics from pure French sources. Over 400 photographs. 183pp. 8⅜ × 11¼.
22824-X Pa. $6.95

THE FOUR BOOKS OF ARCHITECTURE, Andrea Palladio. 16th-century classic covers classical architectural remains, Renaissance revivals, classical orders, etc. 1738 Ware English edition. 216 plates. 110pp. of text. 9½ × 12¾.
21308-0 Pa. $10.00

THE WIT AND HUMOR OF OSCAR WILDE, edited by Alvin Redman. More than 1000 ripostes, paradoxes, wisecracks: Work is the curse of the drinking classes, I can resist everything except temptations, etc. 258pp. 5⅜ × 8½. (USCO)
20602-5 Pa. $3.50

THE DEVIL'S DICTIONARY, Ambrose Bierce. Barbed, bitter, brilliant witticisms in the form of a dictionary. Best, most ferocious satire America has produced. 145pp. 5⅜ × 8½.   20487-1 Pa. $2.50

ERTÉ'S FASHION DESIGNS, Erté. 210 black-and-white inventions from *Harper's Bazar*, 1918-32, plus 8pp. full-color covers. Captions. 88pp. 9 × 12.
24203-X Pa. $6.50

ERTÉ GRAPHICS, Erté. Collection of striking color graphics: *Seasons, Alphabet, Numerals, Aces* and *Precious Stones*. 50 plates, including 4 on covers. 48pp. 9⅜ × 12¼.   23580-7 Pa. $6.95

PAPER FOLDING FOR BEGINNERS, William D. Murray and Francis J. Rigney. Clearest book for making origami sail boats, roosters, frogs that move legs, etc. 40 projects. More than 275 illustrations. 94pp. 5⅜ × 8½.   20713-7 Pa. $1.95

ORIGAMI FOR THE ENTHUSIAST, John Montroll. Fish, ostrich, peacock, squirrel, rhinoceros, Pegasus, 19 other intricate subjects. Instructions. Diagrams. 128pp. 9 × 12.   23799-0 Pa. $4.95

CROCHETING NOVELTY POT HOLDERS, edited by Linda Macho. 64 useful, whimsical pot holders feature kitchen themes, animals, flowers, other novelties. Surprisingly easy to crochet. Complete instructions. 48pp. 8¼ × 11.
24296-X Pa. $1.95

CROCHETING DOILIES, edited by Rita Weiss. Irish Crochet, Jewel, Star Wheel, Vanity Fair and more. Also luncheon and console sets, runners and centerpieces. 51 illustrations. 48pp. 8¼ × 11.   23424-X Pa. $2.00

SOURCE BOOK OF MEDICAL HISTORY, edited by Logan Clendening, M.D. Original accounts ranging from Ancient Egypt and Greece to discovery of X-rays: Galen, Pasteur, Lavoisier, Harvey, Parkinson, others. 685pp. 5⅜ × 8½.
20621-1 Pa. $10.95

THE ROSE AND THE KEY, J.S. Lefanu. Superb mystery novel from Irish master. Dark doings among an ancient and aristocratic English family. Well-drawn characters; capital suspense. Introduction by N. Donaldson. 448pp. 5⅜ × 8½.
24377-X Pa. $6.95

SOUTH WIND, Norman Douglas. Witty, elegant novel of ideas set on languorous Meditterranean island of Nepenthe. Elegant prose, glittering epigrams, mordant satire. 1917 masterpiece. 416pp. 5⅜ × 8½. (Available in U.S. only)
24361-3 Pa. $5.95

RUSSELL'S CIVIL WAR PHOTOGRAPHS, Capt. A.J. Russell. 116 rare Civil War Photos: Bull Run, Virginia campaigns, bridges, railroads, Richmond, Lincoln's funeral car. Many never seen before. Captions. 128pp. 9⅜ × 12¼.
24283-8 Pa. $6.95

PHOTOGRAPHS BY MAN RAY: 105 Works, 1920-1934. Nudes, still lifes, landscapes, women's faces, celebrity portraits (Dali, Matisse, Picasso, others), rayographs. Reprinted from rare gravure edition. 128pp. 9⅜ × 12¼. (Available in U.S. only) 23842-3 Pa. $6.95

STAR NAMES: THEIR LORE AND MEANING, Richard H. Allen. Star names, the zodiac, constellations: folklore and literature associated with heavens. The basic book of its field, fascinating reading. 563pp. 5⅜ × 8½. 21079-0 Pa. $7.95

BURNHAM'S CELESTIAL HANDBOOK, Robert Burnham, Jr. Thorough guide to the stars beyond our solar system. Exhaustive treatment. Alphabetical by constellation: Andromeda to Cetus in Vol. 1; Chamaeleon to Orion in Vol. 2; and Pavo to Vulpecula in Vol. 3. Hundreds of illustrations. Index in Vol. 3. 2000pp. 6⅛ × 9¼. 23567-X, 23568-8, 23673-0 Pa. Three-vol. set $32.85

THE ART NOUVEAU STYLE BOOK OF ALPHONSE MUCHA, Alphonse Mucha. All 72 plates from *Documents Decoratifs* in original color. Stunning, essential work of Art Nouveau. 80pp. 9⅜ × 12¼. 24044-4 Pa. $7.95

DESIGNS BY ERTE; FASHION DRAWINGS AND ILLUSTRATIONS FROM "HARPER'S BAZAR," Erte. 310 fabulous line drawings and 14 *Harper's Bazar* covers, 8 in full color. Erte's exotic temptresses with tassels, fur muffs, long trains, coifs, more. 129pp. 9⅜ × 12¼. 23397-9 Pa. $6.95

HISTORY OF STRENGTH OF MATERIALS, Stephen P. Timoshenko. Excellent historical survey of the strength of materials with many references to the theories of elasticity and structure. 245 figures. 452pp. 5⅜ × 8½. 61187-6 Pa. $8.95

Prices subject to change without notice.

Available at your book dealer or write for free catalog to Dept. GI, Dover Publications, Inc., 31 East 2nd St. Mineola, N.Y. 11501. Dover publishes more than 175 books each year on science, elementary and advanced mathematics, biology, music, art, literary history, social sciences and other areas.